SMITH'S GAZELLE

# LIONEL DAVIDSON
# Smith's Gazelle

*faber and faber*

This edition first published in 2008
by Faber and Faber Ltd
3 Queen Square, London WC1N 3AU

Printed by CPI Antony Rowe, Eastbourne

A CIP record for this book is available from the British Library

ISBN 978-0-571-24293-1

# 1
# All About the Ungulates

A man called Motke Bartov, then engaged in a count of animals in the Wadi Parek of southern Israel (this was February 1957), made the first sighting. It was dusk when he made it and the light was bad, so he wasn't sure what it was. He decided to lay up for the night in a hide he had made and see if he couldn't get another look in the morning. In the morning he got another look, but it was no better and he still couldn't say what he'd seen. It wasn't quite a goat or an antelope or a deer. There was a feeding group of six of the animals, very nervous. When he tried to get closer they fled.

In the course of the day he went to Beersheba and phoned Major General Naftali Mor, who was his boss on the project, and told him about it. Major General Mor, a famous poacher in his day, had a wider practical knowledge of the wildlife of the country than anybody else, but he couldn't say what the animal was either. He thought Motke might have been fooled by the early stages of horn production in fallow deer. Motke swore it was no fallow deer he had seen.

'So wait a minute, Motke, let's have a look,' the general said and got some books down. After a few minutes he picked up the phone and said, 'How did that horn structure go again, Motke?'

Motke told him. He said it was lyre-shaped as in antelopes, but looped as in goats, or it might have been branched as in deer. 'That's how I couldn't tell if it was a goat, an antelope, or a deer,' Motke said. 'Only what I think now,' he added, suddenly realizing the strange tone in the general's voice and worried by it, 'is that all I saw was a bunch of *Gazella gazella* that were feeding on saltbush, and what is making the difficulty with the horns is that saltbush is stuck there. This is what I am now sure of,' Motke said. 'So how is everything there?'

'Where were the terminals of the horns, Motke?'

'Where the saltbush is stuck. At the back.'

'It's important, Motke. Did the loop go forward or back?'

Motke thought about it. 'I don't think there was any loop,' he said, worried, 'I think what there is is saltbush. Whatever it is, it's at the back.'

'Were there females there?' the general said in the same strange tone.

'Yes, there were females.'

'How could you tell the females?'

'They were smaller. They had smaller horn structures. Also they ran first.'

'How big was the animal altogether?'

'It wasn't big. It was small for a gazelle. It's why I thought it was a goat. What is it?' Motke said.

'I don't know. But what I want you to do,' the general said, 'is run out and buy some alfalfa and get back to that wadi with it as fast as you can. Spread the alfalfa and let the air get at it. But don't spread too much. And use gloves. This is a fantastic animal, Motke.'

'What is?' Motke said.

'It's early to say. Is your hide up or down?'

'It's up, on a hill.'

'Make another. Make it low, down in the wadi. Use the upper hide in the evening when the air currents are rising, and before dawn get down to the lower one. It scented you, Motke – this is what made it nervous. The animal has fantastic scent.'

'What animal are we talking about?' Motke said.

'As yet,' the general said, 'I couldn't hazard a guess.' He could, but he thought there was a good chance of making a fool of himself. So all he said was, 'Better see to everything quickly, Motke. Ill try to be with you tomorrow – maybe even today.'

But the general didn't get to Motke that day. Before he went to the Wadi Parek he wanted as much information as possible on what he was looking for, and at the moment he had hardly any. The Nature Reserves Authority, which he headed, hadn't been running long and was short of everything, including books. He'd looked at Tristram's Holy *Land Fauna* and some other works in German and French, Huebschner's and Lepadière's. Tristram hadn't mentioned what he wanted, and Huebschner and Lepadière said it was extinct. He knew it was extinct himself. Everybody knew it was extinct. He saw there was such a good chance of making a fool of himself that when he went down to the Weizmann Institute of Science at Rehovot – which he did about ten minutes after the phone conversation with Motke – he didn't tell them what he was lookmg for, either. He simply went to the zoological section and breezed about the shelves trying not to look like a poacher or a general but a busy student of zoology.

On the shelves of the Weizmann Institute the nature of the Creation was laid out in a scientific and orderly manner. That part of it that was vertebrate was divided into five classes, and the one the general wanted was mammals. There were nineteen orders of mammals. The Artiodactyla was the one required, and, nosing around, he saw that it ran to nine families divided into eighty genera, which were subdivided into 195 species. By this time the general thought Motke was making rather a hell of a lot of trouble down there at the Wadi Parek, but he persevered.

The Artiodactyla comprised the order of even-toed ungulates, hoofed animals, among them the deer. The general didn't think it was a deer now but he had a look, all the same. Then he turned to some other families of the order. He turned to the family Bovidae. This family comprised the even-toed, ungulate, cud-chewing, permanent-horned Artiodactyla: the sheep, cattle, goats, and antelopes. He thought he could skip the cattle and the sheep, but he went through the goats and antelopes with a fine-toothed comb. He came to the subgroup Gazella. There was the Dorcas gazelle, the Persian, the Mongolian, the Saiga, Grant's, Thomson's, Smith's . . .

The general ran into a difficulty. The older classic works did not mention the species he sought. The newer ones said it was extinct. There seemed to have been no golden period for the animal when it was actually observed to be in existence. The general had the exasperating impression of having glimpsed it, as if in a rear-view mirror, just one moment too late, as it sank on its ungulate feet from the battle for survival. And he was aware again, as he'd often been before, that despite the formidable massed volumes of the libraries of the world, knowledge of things was sketchy, scholarship a patchy business.

Yet there'd been an awareness of this animal. He could recall scraps of lore himself – from cigarette cards, perhaps, cadged from British soldiers in boyhood? A phantom image remained with him of an 'artist's impression' of a small beast with racing-bicycle type horns peering from a coloured card. He could even recall the back of the card: 'Game Animals of the World: one of a series of 50.' And under it, 'Issued by W.D. and H.O. Wills, Ltd., Bristol, England.' It had been a rather fabled animal, a slightly improbable animal. Some trace of this impression seemed, indeed, to be hinted at in the academic works that mentioned it. One carried a thumbnail drawing of the bicycle-type horns, cautiously subscribed 'Field Sketch Only.' And the accompanying remarks noted that the species was 'said to have been' this or 'alleged to have been' that. Who had made the field sketch, and who had made the allegations?

It was now quite late in the afternoon and the general was hungry and tired. But he went carefully back over the works consulted in search of any small item he might have overlooked. In only one of them, Boignier's five-volume *Fauna Orientalis*, could he find anything at all worth pursuing. This was a reference to the '*Proceedings of the Royal Zoological Society* [d'Angleterre]' of 1867. The general was rather desolate as he reviewed this solitary item, and he had a feeling, more lowering than ever after his day's labours, that there was something absurd about the research. But to the best of his knowledge he was not known in the library, so as a last throw he went to the librarian on duty and asked if the *Proceedings* of the RZS were kept there. The librarian was a little old man in an alpaca jacket with a wry-neck and bottle glasses and he looked suspiciously at the general as he said that they were.

'I want the *Proceedings* for 1867.'

'No good. Only from 1930.'

The general turned away, strangely relieved.

'What is it? Maybe I can help.'

'It's of no importance. A certain species.'

'What species? There's every species here.'

'A gazelle.'

'Which gazelle? There are lots of gazelles.'

The librarian had a loud voice, and heads had turned. '*Gazella smithii*,' the general said in an undertone, but scientifically.

'Smith's gazelle! What, you think it's turned up in one of your reserves, General?'

The jovial uproar had turned more heads and the general

changed colour. He said, 'It was for comparative work, of no importance, nothing,' and made for the door.

'Smith's gazelle – wait. I remember indexing an item once. Wasn't it supposed to be an animal of the area, after all?'

'Of the Sinai,' the general said.

'Exactly. The Sinai isn't local enough for you, General?' The general had commanded a tank force in Sinai the previous year, 1956. 'I'm almost sure it was in Special Collections.'

The Special Collections index was behind the desk, and the man fingered through it. 'As I thought. Draft notes for a monograph and some other papers. Mendelsohn has them.'

'Mendelsohn?'

'Professor Mendelsohn, next door. It's late now. Do you want me to phone for you?'

'Don't bother.'

'What bother? It's no bother. I can phone.'

'Very kind,' the general said, and waited by the desk while the man did so, at full volume. He learned, and all the library learned, that Professor Mendelsohn was abroad but that one of his research students was still in the building.

The student promised to search out the papers, and General Mor went to collect them. He found that the papers originated in the early 1860s in England. He took them home with him that night and read them.


2


In the early 1860s *The Times* and other newspapers in England raised a considerable outcry at the insanitary conditions and the accelerating decay of several Christian shrines in Jerusalem. The Turkish authorities replied that the ancient underground waterways of the city were to blame, but that to repair them would call first of all for an exploratory survey of almost insuperable difficulty, for which, anyway, no funds were available at the moment.

This reply failed to give satisfaction in England. Charles Dickens interested himself in the matter, and a friend of his, Miss (later Baroness) Angela Burdett Coutts, of the family of the firm of private bankers Coutts & Co., approached the British army to see what advice and assistance it could offer. The army said it could itself undertake the subterranean exploration, but not out of public funds and only at the invitation of the Turkish authorities. Miss Burdett Coutts approached the Turkish authorities and started a private fund. In 1864, the 'Palestine Exploration Fund' was able to send a party of Royal Engineers under the command of Captain (later Sir) Charles Wilson to start the survey.

Captain Wilson set about his task with energy and enthusiasm, sinking shafts and driving tunnels everywhere under the Holy City. (The technical reports of his party, 'models of painstaking accuracy' in the words of a modern archeologist, have formed the basis for most latter-day archaeology in the area.) In the first year enormous advances were made in both sanitation and scholarship, Captain Wilson himself making several notable discoveries, the most important his identification of the so-called Tyropean Bridge that linked the Temple with a forum below – still today known as Wilson's Arch. But his aide, Lieutenant George Lucie Smith, ran him a close second.

Somewhat perturbed by the interest aroused in this part of their empire, and also rather jealous, the Turks in time decided to circumscribe the activities of the Royal Engineers, limiting them more closely to the actual drainage. In the winter of 1865, when rain and extensive flooding stopped work, Lieutenant Smith, by this time bored with drains, asked permission to make a trip into the Sinai desert to see what the rain had brought up there. A keen naturalist, he backed up his request with a letter from the Royal Horticultural Society in England, soliciting information on certain varieties of the plant *sedum* thought to be indigenous to this desert. After some delay permission was reluctantly granted, and in January 1866 Smith set off for Sinai accompanied by two camels, two servants, and a troop of Turkish soldiers.

Smith's interest in Sinai was not, however, wholly horticultural. Disgusted by the corruption of Turkish rule, he had formed the opinion that British would be better, and his main object in visiting Sinai was to survey it with a view to a military operation. In the desert he soon lost his Turkish escort, and for the next nine weeks hurried from one end of the peninsula to the other, mapping it. (His survey, no less accurate than that of the Jerusalem drainage system earlier, was much appreciated by General Allenby and his army when they passed that way fifty years later.)

This energetic young man, not quite twenty-four, still found time to make some observations of the flora and fauna of the region. He collected several varieties of the plant *sedum* together with specimens of its sodden seed which had not germinated from the previous year, and sent them to England, where at Kew and at the Society's grounds, then at Chiswick, half a dozen of the seeds were coaxed into life. (Only one proved to be new to science. Specimens of its progeny, *sedum coeruleum smithii*, the blue stone-crop, are today to be found all over the world in the 'hot, dry positions' recommended by the seedsmen.) He also found a dwarf variety of *opuntia*, the fig cactus, which did not, however, remain dwarfed away from its habitat. And he found Smith's gazelle.

Smith's gazelle, when news of it reached the Royal Zoological Society, evoked much interest. There were several unique features about it, and he was asked if he would address the Society and write a monograph on the subject. By this time (it was 1867), the Turks had had enough of Smith and asked for his recall. Smith went, with his notes. For several weeks in the autumn of 1867, while on leave at his family home at York, and at his club, the United Service in Pall Mall, Smith worked at his compendious notes – for the General Staff Geographical Section, the Royal Horticultural Society, and the Royal Zoological Society. The latter had not yet accepted his new species, which was a matter for the classification committee, who in turn awaited his monograph and his lecture, both announced (in the *Proceedings* of the Society for 1867) for the following April.

Smith was unable to keep to these commitments, however. Relieved for so long from the general list, he was abruptly placed back on it when trouble developed in Ethiopia, where the Negus had imprisoned the British consul. A British expeditionary force under General Sir Robert Napier was sent to the country on January 2, 1868, and Smith went with it. He was killed during the attack on Magdala on April 13, which was also his twenty-sixth birthday.

Smith's notes, left behind in a large War Offiice folder at the United Service Club, were sent by club officials to the War Office, where the contents were immediately given a Confidential classification by the Geographical Section. All requests by the two learned societies for the original papers were refused (Smith's horticultural, zoological, and military observations being, apparently, inextricably mixed). The relevant information was abstracted, however, and copies sent to the societies. This satisfied the Royal Horticultural (who had, after all, received specimens) but not the Royal Zoological, whose classification committee had begun to evince some scepticism. Smith's approach to the animal world, strangely at odds with his sharp eye for a plant or a drain, fell some way short of the scientific. His description of the gazelle, 'a handsome little beast with an expression of Madame Patti,' was found by T. H. Huxley to be 'offensive and, I should say, improbable.' The committee quietly shelved the matter. (But a journalistic Fellow of the Society, in anticipation of the lecture, had meanwhile placed a couple of articles in *Blackwood's* and *The Morning Post*, which duly appeared, the latter adorned by the Fellow's rendering of Smith's rapid sketch of the bicycle horns – thus starting the 'handsome little beast' on its career.)

Smith's original papers remained in the War Office files for fifty-five years, until 1923, when, under the direction of Sir Ronald Storrs, the British mandatory authority for Palestine began organizing the first modem survey of the country. In that year the file was signed out of the War Office in London and signed in by the Survey Office in Jerusalem. It remained there for another twenty-five years, until 1948, when the Israeli War of Independence brought about its further transfer to Tel-Aviv and the Israel Government Survey Department.

Here, with several tons of other mandatory papers, it quietly mouldered until the mid-1950s, when it was finally sorted. Those observations of Smith's that were broadly geographical were retained by the Survey Department, those that were botanical sent to Professor Volcani at the Volcani Institute of Agriculture, and the zoological sent to Professor Mendelsohn at the Weizmann Institute. This was the material that Major General Naftali Mor took home with him.

*A handsome little beast with an expression of Madame Patti – small, I should say, for a gazelle. It tastes of turkey,* Lieutenant George Lucie Smith had reminiscently written, in that year when the leaves began to fall in England and the British consul prepared to get himself arrested in Ethiopia. *It is on this account very enthusiastically hunted by the Badawin who manage to inflict great losses even*

*with their ancient muzzle-loaders. This is the more remark-*
*able when it is considered that because of the animal's*
*highly developed sense of scent, much caution is needed to*
*get within 400 yards. No great foresight is necessary to see*
*that should those Gentlemen manage to lay hands on*
*efficient European weapons, the Species would be wiped*
*out in short order. This arises, in part, from a very curious*
*detail. The Female is the larger of the sexes, and has the*
*larger and more elaborate horn structure. Whether because*
*of it Nature has given her some protective Male functions,*
*or whether the additional weight makes her slower, the*
*fact is that in flight she is to be found in the rear and is on*
*that account very much easier to hit. The Breeding Poten-*
*tial is thus always at serious risk. I was able to observe for*
*myself how, upon a Herd being startled, it was the Male*
*that first took to its heels.*

*To come upon a Herd of the little creatures is a jolly*
*sight. Fifty or sixty of them may be seen at a time browsing*
*on the herbage brought up by the rain in the larger wadis.*
*No larger than a well-grown Alsatian or German shepherd*
*dog, and of about the same colouration as the paler*
*members of that Breed, they resemble nothing so much as*
*a Pack of Hounds at Scent. At the first hint of alarm,*
*however, what a change! Up comes a veritable thicket of*
*horns and in a trice they are springing off, like Macbeth's*
*Birnam Wood – Females unfortunately in the rear.*

*Late winter and early spring is a particularly favoured*
*time of year for hunting them, since the Females are then*
*with young, and a Badawin delicacy is unborn fawn*
*known as ghal. I am informed that Mating takes place in*
*November, and Kids (normally two in number) are*
*dropped in April. The preferred method of cooking . . .*

Smith had gone on to list several tasty ways of cooking
*Gazella smithii*. But he had not, unfortunately, gone on to
list its height, in centimetres, to the shoulder, or the length
of its horns from pedicle to terminal, or the number of its

teeth, or to enlarge further on that 'very curious detail!' of the female having the larger horn structure which had aroused such excitement in the classification committee of the RZS.

On the other hand, there was so much that was plausible in his account that it was hard simply to discount it. Just as quietly as it had been dropped, Smith's gazelle began cautiously to reappear. Some sparse further evidence gathered. The British Arabist St John Philby supplied notes from Beduin sources that tended to confirm Smith's description. Colonel T. E. Lawrence (of Arabia) referred to it in his correspondence with Sir Ronald Storrs. But no other European claimed to have seen it. In 1925, after the *Survey of Palestine* appeared, those authorities who had accepted the animal were in general agreement that it was now safely extinct. Not everybody, however, had accepted it. The RZS, whose 'find' it was, obstinately refused recognition for some years after 1925, and another great European society, the French Zoologique, persisted in refusing for very much longer. The academicians of the Zoologique, as one of them declared in 1948, required more evidence than "*ces details intéressants de la haute-cuisine arabe* 'before accepting a new species into the animal kingdom; and in the case of an animal as suspect as Smith's, they preferred the evidence to come from a Frenchman.

In February 1957, the Zoologique was still listing 194 known even-toed ungulates, not 195.

3

General Mor sped down to the Negev the next after noon with his Hasselblad camera, some high-speed film, and his night glasses. The situation at the Wadi Parek was not encouraging. A pack of jackals had been about and had frightened off the normal feeders.

The general swore. 'Are the jackals still here?'

'They were this morning,' Motke said. 'I think they were passing. They didn't come to the wadi anyway.'

The general looked at Motke and pondered. He didn't want to tell anybody yet. He decided he had better tell Motke.

Motke didn't at first seem to know whether he was being told a joke or not. Then his lip quivered, and he said, 'General, I'm sorry I even mentioned it. I know what it was. I'm quite certain what it was.'

'Something like this?' the general said. He'd made a sketch of the bicycle horns.

'Absolutely not,' Motke said.

'So we'll see.'

'I'm sorry,' Motke said.

The general inspected the arrangements Motke had made with regard to the hides and the alfalfa, and made a few changes. At about five o'clock they went to the upper hide and hid in it.

There was no sound of jackals that evening. During the brief dusk and for an hour or two afterwards several animals appeared silently at the wadi and fed. But the six gazelles did not appear. They waited until eight o'clock and then gave up. The general glumly made coffee. Motke replenished the alfalfa, and later they had a meal and slept for a few hours. An hour before dawn they got up and went down to the wadi.

In the hour before dawn it was cold in the wadi and they sat in the hide with their collars up and their hands in their armpits. The hours after dusk had not been silent. Animals had cried. Rocks had cooled and cracked like pistol shots. But now it was silent and the cold air still. As the dawn came and the tired landscape glimmered back into another day, the animals appeared again. They came in ones and twos, intent backs descending the slope into the wadi. Seen now from below, the creatures showed first against the skyline as shapes from dreams, fantastic conceptions of horn and ear. Watching them, though he knew in his heart he was doomed to disappointment, the general was moved. From boyhood he had been enthralled by the mystery of animals. He watched for several minutes and then he felt the short hairs at the back of his neck bristle and he said very softly, 'Oh, my God.' There on the skyline, descending one after the other, came the unbelievable heads of a troupe of extinct animals. One extinct animal, the general counted, and two, and three, and four, and five. He waited, but there were no more than five. Scarcely daring to breathe, he whispered into Motke's ear, 'You said there were six.'

'There were six.

'There are five.'

'But there were six.'

Moving with marvellous delicacy the five extinct gazelles picked their way between the boulders of the slope and commenced to graze in the wadi. The general raised his camera, but fearful that even the quiet shutter blind of the Hasselblad would go off like a landslide in the silence of the wadi, he lowered it again. Another time, he thought. Not this time. This time he was afraid that if he so much as blinked the whole scene would vanish, the gazelles return to extinction. He sat and stared at them with utter fascination. There were three males and two females. He saw that the horn structure of the female, though in outline similar to the bicycle horns of the sketch, was not, as in the sketch, top-heavy. Some adjustment of muscle and sinew enabled it to be carried by the living animal as lightly and elegantly as a tiara. The lyre shape, instead of ending in two simple upward points, described a forward loop, returning inside the lyre to end in points at the rear. It gave the animal a somewhat rapt and inquiring stance.

General Mor sat in a state of wonder in the Wadi Parek. He couldn't have been more bemused if a small herd of pterodactyl had come to join them. Very softly now, he could hear the sound of the gazelles feeding. They were tugging and munching, gently snorting over the alfalfa. They did this for twenty minutes and ate it all up and went As the wadi lightened, all the creatures went. The general looked after them. 'Motke,' he said, rubbing his temples, 'what a most extraordinary thing! What an unbelievable thing, Motke.'

'It's a dream,' Motke said.

'It's no dream. How many females were here before?'

'Three females,' Motke said, 'and three males.'

'So we are one female short.'

'It would seem,' Motke said. He looked even punchier than the general.

'Are there Beduin about?'

'There are Beduin.'

'Warn them,' the general said, in faint tones of trance. 'A single incident – a single attempt even, and I'll have their cattle. I'll have them behind bars, Motke.'

'It's a dream,' Motke said.


4

Marshal of the air force Jean-Claude de Joinville flew in two days later. General Mor, nibbling his fingers in the control tower, decided there was still time to call Motke again. He picked up the phone and called him.

'How is it?' he said.

'It's the same,' Motke said

'What did you find out?'

'Nothing.'

'What did the army find out?'

'They didn't find anything either,' Motke said. He was

sitting in the wadi with the radio phone the army had given him.

'How in God's name is it possible,' the general said, hanging on to his temper, 'that several hundred able-bodied men, yourself included, can't find out which of just three groups of Beduin is eating meat?'

'Plenty are eating meat. It's a mild winter, there's lambs,' Motke said.

'Motke,' the general said. He knew Motke didn't approve of the operation. He was now heavily dependent on Motke. Who knew what Motke was doing with the alfalfa? 'Motke, I am talking now from the airstrip. The air marshal has already arrived. I can see him!' He could see not only the air marshal but also the air marshal's single piece of luggage, which was just appearing out of the aeroplane with him. Even from here he could see it was a magnificent Schultz & Larsen. 243. He began to sweat again. He said, 'Motke – you know what I've promised him.'

Motke didn't say anything.

'It's of vital importance, Motke. It's important first of all for science, but also for the country. We need this air marshal. It is in every way more desirable that he should have a head than the Beduin. Understand, Motke!'

'I don't make the heads,' Motke said stubbornly.

'Motke, be careful,' the general said, and hung up.

De Joinville was keeping his single piece of luggage very firmly in his hand, so there was nothing for the general to do but embrace him and walk him to the jeep. 'Tell me again,' the Frenchman said.

The general told him.

'You actually, physically, saw them?'

'With these eyes.'

'The female is truly so beautiful?'

'Fantastic'

'Oh, my God,' the air marshal said. 'I haven't slept for

forty-eight hours. I think I'm too old for it, Naftali. Just once in a lifetime, such a female!'

'Jean-Claude, if you live to a hundred and twenty,' the general said, 'you still won't be too old. If you're disappointed on this occasion, then there'll be another.' He explained the grounds for possible disappointment. There had been six of the gazelles. When he had called Paris there had been five. This morning there were four. 'Beduin are picking them off,' he said.

'They've still left a female?' the marshal said urgently.

'Two females and two males.'

'Thank God. So long as there's one.'

'Well,' the general said, 'if there's only one, we'll have to wait for that other occasion. The army is now involved. The prime minister's office is involved. The religious authorities are involved, Jean-Claude.'

'The religious authorities? What in God's name has it to do with them?'

'In God's name,' the general said glumly, 'everything has to do with them. The feeling is that it's a miracle and we're not entitled to interfere. If there's only one left, she's got to be given her chance.'

'What chance? Are you mad? The Beduin will get her. They'll eat her,' the marshal said with shock and horror.

General Mor nodded sorrowfully as he put the jeep in gear.

They got to the wadi in an hour and a quarter and found Motke sulkily laying alfalfa. He contrived to have alfalfa in his hand when the marshal offered to shake it, but he answered questions civilly enough. He said the gazelles were thought to be in a small canyon seven or eight kilometres to the east. He'd given the canyon a wide berth and had asked the army to do so too. There were three encampments of Beduin not too far distant. All were semi-settled and drew the seed-sowing allowance

17

from the government, so he didn't think they were the culprits. All the Beduin in the area had been visited and warned against shooting gazelles of any kind. The gazelles had evidently been moving from west to east – last year's disturbance in Sinai probably having shifted them – when his alfalfa-baiting had halted them. He thought they would have safely moved on by now if he hadn't continued baiting.

'*Safely*?' the marshal said, suddenly seeing how the land lay. 'They'd have fallen to the Beduin.'

'Do we know when a sparrow falls?'

The marshal gave him a sharp look. 'I'll see the hides,' he said.

He made some small rearrangements in the hides and walked around the area. A number of things bothered him. The swiftly changing wind direction bothered him. He said he could smell jackal.

'There's no jackal,' Motke said. 'There was jackal, but not now.'

'I can smell them. Have you got a cold?'

'I get malaria, not colds, and I don't get it in February.'

'Are you coughing? Do you sneeze?'

'I cough and sneeze like a normal person,' Motke said. 'There are no jackal.'

'You need a decongestive. I can hear you. Wrap up warmly,' the marshal said.

They went into the upper hide in the late afternoon. The general didn't see the marshal load his gun, but he caught the glimmer of a white handkerchief in the gloom and an absorbed movement, almost of prayer. He couldn't tell whether the marshal was holding the cartridge against his heart or had merely produced it from his inside breast pocket. The bolt action of the Schultz & Larsen was like a piece of silk.

They sat for three hours, the marshal totally immobile. Several animals came, but the gazelles didn't. About eight o'clock they gave up. Again the general didn't see what happened to the cartridge. He had encountered it before among the most dedicated hunters, the mystique of the single cartridge.

They had coffee and a cold meal and turned in early, the marshal keeping himself and his cartridge a little apart. The general saw all this and understood it, and he hoped the gazelles would appear in the right numbers in the morning.

They rose in the dark.

'How is the man's cold?'

'The patient is in a good condition. He'll survive,' the general said wryly.

'I can hear him. Is he well wrapped up? Has he got a handkerchief?'

'A beautiful one. Embroidered by my wife,' Motke answered for himself.

'Use it if you feel a cough or a sneeze coming on. Have you a second handkerchief?'

'I am in a good position for handkerchiefs.'

'Use two. Muffle yourself with your hat. Keep warm.'

'I am very obliged to the marshal,' Motke said.

General Mor and Motke went down to the lower hide, and the marshal came silently after them five minutes later. The general wondered what new dedication had taken place with the cartridge in the meantime. He felt somewhat dedicated himself in the cold darkness. He had a feeling in his bones that it was the last time for the gazelles and that if they didn't come now they wouldn't come at all, so he set the Hasselblad and wrapped a scarf around the camera body to muffle the shutter action, and waited. He could feel the marshal waiting beside him like a Buddha.

As day dawned the animals came again, in ones and twos. Presently the gazelles came.

The general had kept his eyes on the jagged rim of the wadi where the gazelles had appeared before, and for minutes had visualized the strange and beautiful horns suddenly materializing there, but when they did his heart leapt again.

'Sweet Jesus, it's all I will ever ask you,' he heard the Frenchman blasphemously praying in his ear. But the general had no time for him now. Looking through the reflex finder he carefully squeezed off the first exposure, and turned the film and took the second and the third as the fine heads, one at a time, breasted the rim and stood black against the skyline. There wasn't a fourth head. He looked carefully through the finder as the animals descended the slope, and realized something that the marshal had probably also by now realized. He gripped the Frenchman's arm. He said, 'There is only one female. You can't have her.'

He saw the Frenchman's eyes shining in the hide.

He said, 'Jean-Claude, do you understand?'

'I understand.'

'You can't take the female.'

'I hear you.'

General Mor didn't know what to do. He couldn't jog the Frenchman's arm as he sighted. He felt a pang for him, and for the female. 'You can't have her,' he said again softly, and waited. The animals came on delicately down the slope, and began to browse on the alfalfa. The Schultz & Larsen sighted and swung a little this-way and that. In the poor light against the undifferentiated background of the wadi it was not immediately possible to identify the female. The general knew she was in the middle. He didn't want to use the camera again while they were so close. At the moment of alarm the heads would come up and swing around. That would be the moment to use the camera. 'Take one of the males,' he said. The Frenchman didn't answer, sighting along the long barrel.

It grew lighter in the wadi. The browsing heads of the gazelles came up and down, turned towards them and turned away. The Frenchman waited patiently, and the general knew he'd identified the female by now. He looked at her himself through his night glasses and saw from her rounded belly that she was in kid. The gazelles had now moved and he was afraid to breathe a word. He could hear them munching and snorting, thought he could even distinguish the particular snorting of the female. Above the snorting he was presently aware of something else. Motke was hunting for a handkerchief. He was hunting for two. He crammed his hat over his face as well. Only a very little sneeze came out of Motke, but what followed it came very fast. Three fine heads went up, one fractionally slower than the others, and turned towards them. The Schultz & Larsen fired at the first movement. One gazelle fell – pawing. The other two bounded away. As they did so, the Frenchman threw himself out of the hide with a terrible cry of 'Merde!' and almost bounded after them. General Mor took two exposures, one of the animals scrambling up the slope, and the other of Air Marshal de Joinville in the moment that he threw the Schultz & Larsen in a great arc over the wadi and commenced his dance. Then he went out and threw his arms around the weeping Frenchman.

'Jean-Claude, my warm thanks and congratulations. I knew you'd do as I asked. You have a splendid male.'

The two remaining gazelles ran for most of the day. They didn't stop at the canyon which had proved so disastrous a base. As dusk came on, utterly spent, they lay down to rest in boulder-strewn territory, and here a Bedu who didn't know much about ungulates shot one and carried it rapidly home to dinner. Though ignorant, this Bedu was well aware of the injunction against shooting gazelles and he made haste to dispose of his prey. He skinned the hide and burned the horns while his wife made a stew in one of the tasty ways noted by Smith. Because she was pleased with her husband, but also because he hadn't lately been so satisfactory in all departments, she let him have some especially animating parts all to himself.

It was a tremendous meal and they were still digesting it far into the night.

Far into the night, the sole survivor of Smith's gazelle still ran. It ran in a northerly direction, and it ran like hell.

## 2
# All About Hamud


Twenty-five kilometres from Damascus, in a south-easterly direction (though hardly anybody cared how far or in which direction) lay the village of Kufr Kassem. It was a gruesome little place of fifteen hundred souls, most of whom made a living by toiling, not very hard, on the land. The land didn't belong to them but to a lawyer in Homs, who was a member of his secret revolutionary regional council and a useful man in the liberation movement. The lawyer didn't bother them much in Kufr Kassem; but twice a year he went down to collect the rents and give them a talk on how things were doing in the liberation movement. They were conservatively minded in Kufr Kassem, but they respected the lawyer because despite being a liberator he was pretty sound on religion and tradition, and he promised that nothing very revolutionary would happen in Kufr Kassem while he was landlord.

There was a fair amount of tuberculosis in the village, and most of the people weren't well. This made them unattractive. But even by local standards Hamud was ugly. He only had one eye and not much roof to his mouth, which made him hard to understand, and also Kufr Kassem's best joke. If anything was hard to explain, people would say, 'Go and get Hamud to tell it,' or if a girl wanted a husband, it's Hamud she's after.'

He had a wife, though.

He was a day shepherd.

One evening in February 1957, while walking home behind the sheep and goats, Hamud passed his mother-in-law's house and thought he saw her wearing green. He knew it was only the light but all the same he said, 'There is no god but God.'

Further on a man passed him saying, 'God strengthen you.'

'Why?' Hamud said, but he added, 'According to His will,' as custom decreed.

In the pens where he turned the sheep and goats over to the old nightman, the man said to him, 'God strengthen you.'

'For what reason?' Hamud said. 'What's happened?' But the old man couldn't understand him and didn't answer.

Perplexed, Hamud went home, but found no one there. Then he realized what must have happened: the reason for his wife's absence and the condolences. His mother-in-law must indeed have worn green. They'd had a death in the family. Who could have died? He went into the kitchen and there saw his wife's box on the table. The key was in it!

He looked at it for a long time, trying to think what possible emergency could account for the key being in the box and not around his wife's neck. He had never seen it away from her neck. A death was surely no occasion to wear beads and bracelets, kohl or henna. He had no right to do so but he opened the box. Everything was still in it, neatly arranged.

He couldn't understand this at all and went out of the house to inquire into the matter. In the dusk he saw his mother approaching with a large bundle.

'God strengthen you,' she said.

'According to His will,' Hamud said.

'God blacken their faces.'

'Whose faces?' Hamud said.

'Come into the house, *halaila*. He sees all things. He protects us from the devil.'

'What?' Hamud said, dazed. His eyes were wide in the dusk. 'What is it? What's happened?'

He had a presentiment of what had happened, but his mother didn't answer and went into the house, and he followed her, terrified. His legs were shaking so much he couldn't stand. He sat on the divan. 'What?' he said.

His mother lit the lamp. 'Don't mourn her, *halaila*. She was a daughter of sin.'

'Who?'

'She was with Achmed. Her brother took her, her father took Achmed. They were warned. You weren't to know.'

'Achmed? But I knew, I knew,' Hamud said.

'God protect you, you weren't to know.'

'I did know. I knew. What does Achmed matter? She's mine.' He had given nine sheep, a dress, the bedding, and three hundred pounds for her. She was his father's brother's daughter. She had to have him. He had offered her a quittance if she didn't want him, on account of his ugliness and his speech. But she hadn't accepted it. She was sorry for him. What did Achmed matter in the face of all this?

'Which brother?' he said.

'Salim.'

'Salim.' He loved Salim. Salim was a brother to him.

'Salim's hands are clean. She was a daughter of sin. It was a duty.'

'What will I do?' Hamud said, moaning.

'You'll find another.'

'Who else will have me?'

'If no one, I will. Eat, *halaila*.' She'd brought him soup, lamb and rice, and halva: rare tidbits. 'Your life will be sweet enough, *halaila*.'

He ate everything she gave him, and got up and put his sheepskin on. 'Where are you going?' his mother said. He didn't answer because he didn't know. He couldn't sit in the house.

'Don't go to her parents. Not until a settlement is arranged. Don't go there.'

'No,' he said.

He went out. His sheepskin smelled so badly he could smell it himself. He took it off and flapped it in the night air, and as he did so a black bird flew out of a tree and circled his head before settling again. A single raven! His legs were shaking so much he could hardly walk. He found that he was walking to the coffee house. He rarely went there because nobody talked to him. Tonight the *sheshbesh* players pressed his arm in sympathy and said, 'God strengthen you.'

'According to His will,' Hamud said, and looked for Salim and saw him sitting in a corner, weeping. He went and sat with Salim.

'God strengthen you,' Salim said, sobbing, and showed his hands to show they were clean.

'According to His will,' Hamud said, and pressed the hands to show he knew they were clean.

'I did as my father said, Hamud. I loved her.'

'I know,' Hamud said, and wept himself.

'If I had another sister, you would have her.'

'I know.'

'Take coffee with me, *habibi*.'

Hamud took coffee with him.

'You'll have everything back,' Salim said. 'You'll have the nine sheep and their offspring. You'll have the bedding and her dress, also her box, complete, untouched. You'll lose nothing. As for the money, my father will give you the three hundred pounds or a donkey, whichever you want. There'll be perfect justice, Hamud.'

'Yes,' Hamud said.

'We'll go to my father and settle it tonight. Take more coffee, *habibi*.'

They had more coffee and went. In the lane Salim wept again and Hamud wept with him.

'God blacken his face, I'd sooner have taken him,' Salim said, 'but my father took him. It was a hard thing, Hamud.'

'Yes,' Hamud said.

'She didn't struggle, she didn't protest. It was quick and merciful, with the knife. I weep for her, Hamud.'

'I weep for her,' Hamud said.

'You are my brother,' Salim said, and weeping, put his arm around Hamud's neck.

'My brother,' Hamud said and, also weeping, cut Salim's throat.

The blade was so quick that for a moment Salim didn't feel it. But he looked in surprise at Hamud and opened his mouth. Hamud wrenched the head back to widen the slit, and cut again, deeply, working the knife there and back. Salim's *kefiyeh* and headrope fell off as Hamud did so, so that he looked strangely young and puzzled, as when they had been boys. 'God blacken your face,' Hamud said, '*habibi*.'

Again Salim tried to speak, but now he spoke like Hamud and fell to his knees, clutching his throat. Hamud pulled him to the side of the lane and straightened him out. The moon was in Salim's eyes as he looked, astonished, at Hamud, blood gushing from his throat and mouth. He tried to rise, so Hamud hit him on the head with a rock, and stood on him until he died. Then he went to see Salim's father.

He heard the old man cry out, 'Who is it?' when he knocked on the door.

'Hamud, *ya* Abu Salim.'

'Hamud.' The old man recognized the voice and opened. '*Ya* Hamud, God strengthen you,' he said, breaking into sobs as he held out his hands to show they were clean.

'According to His will,' Hamud said, and pressed the hands.

'You're bleeding. What have you done to yourself?'

'Butchering,' Hamud said.

'Come in and clean yourself. Take coffee.'

Hamud went in and cleaned himself and took coffee.

it's a tragedy, I weep for you,' Abu Salim said, wiping his eyes. if I had another daughter, you'd have her. Ya Hamud, you're a son to me.'

'You are my father,' Hamud said.

'But justice will be done. You won't lose. You'll have the nine sheep and their offspring. You'll have the bedding and her dress and box. You'll also have the three hundred pounds or the finest donkey,' Abu Salim said. He was a breeder of donkeys, it will be whichever you say. We'll go and see the donkeys.'

They finished their coffee and went to the stalls to see the donkeys, 'I'd give you Ayisha, the old man said, putting down the lamp. 'What donkeys you'd get from her! I'd even give her to you. What do you say, Hamud?'

'I'll have her,' Hamud said.

'Then it's a bargain,' the old man said, and embraced him.

'A bargain,' Hamud said, and cut his throat.

The old man was stocky and stronger than his son, and he gripped Hamud tight, struggling with him. Hamud stabbed him deeply in the back until he pulled away and then cut his throat again. On the ground the powerful old man still struggled, kicking the lamp over and starting a small fire in the straw, and even with blood pumping from his throat managed to cry out. So Hamud filled his mouth with earth and stamped on his face until he was quiet. 'God blacken your face, Abu Salim,' Hamud said, and led Ayisha out of her stall.

The donkey was frightened of the flames and shied, but Hamud pricked her with his knife and got her moving. She was a good donkey and moved fast. There was nothing for him at home now so he didn't go there. Jogging briskly on the donkey, he left Kufr Kassem, the village where he'd lived all his life, and with tears streaming down his face cursed it, for he saw now that he'd never had a proper life there, only the life of a dog. He left the village blindly, and took the track to El Harra and then Rafid and Sheikh 'Ajmal, trotting without thought through the streets. He didn't know what to do or where to go, for he knew he was already a dead man. But when he'd reached the hills beyond the valley and looked back and saw the flames burning in Kufr Kassem he was glad of what he'd done and cursed it again, praying that everyone in it, those who loved him and those who hated him, should be blotted out from this world and the world to come, for he was damned himself now and had no part in the future life.

2

The donkey stopped several times in the night, braying and groaning loudly for water. Hamud hadn't seen any water, but he let her rest for a while and crop on the new grass that the February rains had brought up. He kept going all night, skirting the familiar villages, Abu Sharkhi and Kufr Idris and Ghar, that he would never see again. He knew where he was going now. Once, a long time ago, his father had taken him to a Suleibba camp to see if one of the tinker women, a well-known witch, could get him to talk properly. The woman had taken Hamud alone to the head of a nearby ravine, and for several hours had called to the djinns and lost souls who lived there to help take the curse off him. It had been night-time, and all Hamud remembered of it was the answering howls of wolves and his own terror of the ravine. He wasn't frightened of it now. A damned soul would be at home in the ravine. Nobody would hunt for him in the ravine.

Made cunning by his decision, he decided to hide when it grew light, and he hid all day. He had to tie the donkey's mouth, for she was hungry and thirsty and she brayed. He found water after dark and they both drank. But he was starving and he couldn't eat what the donkey ate. So recognizing the lay of the land the next morning and realizing he was near the ravine, he bought a bag of salt from a man on the way and took the donkey into the hills again and killed it and ate part of it then, roasted on a fire, and salted the rest. It was a fine day of sun and wind and he waited for the donkey meat to dry. From the hills he could see a lot of soldiers about, on the main roads and on the hill tracks, and trucks with trailer guns. He thought at first they must be looking for him, but then, turning it over in his mind, realized this was not a matter for the army. He must be near a border, then. Which border? He hadn't gone as far south as Jordan. It must be Palestine and the barbarous Jews who had taken it over. The lawyer from Horns had explained how the Jews had massacred the people and stolen the land. Was it possible that they had taken over the ravine; that he would not now be able to get into the ravine?

He could see, below him but far away, the black dots of Beduin tents. The Bedluin moved about and knew everything. He was tempted to go and ask them. But they might also know about him. He lay and worried about it for several hours, watching the soldiers and the trucks. He'd planned to climb down into the ravine by day, but he saw now he'd better scout the position under cover of darkness. The donkey meat was not properly dried, but he cut it into strips and rubbed more salt in and bundled it up, and when dark came got moving.

He walked for a long time, taking his directions from the pinpoints of light from the Beduin camp, until the moon came up. But it was already declining when the remembered rocks around the ravine came into sight. He'd steeled himself, with the thought that he was already a dead man, against any terror he might feel at going down into the ravine. But when he came to it he didn't feel any, merely strange and momentous at the thought of leaving life and descending into the world of the djinns and souls. He couldn't see whether the Jews had taken it over or not. The head of the ravine was totally deserted on this side, and he couldn't see across to the other; there was merely a rim of tumbled rock, chalky white in the last of the moon, and below it the enormous black chasm of the ravine.

Hamud drew a breath and began to climb down. He wondered if the souls and djinns expected him, if they were even now aware of him, a moonlit figure clambering down from the world above into their world. He couldn't visualize their world. He knew the souls and djinns were invisible and he wondered at what point he would become invisible too; or whether it might be that the souls were invisible only to those above and not to each other. He wondered also what his soul was like and when it would become known to him. He wondered if his soul could speak and if so what language. He knew there were souls here from all time, souls from the time of Abraham, and he had a sensation of returning to some old state, the recollection of which would come over him more and more as he descended. He felt relief now that the sickness of life was behind him, but also disappointment and regret for what it had been. In some way as he sprang into the world he had become damaged, so that he couldn't speak, and so his one life had been the beggarly one of a dog – without achievement, without merit, not deserving of reward. In a stoical arid resigned way he'd always known such a mean identity could never aspire to Paradise. What would he do in Paradise, how entertain his assigned *houris* in the garden of delights? Some other soul, some handsome talking soul like Achmed, would inevitably attract his *houris*, and the whole familiar pain would begin again. Better to have done with it, to shed the hurt of identity and return to the primal limbo. If he had damned himself, the Compassionate, the Merciful would surely not leave him damned forever.

He clambered down out of the moonlight, still trailing his failed and painful identity, and waited for the moment when it would slough off and pass out of recollection as his soul emerged once more. He stepped carefully in the blackness, every part of him tingling and alert for the first contact with souls, and between one step and the next heard a small sound, and stopped, and presently heard it again, and realized it was only a wolf. A wolf had scented him – had more likely scented his sheepskin or the bundle of donkey meat. He took his knife out and continued. But the wolf, if it was a wolf, must have sighted him and realized the presence of a human, for it didn't approach.

He climbed steadily down for a long time, until the blackness went and a grey dawn began to seep, and he reached what he thought was the floor, but which turned out to be a shelf of rock, exceptionally wide, fifteen metres at least. Rain had brought soil down, and trees and bushes grew quite luxuriantly – almost screening the slit in the sky above, as he found, looking up, when at last he came down from the shelf and found the true bottom, ten metres or so below it.

Daylight was now coming strongly from above, and Hamud looked with weary disappointment about him. He was stunned with fatigue. He didn't seem to have slept for a long time. He couldn't remember when he had last slept or the sequence of crazy incidents in between. He wondered if this forgetfulness was the first sign of identity being shed, and he thought he'd better sleep and that the whole thing might happen during sleep. He couldn't sleep on the floor of the ravine, for water was running there, so he looked for somewhere dry. He'd passed the cave without seeing it when a sound drew him back, knife in hand.

Stupid with fatigue, he forgot to stand to one side and instead blocked the mouth as the animal came bolting out, butting him in the middle and tumbling him over. He hung on to its horns. He thought it was a goat, and then saw it wasn't a goat. He didn't know what it was. It looked like a gazelle, but not like any gazelle he had ever seen before. But a gazelle was meat, so he gripped his knife more firmly, and then saw that the gazelle was in kid. Why should he take one gazelle when he might have two?

# 3
# All About the Kibbutz

Amos finished the row of Parson Browns and got down off the platform and moved the tractor over to the Golden Wonders. He pruned his way down the Golden Wonders, worrying about the filtration plant in the pool. He knew he'd been wrong to back the Armstrong. A few lousy pounds more and they could have had the Weston-Firbank: replaceable flat filters, metered chlorination. Just a few lousy pounds. He wondered what ought to be done about it now.

He wondered all down the first row of Golden Wonders and stopped and took his dark glasses off and wiped his eyes and his face with his hat. Then he wiped his neck and his red beard and wrung the hat out and put it back on his head. It was hot in the orchard. Even the breeze was hot. He could feel sweat trickling under his shorts. How many of them would bother to shower off the sweat before going into the pool, a day like this? They would just go into the pool. It needed a big trouble-free workhorse like the Weston-Firbank to cope with all that sweat. There were over two million litres of water to shift around there: a full-size Olympic job. The children were in and out of it all day, little babies were in and out of it, old people. The whole kibbutz got value out of that pool. To try and economize by a few lousy pounds in a matter of hygiene! It wasn't even the only economy. There was the tiling, the pump, the algaecide distributor. What did they know of the problems of running a big pool? They just enjoyed it and thought it ran itself. Amos put his glasses on and shook his head, and was still shaking it when Rina called over from the winesaps. She was asking the time. The time. He looked at his watch and saw it was a quarter to twelve. He came down fast off the platform. Worrying about the pool he'd nearly missed lunch again.

It was so late he took the tractor right down to the dining hall and parked it outside and they went in. He saw his wife, Pnina, and waved to her, but there was no room at her table so he sat elsewhere and had his lunch silently, still trying to figure it out. The food was stodgy, too much starch. That would have to change when they got down to training. High-protein stuff would be needed then. He knew it was early to worry, but he worried. Amos was thirty and very wiry, but a fantastic swimmer.

Pnina came over when she'd finished her lunch, and stroked his hair. He'd been worrying about it in bed. 'Leave a little for somebody else to worry over,' she said.

Amos nodded ironically. There'd be something for them to worry over, for Chrissake, when the lousy Armstrong broke down. 'Go and have a rest,' he said.

'Today I can't. I want to be sure you have one.'

'I'll have one,' Amos said.

He finished his lunch and went to the apartment. He couldn't manage to rest. He got up and took the file out and went over the papers again. He was still going over them when he heard the tractor. He looked at his watch. Rina had brought the tractor.

'Listen,' she said angrily when he went out, 'what the hell is the matter with you? Give me the watch if you're going to stay in a trance.'

'What's the matter, your time's so valuable?' Amos said, but he gave her the watch.

They put in another hour and a half with the apples and knocked off sharp at half past two. Rina gave him the watch and they rode down to the kibbutz without speaking. He went to the apartment and took a shower and walked out of it into the room. Pnina was already asleep in the room, with her mouth open. He didn't disturb her. He lay down still wet on his own bed and drew a sheet over him. He managed to drift off.

Pnina wasn't there when he woke up. He knew where she'd be, so he showered again and put on a clean shirt and shorts and went there. Half a dozen children were on the baby-house lawn. Jonathan saw him from a long way off and came running on fat legs. Amos picked him up and bit his bottom. '*Nu*,' he said, 'how is it?'

'Swim,' Jonathan said.

Amos's heart glowed. It was one of the first words he'd taught him. He supported Jonathan under the chest and thighs and spun him around. The child did a perfect breast stroke: perfect.

He played with him for half an hour, but he was worried, so he left him to Pnina and took a stroll to the pool.

The little bastards were playing soccer on it again. He'd told them a hundred times. There were plenty of places for them to play. They'd also moved the boundary stones to make goalposts. He chased them off and replaced the boundary stones and stepped back and had a good look at it. He'd shifted the loose stuff himself and what was visible now was smooth table rock, gleaming dully. Looking at it, Amos felt his heart sinking again.

2

When the fifty of them had got off the trucks, around about 1949, and had a look at the place, all their hearts had sunk. They'd seen it before, of course. They'd made several trips in the course of the year. But they'd thought it would look a bit better when they actually got there. If anything, it looked a bit worse. The land was all bare there. Gigantic flanks of the bare, seared stuff sat doomily under the sky, pitted with rock.

A work party of ten had gone up the previous week to lay out the camp, and as the trucks creaked to a halt they came running and shouting. The work party had levelled a patch of ground in the week and had pitched fifteen tents on it, plus a latrine tent and a couple of prefabs for stores and a dining hall. Everybody showed a lot of enthusiasm for the lines of tents and the prefabs, and while they pointed out the rue de la Paix and Piccadilly and Dizengoff Street to each other, the Jewish Agency people and the Ministry of Agriculture people and various other kinds of people who'd come along for the ride nodded and smiled and looked thoughtfully around at the view. There was plenty of view. The view extended a good way into Syria, and behind them into Israel, and to the west into Lebanon. There was not much in the way of the view. A patch of dusty olives and an abandoned Arab village was folded into one hill, and another Arab village, not abandoned, for woodsmoke was coming out of it, was folded into another. Across a valley was a third village, but that was in Syria. All the villages grew almost imperceptibly out of the decayed flanks of the hills, themselves looking like so many patches of mange.

When the enthusiasm was over, the group unloaded the trucks. They took down food and gumboots and clothing, and sacks of seed and fertilizer and tools. They also unloaded books and a gramophone and a spare receiver for the brand-new telephone line. In case anything happened to the telephone line, they'd brought along ten rifles and a case of hand grenades as well. There were thirty-six boys and twenty-four girls in the group, aged from eighteen to twenty-two, and they'd trained together for a year.

(Trained, sweated, planned together; some had made love together.)

When the Ministry and the Agency people had gone they started the generator and lit the place up and built a campfire with material the work party had laboriously gathered. They became very high-spirited around the campfire. They ate and sang songs in the tiny patch of light in the enormous area of darkness, and those who'd made love felt a rather urgent need to make it again. There were difficulties in the way of making love. It was impossible to make it in the tents and unseemly in the public prefabs. Out in the bare rocky darkness it was possible but painful to make love. But for about the next year they were too tired, anyway.

They were so tired they never managed to sleep out the tiredness, and they were tired again when they woke up. They awoke at three, and by half past were out clearing rock. They elected an agricultural committee and a work committee and several other committees, and they knew from the roster in the evening which task they'd be engaged on next day. Whatever the task was, they knew it only meant shifting rock: it was simply a question of where.

A couple of thousand years before, all this bare rotted land had been fertile with farm and forest. The hills had been plump with villages, the land to the south famous with towns. There'd been an obsessive love of and pride in the place then. Since then nobody'd had love or pride in it. A succession of spoilers had spoiled it; centuries of the listless had taken what was left. God sent the olive and they shook it from the tree. God sent the grass and their sheep ate it. The sheep ate the grass, and the goats ate the trees, and the rain leached the soil so that by 1949 there was just the fine view, together with plenty of rock.

The group knew all this. They were stuffed to the eyeballs with it. They'd dreamed the Paradise they would re-create here, a detailed fantasy of milk and honey and fine rich vine. The Settlement Department of the Jewish Agency in conjunction with experts of the Ministry of Agriculture had tempered this fantasy with science. The 5,000 *dunams*, 1,250 acres, were basically suitable for a mixed sheep and wheat economy. The sheep could graze among the table rock and the wheat could be dry-farmed on most of the rest. Under irrigation the upper land was capable of producing deciduous fruits, and the lower ground, because of a change in soil chemistry and a temperature differential of several degrees, was marginally suitable for acid citrus, lemon or grapefruit; a small perennial spring here allowed easy irrigation. The presence of the spring and a number of regular depressions in adjacent ground also suggested the establishment of fishponds.

But all these fine things were for the future, the Agency said, and meanwhile the group ought to get on with the sheep and the wheat. While they were at it, they could pick up a little ready money with cash crops. Everything could start to happen just as soon as the land was cleared. So the group started clearing it.

They cleared first the sheltered lower area where the citrus was due to go, but where the cash crops were going first. They cleared enough to get a flatcar in, and then they piled rock on the flatcar and manhandled it out. They cleared fifty *dunams* in this way, with pick, crowbar, and flatcar, levering, straining, stumbling. Then they fertilized, ploughed, and sowed where they'd cleared, and moved on to another area. They moved to the area where the winter wheat would go. Several more thousand tons of rock were in this area.

They cleared rock from early in the morning until late in the afternoon, and fell into the dining prefab in such a clapped-out condition that they could hardly raise their voting arms. They managed, though. They'd always managed to give their votes plenty of exercise. They drew up agendas, conducted debates, passed resolutions. They debated future crops, and future children, and their future education; the future kibbutz, its buildings, institutions, and amenities; and they elected numerous further committees to deal with all this. They'd always debated quite passionately among themselves. They'd debated the name of the place, to begin with. A majority had favoured Beit Ha-Emek, the House in the Valley, but then it turned out that another kibbutz had registered the name a few months previously. So they settled in the end for Kibbutz Gei-Harim, mainly because it sounded good in Hebrew, but also because its meaning, the Kibbutz of the Ravine, was appropriate. A deep ravine lay on the borders of their land. It separated their land from Syria.

3

They didn't know what to do about the olives. The shagged-out though picturesque old trees stood on a part of the land destined for the deciduous fruits. The olives had belonged to the inhabitants of the abandoned Arab village – at least had been picked by them. In fact they'd belonged to a man in Beirut, who had also owned much of the surrounding land. The land had been bought by the Jewish National Fund on the understanding that part of the inflated price would go towards compensating the villagers for the loss of the olives. The man said he'd do this, but then he hadn't. This desolated the villagers, and the Fund had revised its plans for the land and pointed out to the villagers that although their former landlord had welshed on his bargain, their traditional practices would be contractually guaranteed by the new owners. They could continue to pick the olives and also to graze their sheep where they'd always grazed them before. In addition they would no longer have to pay rent or set aside a proportion of produce from their allotments.

The villagers had successfully cheated the man in Beirut for years, and this was no great financial prize. Still, they'd never been offered a contract before. Dazzled by it, they sent their *mukhtar* to Acre to consult the local Sha'aria court. The Sha'aria advised the *mukhtar* that he had got quite a good deal, but on the way back he thought of an even better one. It would be better, he told the new owners, if the rights offered were those of ownership rather than usage, and better still if they were offered to him rather than to the village council: he could then rent out the land himself, and on a much-improved rental scale, in consideration of which he would be able to make a handsome annual present to the Fund, which under the terms of the offered contract would get nothing.

This proposal was declined by the Fund, and the original contract was drawn up and signed by both parties. A few months later a new settlement was started on the far side of the olives, and the Arab villagers burned it down. Much incensed, the Fund asked for a meeting with the village council and inquired why they'd done it. The *mukhtar* sadly shook his head and said he'd expected something of the kind. The villagers were disturbed at being made to sign away their natural rights in exchange only for user rights, and were nervous when they saw new settlers coming to usurp them.

The Fund said that nobody was being usurped; the contract had been offered to guarantee against this. They also pointed out that the villagers had previously had no rights at all. The only rights they'd ever had were those freely offered in the contract. The *mukhtar* agreed that the situation might appear that way to shrewd legal brains, but he said the people in his village had simple brains which looked at things in a simple way. The answer was probably to give him the rights and then all the brains would know where they were and would have no cause to be nervous.

The Fund again declined this proposition and warned that a contract was only valid if respected by both sides; but the whole discussion was conducted with such amiability and reasonableness that they felt they could safely recommend the re-establishment of the settlement. Some time later the settlement was establishd again, and shortly afterwards the Arab villagers burned it down again. To underline their nervousness they also murdered two of the settlers.

By this time similar nervousness was being exhibited all around and the 1948 war broke out. Brains from several surrounding states discovered they also had natural rights in Palestine. Syria discovered that the place was not so much a state as a province of Syria, and sent their General Kawkji down to collect. Kawkji came down like a wolf on the fold, his cohorts including tanks, artillery, and several motorized brigades. He was joined by, among others, the simple villagers who'd burned the two settlements, who now looked forward to burning several more. The settlers, however, though lacking tanks, artillery, and motorized battalions, had provided themselves with gasoline bombs, rifles, and bayonets, and dug in to meet Kawkji, halting his advance and counter-attacking with such brio that his battered force turned around and took off, setting up some new kind of local record not to be equalled for several years. The simple villagers, much astonished by the strange way things had turned out, also took off, in the same general direction, not stopping at their village or at the olives that they had been licensed to pick.

These were the olives that produced the headache a year or two later.

They were horrible little olives, bitter and dry, no proper cultivation having been carried out for generations, possibly centuries. The kibbutz took a sounding from the

Ministry and were told that even if brought to full yield the olives wouldn't work in a kibbutz economy. Olives worked in a peasant economy. Though undemanding in terms of water and fertilizers, the small fruit took myriads of hands to thin and pick. What the peasants got for the resultant oil and the few edible fruits would keep them in the full standards to which they were accustomed, but it wouldn't keep the kibbutzniks, not if they wanted schools, libraries, concert halls, and the like. What this rural intelligentsia had to do was to get the land going under low-labour mechanized crops or high-labour high-yielding ones, such as the deciduous fruits advised, and forget the picturesque olives.

The group had a debate about it and thought the Ministry was probably right, but they still didn't like to dig up the shagged-out olives. While they were thinking about it a man came down from the other Arab village and asked if they wanted anyone to look after olives. He said he knew those fine old trees like the back of his hand. He conceded they'd gone off a bit of late, but said all that was needed to get the loads of lovely fruit that had been such a feature of the area in former years was the touch of a friendly expert. He could also promise to use his influence with a few of his relations who wouldn't be above helping out at harvest time.

The kibbutzniks went into immediate conference about this. Though opposed in principle to allowing anyone else to work their land, they saw in the offer a way out of the dilemma. They could keep the old trees, which would still be doing a useful job in the way of cementing relations. They weren't, after all, money-grubbing farmers, but a community. This way they could start having communal relations. They came out of conference to tell the Arab it would be perfectly all right for him and his relations to pick the trees, and they could keep half the crop for themselves. The old fellow thanked them kindly but said he hadn't quite meant that. The fruit, though lovely, wasn't needed in his village, which boasted several fine old trees of its own. It was a matter of money really, he said.

The kibbutzniks had a graver, yet more urgent debate. The *hiring* of labour, the exploitation of fellow workers on a cash basis, was an offence against their principles of mind-reeling proportions. Also they didn't have any cash, the cash crops as yet not having produced any. The old Arab plainly needed some, though, and the wickedness of the world was not to be changed in a day. So they told him all right and settled the deal, and after he'd gone wondered what they'd do with the loads of olives, and also where they'd get the money.

They didn't have any money. The Jewish Agency was paying them for clearing the land, but that went immediately for food and essential supplies, and would shortly be needed for rent. They'd leased the place on the standard Agency terms, at a rental of two per cent of their income (a notional income based on the number of workers). The Agency would advance money for all buildings, stock, irrigation, and machinery that had been approved in the plan, and when everything was installed the group would start paying it back, over thirty years at interest of three and a half per cent.

This low rate of interest applied only to the approved plans. The group had been advised not to go in for others. Further approved plans would be considered for further Agency loans, but 'unapproved' ones would take them to banks or even 'finance houses' at short terms and frightening rates of interest. A kibbutz that did this was a kibbutz in trouble: to pay off the old it would have to take out new loans, hopelessly encumbering itself for ever. The Agency said that what the group had to do was keep away from all the other kinds of plan and just make themselves expert at this one.

The group went into it in a lot of detail, but they were

bored with the finance and they agreed with the Agency. They didn't think they ought to go in for anything unapproved. They thought that what they ought to do was get expert at making the wilderness bloom.

So they put in a hundred *dunams* of citrus and a hundred of apple, and increased the wheat acreage, and got the sheep grazing. They had a go at the fishponds and they tended the cash crops. They also commenced building the kibbutz. Quantities of cement began to pour in, and they got an architect and a master builder, and under their direction laid the foundations for the one and a half-room apartments and the dining hall and the library; and when a couple of the girls became anxious, for the baby house as well. In this period, the walks and the gardens were laid out, and the pines, pistachios, and Judas trees went in (also the fine shrubs, myrtle and hibiscus and virgin's bower).

The Arab laboured spasmodically in the olive grove throughout this. He brought in loads of fruit, but it wasn't very lovely. They still didn't know what to do with the fruit, but they kept on paying him. The name of this Arab was Abdul.

Money had been so short when they moved in that they hadn't got a swimming pool in the approved plans. The Agency said it was best to wait until the situation eased. They were so eager to get the wilderness blooming that they didn't fight about it. But whenever they asked for a pool afterwards they heard the situation was about the same.

By 1957, the situation had still not changed, but they noticed that a lot of other kibbutzim had got pools, having fought for them in their approved plans.

This made the group edgy.

They were edgy, anyway, but this made them even edgier. They'd become aware of some paradoxical problems. Some of the problems were so paradoxical they didn't even know how to explain them.

They knew they'd worked very hard and had become expert. They were expert at practically everything. Prize apples grew in their deciduous orchards and mammoth grapefruit in the citrus. The wheat fields bulged with their produce, and so did the baby house, the kindergarten, and the schoolhouse. Over the eight years, several of the girls had left to marry into other kibbutzim, but more had arrived to marry into this one, so that forty-five children now created varying degrees of uproar about the place. With the addition of new members and elderly parents the population had grown to 150.

With all this going on, they were poorer.

They were much poorer than when they'd started. They owed more money.

There were reasons. There'd been two years of natural disaster. In one of them floods had drowned the wheat and carried off the carp from the fishponds, and in the other frost had destroyed the fruit. In those years they'd eaten their own cash crops and taken out new loans. But there were other reasons. There was the increase in the population. The population had multiplied two and a half times, but only half of it earned any money. The children didn't earn any, and neither did their nurses or teachers. None of the people who ran the increased services of the kibbutz could be said to earn any. The old people couldn't be said to earn very much. But they all had to be fed and clothed and looked after.

The group saw that while eight years of hard work had made the area younger and richer, it had paradoxically made them older and poorer. There seemed to be something wrong with this. They appreciated the fact that they were making a fine place for their children, and were not averse to the general proposition. But they thought they ought to get something, too. In particular, they thought they ought to get a swimming pool.

The one who thought this most was Amos. Amos had been chairman of the swimming pool committee for eight years now. He had practically every piece of literature on swimming pools. He had fourteen estimates for swimming pools. Not actually having a swimming pool humiliated and frustrated him, and by 1957 it brought him to a decision.

He decided that they had to get the materials for a swimming pool, and that if they couldn't it would be best to scrap the committee because they would never have a swimming pool. He decided this after looking over the last of his estimates. He saw that the price of materials in it was six times that of the first. In the same period, their own income had gone up three times. He saw that it would go on like this.

Once Amos had made the decision he felt liberated. He thought that if the vote went against him he would drop swimming pools. He would take up something else. Or if it seemed to him, on reflection, wasteful or even socially negligent to keep so much swimming pool talent on a kibbutz that would never have a swimming pool, he might join another. Either way, daydreams would be over.

He outlined a resolution, but before presenting it, prepared a specification of the materials. He sweated over it for a month, with all his swimmmg pool catalogues around him. It was a fantastic specification, down to the last nut and bolt. He put together stunning and economical combinations that would make the kibbutz a byword for functional elegance, if they could only rise to it. He had to throw out some good things. He had to settle for things he wouldn't normally have considered. Economy had to be the watchword. But he'd got it to rock bottom now.

# 4

Amos walked home from the pool, and found Pnina at home. She gave him a glass of coffee.

'Is it all clear in your mind?'

'It will never be dearer.'

'Just keep calm. Don't get excited.'

'Why should I get excited?'

'Everybody knows you get excited. Try and make it sound rational.'

'What do you mean make it rational? It is rational. You think it's more rational to have a swimming pool committee for eight years without any prospect of a swimming pool?'

'All right. Don't get excited.'

Amos opened his mouth, and shut it again. Eight years had taught him patience. He took his coffee and the list over to the divan. He crossed out 'one Armstrong filtration unit' and carefully wrote in over the top 'one Weston-Firbank fully automatic filtration unit with chlorine metre.' For a few lousy pounds they'd have hygiene in that pool.

Meetings were held in the dining hall, and there was a full house for this one. Amos was quite relaxed. He sat with the members of the swimming pool committee at a table at one end, and when everyone was in, he got up and told them all about the swimming pool. He told them how they were never going to have one if the situation stayed as it was. He told them how they could change the situation. He said they didn't have to worry about getting the pool built. What they had to worry about was getting the materials for the pool. He read out the list of materials, and said they had to get them now.

'How?' someone said.

'Take a loan.'

'Who'd give a loan for a swimming pool?'

'Don't take a loan for a swimming pool. Take a loan for something else and use it for the swimming pooL'

'That's fraud!'

'Shmaud!' Amos said. 'We'd pay the money back. Who cares how we use it?'

'They care. You only get loans for productivity.'

'For *productivity*? Amos said. Some of his relaxation went. 'What do you think I'm talking about? What do you think you're going to get out of that pool? You're going to get health out of it. You're going to get *extra* productivity. A good, fully filtered fifty-metre pool is going to give you not only health and productivity but the most beautiful feeling of well-being. With that feeling,' Amos said, 'you can move mountains.' He pointed to one out the window, Mount Hermon. 'Mountains! And without it, you know what you're going to get? You're going to get unhealthy and *un*productive, and with every single stinking summer that passes, older and slower and duller and finally,' Amos concluded, 'dead.'

He refused to get excited, though, so he sat down and looked over his list. He heard the larger items on the list called into question. He heard the suggestion that in view of all the difficulties, they should scrap earlier plans and start thinking of a smaller pool. He heard the suggestion that they should think of a canvas pool. He still didn't get excited. He simply got up and resigned from the committee.

His resignation wasn't accepted and the meeting passed to a discussion of economies. He'd heard it all before. There were no new economies that could be practised on the kibbutz. They discussed the old ones again, though. They discussed firing the Arab, and decided they couldn't. Then they discussed the lemons. The lemons came up about every three months. They were losing money on the lemons. A man called Yoel looked after them. Though taking large crops from his grapefruit, he'd got nowhere with lemons. He'd budded, hand-pollinated, intoned over them, without improvement. Anyone else would have made a sensible switch to something else. But Yoel was not sensible about lemons. He was slightly hysterical about them. He warned that if the lemons went he would have to go too, and in emotional terms depicted the future that awaited the successful lemon grower. He said nobody had any conception of the quantities that would be needed by, for instance, the lemon squash interests for the huge immigration of the future. What couldn't be sold as fine kitchen fruit would be snatched up by these interests. Anything they gave the lemons now, he said, the lemons would give back a thousand fold, and he recited Psalm 126: 'They that sow in tears shall reap in joy.'

The meeting listened to Psalm 126 and passed a moody interim resolution allowing Yoel to continue with his lemons, but it didn't help with the swimming pool. So they moved finally to a new resolution, after hearing some close argument.

This was that while it would be fraudulent to misapply the proceeds of a loan, it would not be fraudulent to apply for a loan for some fast-earning scheme the proceeds of which would be immediately earmarked for the swimming pool. If this meant taking out another loan in order to repay the first, it was a burden the kibbutz should bear in view of Amos's expert forecast with regard to the long-term benefits to health and productivity.

Amos was quite pleased about this, and all he had to think of was a fast-earning scheme.

The following week he came up with cotton.


5


There was nothing new about cotton. A few of the more established kibbutzim had been growing it experimentally for two or three years. Enthusiasts at Gei-Harim had even argued for growing it themselves. The difference was that pool-maddened Amos now argued it. He argued in fantastic and up-to-the-minute detail. He said it was true cotton needed a big investment, but it drew a big return. A *dunam* of cotton produced 400 kilos, for which the Cotton Board paid 90 *agorot* a kilo. This gave a return of 360 Israeli pounds a *dunam* or 36,000 pounds per hundred *dunams* – a better return than any industrial crop they could think of.

'We've heard it. Who's got the labour for hand-picking cotton?'

'Don't hand-pick it.'

'What?'

'Machine-pick it.'

'A machine picker costs a fortune.'

'Thirty-five thousand pounds,' Amos said.

'Madman!'

'For a single-row picker. Sixty thousand pounds for the double. We're going to need the double.'

'Get his wife!'

'Lock him up!'

'Which makes economic sense with anything over five hundred *dunams*. We'll need six hundred or even seven hundred to get the maximum benefit. Other costs go up hardly at all –'

'Give him a sedative!'

'Give him a good hiding!'

'Where are you going to get six hundred *dunams*? There aren't even fifty to spare!'

'Under lemons,' Amos said, consulting his notes, 'which are losing us money, we have two hundred and fifty *dunams*. Of the least productive grapefruit, fifty *dunams*. Plus another three, four hundred, whatever we want on the farther ground towards the ravine.'

'Towards the ravine is table rock! It's immovable.'

'Which we blast and bulldoze. I've got the figures. With regard to cost –'

Yoel, moodily reading a report in Italian of the Sicilian Lemon Growers' Association, was not immediately aware of the enormity of what was being suggested. When it struck him, he rose to make a brief personal statement which incorporated his resignation. Half an hour later he retracted it when the meeting, stunned and almost hypnotized by the flow of figures coming out of Amos, moved itself towards a resolution. The resolution was in two parts. The first said that no ground at present under cultivation would be affected by Amos's scheme; and the second that the scheme should be placed before the Jewish Agency for an opinion.

Amos placed it before the Agency himself. The Agency said that the scheme was basically sound though overambitious. But cotton was a crop that should be encouraged in Israel, and though, because of a large penniless immigration recently arrived from North Africa, it couldn't make funds available itself, it was passing on the scheme to the State Agricultural Bank with a recommendation for approval.

Amos and a deputation from the kibbutz attended a meeting at the State Bank. The bank also found the scheme basically sound. But it said a careful study of the kibbutz's balance sheets showed it to be heavily in debt. The heavy expenditure on the double-row cotton picker could not therefore be justified, and the bank recommended the kibbutz, if it could not manage to hand-pick the cotton itself, to hire labour – in particular the newly arrived North African labour: the bank had a duty to make loans that would promote agricultural employment.

The kibbutz replied that its principles would not allow it to hire labour; and not only its own principles, but the principles of the movement to which it belonged.

The bank said it was sorry about the kibbutz's principles, and also the kibbutz movement's principles, but it couldn't provide funds for a double-row cotton picker. The most it could promise was to meet that part of Amos's scheme that didn't include the cotton picker. It would meet it to the extent of eighty per cent. It would advance the money for ten years at interest of nine per cent.

Amos commenced running. He ran tirelessly. He ran back to the Jewish Agency and managed to wheedle the extra twenty per cent out of them, over eight years at three and a half per cent. He ran to every bank in Jerusalem and Tel-Aviv and Haifa. He found some that would advance most of the cost of a single-row picker, and some that would advance up to seventy per cent of a double-row picker. He finally found one that would advance all the cost – at eighteen per cent, over four years, with a lien on the cotton picker.

The kibbutz held a rather awesome general meeting to discuss these frightening arrangements. They were dazed by the nine per cents and the three and a half per cents and the eighteen per cents, and by the varying terms of repayment. They were also stunned by the near impossibility of ever being able to repay.

Amos talked. He said the hard years without a swimming pool had robbed them of mental and physical energy. He said of course they'd be able to repay. Hard-headed organizations like the Agency and the banks wouldn't advance money if they didn't expect to get it back. For a few years, certainly, they'd have to work harder. They'd have to pledge themselves to give an extra hour's work a day. But the work would be worth it. They'd have the swimming pool to show for it. They'd have the enormous income every year from the cotton.

'So what if it fails?'

'Why should it fail?'

Why had the wheat and the fish failed one year, and the fruit another? They were still paying for these failures, which would be as nothing compared to a failure with the cotton. Behind a failure with the cotton would still loom the enormous debt. The debt would flatten them. It would flatten their children.

'All right,' Amos said. 'So there are risks. Where do you get without taking risks? With proper mental health, with real bodily vigour, a person can *take* risks. Aren't there risks with fruit? At least this is a crop that doesn't go bad. It's an ideal crop. We take the risk and put in the work, and the kibbutz, the children, get the future benefit. But meanwhile we also get something. We get a swimming pool.'

In a hushed way the meeting gave its approval to the scheme, with the proviso that all the land must be found in the area by the ravine and not at the expense of the citrus. Amos cautioned that this proviso would mean extra costs. Irrigation pipes would have to be expanded. Vast quantities of rock would have to be blasted and bulldozed into the ravine. But the costs were already so great that nobody could be bothered about the extra ones. They went off to bed with the momentous feeling that something historic had been entered into. One bad year now, and two generations would pay for it.

This was the kind of thing that had been going on at Kibbutz Gei-Harim up to about 1958. On a dull drizzly morning a few months later, a number of thunderous blasts went off in the area beyond the citrus groves, and after they'd died down, three hired bulldozers, waiting in the groves, trundled forward. Amos, in the first, lost no time. Large quantities of shattered rock lay between him. and the ultimate fully filtered job. He got the business end. of the bulldozer down to it and made rapidly in the direction of the ravine.

# 4
# All About the Ravine

Hamud heard the thunder in his sleep and he stirred pleasantly and thought, '*Now* some rain will come down,' and congratulated himself on having moved his sleeping quarters. A few weeks before his sleeping quarters had been all but carried away. He'd wakened to find himself drowning. The gazelles had been drowning too. They were hobbled, of course, and in his panic he hadn't been able to find the knife to cut them loose. He had managed to untie the mother gazelle and one of the kids, but the other had been washed away. He'd gone out immediately into the torrent and found the kid wedged (by the grace of God) in a cleft of rock at the far end of the ravine, with only a leg broken. Hamud had set the leg. Afterwards he had moved his sleeping quarters.

He turned over under the sheepskin and waited for the rain to come down. No rain came down. Something else started coming down. Hamud got up and poked his head out. He was half asleep and not thinking too fast, but fast enough to get his head back in again. An enormous boulder hurtled past, missing it by a hairsbreadth. Hamud sat back on his haunches, quivering, and his first thought was that the djinns had discovered him, and his second that the Jews had discovered him. He discounted both ideas immediately and sat quietly cerebrating while the boulders exploded all about. Djinns didn't throw stones down – how could they? – but up. Everybody knew that.

Similarly, if the Jews had found him they wouldn't wait until he was out of sight to throw stones. They'd come down and kill him. He knew about Jews. He'd been up and had a look at them during the summer. He'd seen one shouting at a lemon tree and kicking it. The man had plainly been mad or bewitched, probably both. There'd been a satanic look on his face as he'd kicked the lemon tree.

He didn't know what other explanation there could be for the bombardment. It wasn't a landslide. Someone was up there throwing the stuff. It was coming down in single large lumps. It was coming down over a wide area. Hamud remembered the look on the face of the man who'd kicked the lemon tree, and he thought it might be some mass act of rage. He thought the only thing to do was to wait for the fit to pass.

The fit took a long time. It stopped about noon and started again about two. It finally knocked off in the late afternoon.

Hamud stayed where he was for a while in case the artful swine were watching for signs of life. But when the light began to go he went out and had a look. He left the gazelles hobbled.

Hamud quite liked what he found. A nice lot of stones had come down, of excellent shape and size. There'd been a surprising shortage of really nice stones in the ravine. Most of the stuff was debris, much too small. The larger stuff was too large, very complicated and tiring to shift. He hadn't liked to shift too much in case he gave himself a rupture. But the work had to be done, of course. A very great deal of work had to be done. The whole thing was going to take years, and would need vast quantities of rock.

Hamud examined the rock that had come down to him, and he saw right away that it was exactly what was required: excellent stuff in a wide range of grades and sizes. There would be no difficulty whatever, for instance, in laying proper stepping stones. The ones he'd laid had been of very inferior material and already most of them had washed away. He had to cross the ravine quite often and there was water in it. He didn't like getting his feet in the water, quite apart from the danger to the gazelles.

While he was at it, and with a careful look upwards, Hamud crossed the ravine and examined his traps at the other side. He collected a couple of conies and a bit of fodder for the gazelles and returned, whistling softly in the dark. The gazelles sensed him from a long way off and he heard their affectionate whinnies. They hadn't been out all day. He had another upward look and decided to keep the fodder and let them out. The fodder might be needed for tomorrow or some other day when the Jews had a fit. A proper store for fodder was another of the things that had to be seen to. A sudden burst of happiness exploded inside Hamud, almost lifting him off the stepping stones. He wanted to sing and skip as he thought of the enormous number of things that still had to be seen to. But he continued on home carefully, occasionally having to lower himself from the stones into the water.

The gazelles nuzzled him as he untied them, and he nuzzled them back and adjusted their ropes so that they were only half hobbled and sent them out. Then he lit a fire and cooked and ate the conies, and afterwards sat out on the step, quietly belching in the dark and turning over his schemes in his mind.

Hamud was terribly happy. He'd never been so happy in his life. He didn't regret having left his life. He knew now that he'd never really been happy in it. More than ever he saw that it had been the life of a dog, always at a disadvantage, dependent on the whim or sympathy of others for every crumb of pleasure. Here he was at no disadvantage; on the contrary. Here he was master, and very little happened that he wasn't aware of, even in control of, and none of it needed speech. He'd developed amazing proficiencies in the lower world. In the early days he'd had to learn to shoot his food with a sling made from the donkey's guts, and quite soon had been able to pick off even the smallest creature at a hundred metres. But that was a chancy method of survival. The traps he'd invented were much less chancy. But even the traps left something to chance. Among his teeming ideas, Hamud was working on some that would make him still more the master of this world.

He'd been in it for a year now. For the first months he'd waited for the djinns and souls to make contact, and only slowly had realized that he must be on some kind of probation. For he hadn't changed in any way. He'd watched himself for change. His fingernails had continued to grow, and his toenails. His hair had continued to grow. Nothing was changing! He realized he must be in some interim state, and that only when he'd passed out of it would the souls be able to contact him. He'd wondered for weeks what he was supposed to do in the interim state. He'd prayed and fasted until one starving day, looking with longing at the succulent gazelle, he'd suddenly understood.

*The gazelle wasn't real.* It was like no gazelle known to men. It was a gazelle that had been sent. Why had the gazelle been sent?

Everything else in the ravine was real – the other animals, the birds, the vegetation. Everything was as it should be except this. One tiny part of the total scheme had been changed to show that the scheme itself was not as it seemed. It was a cunning fabrication, containing an enigma which had been designed for him to solve. What could it possibly be?

Hamud fasted again, and one morning awoke to find the gazelle licking two new-born kids. The gazelle was looking at him and the kids were looking at him. His head spinning with hunger and exaustion, Hamud looked back trying to plumb the meaning in these looks. There was a male kid and a female one. Male and female. Suddenly, finally, he'd got it. Male and female. The animals had been sent to breed and multiply. They were to be preserved, not eaten. All other lawful animals he could eat. These he couldn't eat. He remembered the story of Adam, given all things except the fruit of one tree. Adam had eaten the fruit of the tree, and had met judgement. Could it be that this situation had been devised for *his* judgement?

Hamud broke his fast and thought about it. He thought it very likely. He recalled a *hadji*, returned from pilgrimage, who had rested a night at Kufr Kassem. The *hadji*, after seeing everything, had given his opinion that the world was nothing but a dream in the mind of Allah. Hamud had been much struck with the opinion, though aggrieved at his own mean part in the dream. But he saw now there'd been no injustice. God created all dreams. Perhaps his former life had been a part of somebody else's dream.

The more he thought about it, the surer he was. He'd always known there was more to him than the character whose part he'd acted out in Kufr Kassem. His soul didn't have only one eye and no roof to its mouth. Perhaps that had been something necessary to his wife's dream. His wife had been given beauty in her dream and also compassion, but the compassion had brought her Hamud and the beauty her lover, and between the two her fidelity had been tested, and she'd failed. Everything that had happened since had flowed from the failure. Hamud had killed her father and her brother, and so had found himself here; and as he thought of it, he got up from his meal and with outstretched palms recited:

'*King on the day of reckoning!*
*Guide us on the straight path,*

The path of those to whom Thou hast been gracious;
With whom Thou art not angry,
And who go not astray.'

He recited it several times, tears streaming down his face, marvelling at the way in which the contents of one dream were instantaneously fashioned by God to make another. He saw now that he was in a dream made entirely for him. He didn't know why the animals had to be preserved. He only knew this was his test; and from that moment had started to plan, on a large scale.

The gazelles would multiply. His sheep and goats at Kufr Kassem had reproduced in their second year, and he thought the gazelles would do the same. So in two years he could expect new kids, and the year after more, and the year after that more still – not only from the original kids, but also from the second generation of kids, who would no longer be kids. And so it would go on. The numbers could proliferate in an amazing way. It would need amazing quantities of food. It would need accommodations for the food, and for the gazelles, and for himself, and for his own food.

He saw that the interim state could last a long time, and he was glad about it. He liked the interim state. One test he knew he'd passed already. He hadn't sought safety for himself at the time of the flood, but had gone out immediately after the lost kid. It was the male that had been lost, and he'd realized right away the special nature of the test, for if the male was lost all hope of continuity would be lost, and he would have failed. But God had spared the male. God had spared the gazelles.

Hamud belched quietly in the dark, and he knew that God would spare him too. He felt the eye of God on him in the dark.

There were aspects to the dream that were not dear to Hamud. He couldn't be sure whether events came about

in it because he willed them or because God did. He'd
certainly needed the rock. But the rock hadn't come down
just because he'd willed it. Other events had been necessary. The vast mechanism of God had instantaneously set
in motion these events. It seemed to Hamud that anything
he really needed for the dream he could will, and if it was
legitimate, God would grant it. It struck him as a sound
explanation. It seemed to make him a partner, at least an
assistant, of God.

He had another look at the rock before going to bed,
and remembering all that still had to be done, he thought
he had better will a bit more.

More arrived the next day. It continued to arrive for the
next six and a half days, with a one-day interval in the
middle. Arrivals were always preceded by thunder, so
when the thunder finally stopped, Hamud knew that the
deliveries had too.

He spent a whole day inspecting his stock, and on the
next one he got back on schedule.


2


His schedule was so enormous it often made him feel faint
to think of it. Sometimes, if it was going well, he felt drunk
and laughed aloud. It was quite an elastic schedule. Some
part of it could be tackled at almost any hour of the day
or night. He was building a village and a farm. He was
building two villages and two farms, one on the floor of
the ravine and one on the shelf. The one on the shelf was
for winter, but winter was nearly over now, and the really
urgent work was going on below. Hamud was building a
cistern there.

There was plenty of water in winter but none in summer,
for all of it drained away at the far end. He'd thought of
building the cistern at that end, but there was no cover

there. He had to have cover. Surprising numbers of people were about. In summer it had been Beduin, who had pitched with their flocks on the eastern side. In winter it had been the Jews. Groups of them had come, day after day, to peer down into the ravine. One, with a red beard, had even begun to climb down, and in a panic Hamud had waited for him with his knife. But the man had only climbed halfway, to see if it were possible to observe what was below the shelf. (It wasn't, and this had persuaded Hamud to put his cistern there.)

He went out and inspected it right away. Ideally, the cistern should have gone in a pit in the ground, but there was no pit and he hadn't devised a way of excavating one. For the time being he was using a cave and building a retaining wall across its mouth. Suitable rock for the wall had been one problem, and some way of sealing the joins another. He thought he'd solved the sealing with the discovery of a large deposit of clay at the far end of the ravine. But he saw now that he hadn't. The cistern was leaking.

He poked his head in to find out why. There was nothing wrong with the clay. There must be something wrong with the rock. He saw that there was. The poor-quality stuff was already damply crumbling away inside. He had a further pile of it already shaped and squared off for the next course, but he saw at once he'd have to scrap the lot and start again with the new stock. It meant delays, of course. It meant emptying and refilling the cistern. But there was no way out of it. He straightened up and lowered himself down into the ravine, to inspect his operations at the other side.

He found his traps had done well: ten fine conies to show for the week – none, unfortunately, alive. Hamud had plans for live conies. But he threaded the catch and carried it with him on his way to the trial grounds. The trial grounds were further along the shelf. He had alfalfa growing there, and barley and onions, also cabbage, radishes, and grapes. He thought this was what he had growing. He couldn't be certain. He'd never done any growing himself before. But exploratory trips around the ravine had disclosed plants that bore a resemblance to these remembered crops.

Hamud had racked his brains to try and remember how they'd gone about things in Kufr Kassem. He recalled that his wife used to pick out the best plants and save the seed or pull off bits of the plants and get the bits to grow. He'd tried it himself and found to his astonishment that the seed and the bits did grow. It was a mystery to him how they grew. It was a mystery how anything grew. He hoped to grow practically everything on his future farms and was still carrying out explorations of the ravine.

He found that his trial grounds had also done well. No rock had fallen there, and a week of sun and rain had bushed up the rows. He pulled up what he hoped was an onion and examined it. It was certainly more of an onion than it had been the week before. The cabbages and radishes were more as they ought to be too. He couldn't be sure about the alfalfa or barley, and as for the grapes nothing was to be seen at all. But he knew he wasn't wrong about the grapes. He'd seen the fruit last summer: the jungle of vines had wandered from a blackened stump half a metre thick.

It had puzzled him how the vine had got there, how any of the stuff had got there. Apart from the recent settlement of Jews it was obvious that nobody had ever engaged in agriculture in the bare hills. But then, awaking from sleep, he'd suddenly remembered something his father had told him long ago when they'd gone to the Suleibba camp. They'd taken their direction from a hill known as Khirbet al Yahud, the Ruin of the Jews. When he'd asked his father why it was called that, his father had said that thousands of years ago the Jews had had cities and villages all about here, until a series of miracles had destroyed them and driven them out so that the Beduin could freely roam. Many thousands of them had been hurled by God into the ravine, thus originating its haunted character; and indeed Hamud had since found several interesting objects that supported his father's story. He went and collected one of them now from a little store he had made nearby, and commenced hoeing between the rows of the trial ground with it.

Hoeing between rows was an essential part of growing, Hamud knew; it was his strongest recollection of Kufr Kassem. With a long branch tied to the thing, he found that it hoed very nicely. He'd come on it some weeks before, had thought it at first a Christian relic, for it was in the shape of a blackened cross with white encrustations across one of the bars. The encrustation, on inspection, had proved to be the remains of a hand, and the cross the upper part of a sword. He had since found the remains of several other hands and swords and other parts of bodies together with much rusted ironwork; and further along the shelf quite a large collection, as though a number of individuals had alighted there in rapid succession from the same position above.

Hamud had retrieved the ironware from the pile of bones and was keeping it, well smeared with fat, in his store for future use. One interesting piece, whose original purpose he hadn't yet divined – it seemed to be part of a wheel with a curved sword sticking out of it – he particularly looked forward to using. He thought that if the wheel were reconstituted and the sword beaten out it ought to make a very useful and ingenious ploughshare. He wondered if anybody had ever thought of this before, and marvelled again at the amazing number of ideas and plans that came to him in the lower world.

But there was no time for marvelling today. He hoed the ground in fast time and sped on to his other operations, coming at length to the last, his main growing areas for the future. The growing areas had been picked in positions that gave the maximum light below together with minimum observation from above, and he'd scrambled about for weeks to check that he'd picked right

No rock had fallen in the growing areas, and this was something of a mixed blessing, because plenty of it was going to be needed. The shelf sloped here and the ravine bed dipped, and all of it needed building up and terracing. But he gave thanks for now having the materials to do the job, and he climbed to the highest terrace and looked about him in the ravine. He saw all that he'd done so far, and he saw that it was very good. Then he hurried home for the next stage of creation.


3


Hamud worked hard at his schedule through 1958 and 1959, building terraces and planting out selected plants. He improved the cistern and had water to spare. He pulled up rooted bits of bushes that the gazelles seemed to like and transplanted them all about the ravine, and he collected live conies and bred from them. In his spare time he made pots. He became an avid potter. He made nearly a hundred, in a variety of shapes and sizes. The failures he made into plates and markers, and he wrote the name of God on them in wet charcoal and baked it in, and placed them in all the areas where he lived and worked. He placed them at the ends of rows and in the enclosures for the gazelles and the conies.

A strange thing happened in the summer of 1958. The mother gazelle detached herself from the kids and joined him. When he left her in the evening, she whinnied after him, and one night whinnied so long that he went out the gazelles' enclosure and released her and she followed him to his own quarters. Because of the broken night it was hours before Hamud slept again, and he was heavily asleep when it was time for the dawn prayer. The gazelle woke him for the prayer, and when he thought about it Hamud realized God must have appointed the gazelle to this duty, so after this he let her share his quarters.

Sometimes the gazelle would lie and look at him for hours in the firelight. Hamud thought it was the most beautiful animal he had ever seen, certainly a dream animal. Real gazelles showed grace only from a distance: dose up, they were gawky, twitching beasts, spindly legged, rat-faced, ill-proportioned. This gazelle was none of these things. It was compact, even dainty, with precise, measured movements and the head of a queen. Often as it sat on tiny folded hooves gazing at him, Hamud marvelled at the regal perfection of the head, the symmetry of the curving horns. They reminded him in some way of the flowing lines of the name of God. He kept careful watch on the kids to see if they were developing in the same way, and saw that the female was, but not the male. The male lacked the length of horn and the beautiful loops of the female. It was also smaller and more nervous, the first to move at any hint of alarm. Its leg had mended, but the bone had set at an angle so that it was lame. As it grew older, and more venturesome, Hamud kept it close-hobbled and fed it by hand, fearful that it might take alarm some day and fall and break its neck. Important duties lay ahead of the little runt and Hamud was taking no chances until it had accomplished them.

Already he'd found that breeding had its problems. There'd been trouble with the conies. The cony was a species of rock badger, and unsociable. The males fought when placed together and the females refused food. He'd had to build separate cubicles for them, but even so the captive animals were sickening and dying. Hamud persevered. He meant to breed a race that wouldn't sicken and die. He needed conies. He needed the skins for covering and ropes. It took five cony skins to make a decent hobble rope, and who knew how many hobble ropes he'd ultimately need? He also needed the meat, but this was less important. He had plenty to eat apart from meat. Sometimes in the winter when the air was too damp to light a fire he lived for days on bread and onions, washed down with gazelle milk, and couldn't remember eating better in his life. The barley bread, baked with saltbush, kept well in his store, and the onions, selected and reselected, were the finest he'd ever tasted.

It tickled him that the ancient crops of the Jews should have awaited him over the centuries, seeding and reseeding themselves until it was time for him to come and select them. Everything about the situation tickled him. He'd scaled off the rust from the Jews' old ironwork and found the metal underneath still good. He'd burnished and sharpened several fine blades from it, and had them constantly in use. He'd also beaten out the curved sword and rebuilt the wheel, and found that the ploughshare gave excellent and rapid service in the growing areas, leaving him with much extra time for his many other stimulating duties.

Everything about the lower world stimulated Hamud. Through 1958 and 1959 he worked hard in it, inspired by the richness of his life, exalted by its purpose.

Hamud began his experiments at gazelle breeding in the autumn of 1958, and by early winter saw that both females were in kid. He gave two days of thanks for this, and when the mid-season rains set in, moved up to the shelf. He remained on the shelf for the rest of the winter. He was still there in April when the gazelles gave birth. The mother gazelle gave birth to a male and a female, and the daughter to two females. Hamud came down off the shelf and put in a summer of hard work.

He had seven gazelles to work for now.

In the autumn he commenced breeding again, and when the winter revealed the two older females to be in kid, he again gave thanks.

It was a hard winter. There were blizzards above. No snow fell in the ravine, but there was ice everywhere. Sheets of it hung from the choked wadis above and shattered in the ravine from time to time. An ironhard wind blew, and Hamud moved his livestock into the caves, and lit fires there. He had to get up in the night to refuel the fires, but in the morning still found ice on the floor and on the walls. The wind howled so loudly at night that the restless animals were terrified, and Hamud wasn't very happy himself. On the fourth night of the freeze-up (it was in January of 1960), the mother gazelle showed such agitation that Hamud muffled himself up and went outside. He saw two wolves outside. They were eating the conies in the next cave. Hamud ran back and got his sling and his knife, but had no chance to use the sling because one of the wolves jumped on him. Hamud fought the wolf and stabbed it several times, but it got away. Both wolves got away, their mouths crammed with conies. Over thirty dead conies were left behind.

Hamud had been painfully torn by the wolf, and his right ear was almost torn off. But he saw a fresh test here. He thought the wolves would be back. A pack of them would probably return. He prayed a good deal that day, and in the evening made up the fires in the caves and went out into the ravine to meet them. He saw that what he had to do was get the wolves long before they got to him, so he took a good pile of stones with him. He prayed while he waited for them, and he had to wait a long time. The moon was well up before the wolves came. With a sinking heart he saw six of the lean black shapes flow one at a time down the eastern side of the ravine and gather at the bottom. The small pack moved towards him in an ill-defined blur.

He let them get well within range before he loosed off, aware of the danger of them scattering and coming at him from different angles. He prayed very powerfully as he got his first shot off. It caught one of them squarely in the muzzle and it dropped as if pole-axed. The wolves didn't scatter. They seemed a bit bewildered. Hamud hit another two, and the rest took off. He waited where he was for a bit, and presently the three returned. Hamud hit another one. The other two went, and didn't return. Hamud waited a while and went and cut the throats of the wolves he had hit.

He kept up his vigil for another few nights, and after that didn't need to.

Hamud was a bit diminished by his test with the wolves. He had lost a piece of his nose and some of his ear and for a few weeks the full use of his jaw. But as his wounds healed, he had a marvellous feeling of relief. It was an enormous test to have survived, and he didn't think there could be a worse one. He thought he'd probably done all his tests now.

The wounds, it was true, took a long time to heal, and hurt quite horribly while they did so. The ear didn't seem to be healing at all. This worried Hamud. He had tied it back to its former position, but it showed no sign of growing there. He didn't know what to do about it. If the ear wouldn't grow back where it used to grow, it was evidently not intended to grow there. He wondered in that case what it was intended to do.

No solution had occurred by April, but the gazelles gave birth again then, so Hamud came down from the shelf and gave thanks once more. There were four new kids.

That April Hamud had eleven gazelles to show for his original one.

# 4

There were certain religious injunctions against forecasting natural increase, which lay within the gift of God alone. But as a steward Hamud had his duties, so he tried to calculate. He got about far enough to see the problem.

He had eleven gazelles now, two of them mature females. In the course of the year three more females would become mature. The five females would produce ten kids. Total herd: 21 *gazelles*, Hamud wrote with his charcoal.

He couldn't tell how many of the new gazelles would be female. But if his five adult females increased only to eight, they would give sixteen new kids. Total: 37 *gazelles*, Hamud wrote.

After that he gave up. He couldn't calculate any more. The numbers frightened him, anyway. How was he going to provide for such a fantastically *multiplying* herd? In a few years it could be *hundreds*. There was the problem of water. Each animal needed two litres a day at least. Two litres a day for seven dry months for hundreds of drinkers . . . Hamud went frantic with his charcoal. He knew he didn't have that much water. Even if he had, his cistern couldn't cope with it. Even if it could, how was he going to fill it? It meant running up and down thousands of times. Even if each journey took only five minutes, if he could do ten in an hour, eighty in a day, two thousand a month; if he could do all this and nothing else, without stopping – Hamud wrote and rubbed out and wrote again – he still could not carry all the water that would be needed.

Hamud saw that his cistern wouldn't do. He couldn't think of any cistern that would do. He saw that what was needed was a sign from God. When the water finally went down in the ravine, Hamud went out and looked for one. Right away, God sent Hamud a sign.

There were still pools in the ravine, but the flow from the wadis had stopped. Hamud noticed something he'd seen the year before. One pool, by the wall, was full every day he passed it. The bed of the ravine sloped, so that the other pools drained away. Why didn't this pool drain away?

Hamud investigated. He found that the pool did drain away. The water was trickling out and running off down the ravine even as he looked. How could a pool continually drain away and yet remain full?

Hamud investigated more closely. He found that the pool was below a cleft in the rock. The wall at the rear of the cleft was wet. Hamud climbed up it, following the water mark. He found the water welling quietly out of a hole in the rock. It was a small hole, no bigger than his hand, and not much water was coming out of it. But it was coming out very steadily.

Hamud looked at it for some minutes. Then he climbed right up the wall of the ravine. He climbed cautiously and he took his time. The Beduin camped almost immediately above, at the beginning of every summer, and he couldn't be sure that they hadn't arrived yet.

There were no Beduin there when he got to the top, but he found the source of the water, and also the reason for the Beduins' annual visit. There was a large pool at the top. The winter rains had collected in a shallow rocky basin, which did not, as in the wadis, fall away into the ravine. The basin was surrounded by vegetation. And he could see the reason for the vegetation. The upper rim of the pool was composed of a different kind of rock, soft crumbling stuff, still wet, although enclosing no water. A good metre of damp rock showed where the water had been. It had seeped away through this poor-quality stuff, as it had seeped away through Hamud's first cistern, and some of it had gone to the vegetation.

Hamud knew where the rest had gone.

He climbed down and had a look at it again. There was no flood of water through the hole, just a steady trickle, two or three litres of it a minute, filtered through several hundred metres of rock. What was needed was a bung. Given a good bung, he could have water at will. He went home, still turning the matter over in his mind.

He began to make daily visits to the pool. He found that from the time he first noticed it to when it dried up was just over seven weeks. The flow slackened in the last few days, but he saw it was still giving something like a litre a minute.

Hamud worked out the figures with his charcoal. He worked them out several times, and he stared in fascination at the figures. Then he gave thanks for them. Something well over a quarter of a million litres of water must have trickled out of the hole, no bigger than his hand, since he'd first seen it. God had made a cistern out of a mountain for him. Hamud fell on his face. While there, he thought about his bung.

During the summer of 1960 Hamud fashioned several types of bung, and also worked out the way to keep one holding back a quarter of a million litres of water. Leading up to the hole was a series of excellent toeholds, the last a small shelf. By cutting a sloping groove in this shelf, Hamud saw that he would be able to build a pillar, inclining inwards. The last few stones of the pillar he could shape in such a way that while no amount of longitudinal pressure would shift them, a simple sideways blow applied to the key one would dislodge it, thus releasing the bung and whatever quantity of water happened to be desired.

He worked on this in spare moments for a good part of the summer. It was another splendid summer, hard-working and creative, and he was very happy. He was bothered only by the question of what might be intended with regard to his ear. Very little of the ear was attached to his head, and it bothered him a good deal. As though to make up for the severity of the winter, the summer was exceptionally hot, and owing to sweat Hamud found it difficult to keep his ear on. However he adjusted the rope, it slipped. There was now nothing wrong with the ear. Although it had taken time, the thing had healed beautifully. So far as Hamud could judge it was in first-class condition. It had simply become dislodged from his head. He didn't let it interfere with his work; but it bothered him, and he couldn't help wondering.

It was a long summer, of 1960, and there was no break in the heat. By October there should have been rain, but there wasn't, and by November there was still no rain. Hamud worried. The level in the cistern was low. He rationed himself, and he rationed the gazelles. He lost many conies that summer.

By the first week of November he had his pillar and his bung quite ready and only awaiting assembly. His intention was to wait for the rains so that the bung could swell naturally inside the hole and he could see what changes might be needed. But by the middle of the month he was so impatient to try the system that he soaked the bung overnight and took it along the next morning to the hole.

The bung was a tight fit and had to be hammered in. Hamud placed the final arrangement of stones at the top of the inclined pillar, and hammered in the keystone to complete the assembly. The thing held beautifully. He pushed and tugged quite hard. Everything held. All that remained was the final test to see that the sideways rap at the critical point would unlock it. Hamud placed the point of his tool critically against the keystone and gave the sideways rap. The keystone fell out and the bung support fell out. The bung didn't fall out.

Hamud sat and looked at the bung. The pressure of water would probably force it out, when there was any water. He didn't want to force it out now and risk breaking it, even though he wasn't sure of the shape. He thought that if he left it in, it could probably be released quite easily when it had dried out. This seemed the soundest thing to do. so he set about replacing the assembly, and was still doing it when the sheep fell on him.

Hamud was so shocked that he fell off the ledge, and the sheep ran away. It ran in panic down the ravine towards the gazelles. It didn't run very far. It had been shorn, but it was a starved, runtish little creature, and Hamud picked himself up and caught it quite easily. A single glance showed that it was a buck and useless for breeding, so he killed it. He was still very shocked, and as soon as he'd done it – and it all happened in a moment – he knew that what he had done was not wise.

He had slit the sheep's throat, and he squatted on his haunches and watched the blood stream and the little legs kick, although the animal was already dead. He thought of all the consequences of this unwise action.

The sheep was undoubtedly someone's sheep. After such a hard summer every sheep counted, and was counted. The owner of the sheep would not rest until he found it.

Hamud watched the kicking finally cease. The live legs of the animal would have carried it back up to the top of the ravine, where Hamud should have chased it. It was still possible for him to take it there. The owner would find the sheep with its throat slit and assume that some enemy had done it. This would lead to dissension among brothers, which was bad. On the other hand, the owner might come down looking for it while Hamud was taking it up, which would be worse. It seemed best, on the whole, to get rid of the sheep.

Hamud took the sheep home and ate part of it for his supper. He thought about it while he ate. It was unlikely that a Bedu would come down into the ravine at night. The Beduin were even more afraid of the ravine than civilized folk; ignorant, superstitious people, the Beduin. He was safe enough for the moment. And once the rain started, the Beduin would go away. How long could it be before there was rain?

Hamud said his prayers, and watered and fed the livestock, thoughtfully. He didn't sleep very well, and when he looked at the sky in the morning could find no encouragement there. He watered the livestock again, even more thoughtfully, and then tied them up. He tied up the mother gazelle as well and quieted her. 'I'll come back,' he said.

He went off to the pool and hid there, with his knife and his sling. He felt weary and unrested, but even when the sun came roastingly up he kept himself alert. He saw a little cony near the site of one of his former traps, and knew he could pick it off with ease although it was well over a hundred metres away. Hamud stayed very still and the cony didn't see him. He watched the cony most of the morning. About noon, when the sun was high and he knew the Beduin slept, he was wondering if he should go back to the gazelles, when he saw the cony's back go up and it disappeared.

Hamud felt his own back stiffen and his hair prickle.

A little stone fell into the ravine.

Hamud saw where it fell, and looked all the way up the wall of the ravine. He couldn't see very far. Bushes and shrubs hung toughly to the wall in the line of descent. They were quite still in the heat of the noon. Hamud felt his ear slipping in the sweat that poured from him. Heat dislodged stones. He prayed that no more stones would fall, and that presently he could go back to see to the gazelles.

Another stone fell, and then several more. Something was undoubtedly coming down.

Hamud had a good pile of stones with him, and from his hiding place he threw some in the air, and gave the small shriek of a djinn.

The movement of stones stopped. Nothing happened for

quite a long time. Then a single stone fell. It did not tumble down the side of the ravine. It fell in the middle of it. Somebody had tossed it.

Hamud didn't do anything about it. Whoever was there had not fled at the presence of a djinn. This was very bad. Whoever was there was a calculating person who was trying to get him to reveal his position. He had no intention of revealing it. He remained quite still, intently watching the line of descent, and waited for the other person to reveal his.

Presently he did. Hamud quite distinctly saw the stone come arcing out of the bush. It seemed to come from the very centre of the bush, and Hamud could place the man exactly. He knew the bush. He'd had a trap there, too. It was a juniper bush and the conies had fed on the berries that fell into the tangle of roots. The man would be standing on the roots, holding himself in position with one hand on the main branch of the bush; Hamud had done it himself many times. From that position he would have a perfect view of the ravine, and of Hamud himself, if only he knew where Hamud was. The man was evidently very skilful, a good hunter who kept himself well braced. There was absolutely no movement from the bush, and there had not been when the stone was thrown.

Hamud saw he was going to have to kill this skilful and calculating person.

As he thought this, he felt his ear drop out of the rope. He didn't move to put it back. He didn't move at all. Sweat ran into his eye but he blinked it out and kept watch on the bush. A line of foliage ran down from the bush, following the course of a runoff of water that came during the heaviest rainstorms. For much of the way down the man would be in good cover; but some dappled part of him was bound to show. All Hamud wanted to know was his height, and where his head was.

The man stood immobile in the bush for the best part of

an hour. Hamud sat him out, equally immobile. Slowly the sun moved overhead, and the man moved. Hamud caught the glint of a buckle: a sandal. The pale blur of a *kefiyeh*: a head. Quite a small man, smaller than himself – thin as a snake.

As he descended he would have to take his eyes off the ravine and watch his feet. Calculating on it, Hamud very slowly took up his sling and fitted a stone. The man would stop again at the next bush down, and once there, Hamud knew, he had him. In cover, out of cover, he knew where the man would have to place his feet, and how he would have to hold himself, and where his head would be.

As the man moved, Hamud slowly placed the sling in position and tensed it, and waited again for all movement to stop, and when it did, gave it some seconds more, and said in his mind, 'In the name of the Merciful, the Compassionate,' for he had nothing against this man, and loosed off.

The man fell at once out of the bush and tumbled through three or four more to lay prone, his legs caught in foliage and his head and shoulders on a small shelf. Hamud waited a while. Then he thought he'd better knock him down, so he picked up another stone and aimed and hit the man in the head again. The force of the blow jolted the head, but it didn't knock the man off the shelf.

Hamud got up and wearily stretched himself and wiped the sweat from his head and neck and tied his ear on again. He saw he was going to have to go up and make certain of it. He had a good drink out of his water bottle, and climbed up. It was craggy ground below the bushes, and Hamud was tired and also sorry for the Bedu – a poor thin little creature, evidently a man in his twenties.

It had fallen to Hamud to cut a good many throats in the past few years, of sheep and goats in his earlier life, and of men and other animals since. But he felt a revulsion against cutting this poor thin throat. A Bedu's life was so hardly won: to end with a single stroke what had been preserved with such endurance! But Hamud knew he was not doing it for himself, so he sighed and felt his ear drop out again as he climbed and he thought he wouldn't bother to put it back until he'd finished the job. But he still paused a short distance from the figure and watched it very closely for any sign of movement.

There was no sign of movement so Hamud perched himself and turned the small head in position, at the same time murmuring again, 'In the name of the Merciful, the Compassionate,' and had bent over it, when the eyes in the head opened, and the teeth in it sank into the nearest part of Hamud, which was his ear.

Hamud was shocked, and his free hand went to the ear, one finger actually going up the Bedu's nose, so that the man had a moment to wriggle around and take the knife from him. Hamud grappled with him, frantically trying to free himself, and the Bedu bit his ear off. With amazement and horror, Hamud saw the whole of his ear in the Bedu's mouth, and the man himself was so surprised that Hamud took the knife from him and stabbed him with it. The Bedu didn't release the ear, so, snarling, Hamud put his knee on him, and cut his throat, across and across, and the Bedu's mouth fell open and the ear fell out and Hamud picked it up.

In a paroxysm, the Bedu got his legs out of the bushes and managed to get one around Hamud. Hamud lifted himself half off the man, in time to receive the Bedu's other foot, hard, in the face. He went backwards over the leg that was behind him and fell off the rock. He fell heavily down the ravine and landed on his back on another rock.

He was very badly winded, and he couldn't get off the rock. He waited a few minutes, feeling very sick, and tried again. He still couldn't get off it.

The Bedu was dying above, and Hamud could see him.

The man was trying to raise himself on his arms, but the arms would not support him. Blood was pouring from him. The body sank powerlessly forward, so that the head hung over the rock gazing down at Hamud. Hamud could see that the Bedu was scrabbling to find stones. But he had no strength to throw the stones at Hamud and they rolled loosely down. The mouth was moving, although no words came out, but Hamud knew the Bedu was cursing him and praying for God to blacken his face.

Hamud saw him die, and he tried again to get off the rock, but he still couldn't. He knew now he must have torn muscles and broken bones. He thought he would wait until he was less shocked and more in control of himself and then try to roll off the rock. He could feel a bit more control in his limbs. He couldn't feel the knife, and he knew he must have dropped that. But he could feel something in his other hand, and he knew it was his ear.

Hamud tried several times in the course of the afternoon to roll himself off the rock. There was no feeling in his legs. He could move his head from side to side and raise his arms a little, but not as high as the rock on which he was spreadeagled. It was quite a large rock, a boulder, and his body was arched backwards over it. He could find no purchase along the sides of the rock to lift himself up or to roll his body to one side or the other. He thought he must have broken his back.

His face was quite badly burned by the sun and he kept his eyes closed. He was very worried about the gazelles. He wondered what could possibly be intended with regard to them. He had left them tied up. They couldn't get at the water. He was terribly thirsty himself, and he'd already had a good drink before he'd gone up to finish off the Bedu. What must it be with the gazelles?

The sun went, and Hamud said his prayers. He could hear the gazelles whinnying, could even pick out the distinctive call of the mother, but he concentrated simply on his prayer, keeping himself very still on the rock, knowing that when he'd finished, having conserved his forces, and strengthened by prayer, he would make one more powerful attempt.

Hamud finished his prayer, and lay still for a minute or two, and made the attempt. He willed his legs to move, but they didn't move. His head and his arms moved, but nothing else did. Hamud tried again, and wept.

He didn't sleep during the night, and when dawn came he prayed again, and tried again, and again wept.

The sun came up and he saw the Bedu still staring at him with his throat cut. The Bedu's mouth was still slightly open with his last curse, and feeling the sun begin to burn his face again, Hamud wondered if God had heard this curse, if perhaps the presence of God in the ravine had simply accepted the curse of the Bedu and granted it, thinking that it came from his servant Hamud. This couldn't be – Hamud knew the reasoning was in some way confused, and tried to put it right. But even behind closed eyes the sun looked through him and there was no shade where his thoughts might go to assemble themselves into meaning.

Hamud could not find meaning anywhere in the white torchlight that thirsted and burned. He heard a voice crackling like burning paper blackening in a curse. He looked everywhere for the Merciful, the Compassionate, and from somewhere behind the blackening light, the Merciful, the Compassionate, faintly answered, but so far off, its whinny a mere recollection, fading, fading.

Seeing it fade so fast, Hamud from his very being asked why he had been forsaken, and pleaded for a sign. But the sign when it came was one that he couldn't read. He tried to read it in the blackness. He tried to read it several times, as it repeated and also spoke itself. He knew the name of God was somewhere written there in the sign, but it was too quick and he was too slow and too unworthy, and he wept. He wept so much that his face was wet. He wept so much that he was soaked. But still he could not read the sign.


5

The sign came much earlier at the top of the ravine, for it came from the east, and it was read immediately.

'Oh, by God, it is very excellent. Hurry, my children! It's not a moment too soon,' Musallem said. He was eighty-one, but still very sharp-eyed. He had been watching for the sign for a couple of days, and had spotted it first. For the past hour he had been exclaiming about it, still looking keenly towards the east, while everybody else bustled about.

'Oh, by God! Again. Only look! Truly excellent. Again, again! Oh, He is good. He will give us, my children, you'll see. Only hurry!'

He wasn't getting in the way very much, so nobody had to shove him out of it. But he was running about and jumping up and down a good deal, frightening the camels. His youngest grandson, Yasir, under direction, took off a few minutes to roll him a reefer and calm him down.

The old man always calmed down with a reefer; and he smoked it sitting fairly quietly on a rock above the scummy puddle that was all that was left of the pool, still peering intently towards the east and cackling a little from time to time at the lightning that flashed there. The sheep and the goats, with the milk camels, were already disappearing in that direction.

All twenty-five of the black tents were down and most already loaded on the bull camels. The camels were in poor condition and groaning horribly as the loads went on, several of them coaxed to their feet only by a handful of dates or the occasional boot. But many of the big tents were still unfolded on the ground as the thunder rolled in.

All the same, Afra still found time to come weeping to the old man, having tried everybody else. 'Who can think of going without him? Grandfather, only speak to them!'

The old man didn't take his eyes off the east, but he had a little drag at his reefer before answering absently, 'Don't interfere with the men, child. There's no time. He was never any good. Who didn't tell you? By God, only look – God's bounty!'

'He's lying injured somewhere! He went after the sheep. I won't leave him. He was the only man here, and now there are none.'

The old man took his eyes momentarily off God's bounty to look with some displeasure at his granddaughter. 'Your mother was a hard-mouthed slut, now roasting, and you're another. Who asked you to take a Ma'ara? What traditions have they? What do they believe? He ran off somewhere. He ran off with the sheep. You're well rid of him, and God will certainly blacken his face. Depend on it.'

'Oh, my children! Who will help?' asked the distraught young woman.

'God will. Idiot!' the old man snapped. 'As he helps all. He'll find you another. *We'll* find you another. What is there to it? Meanwhile go and help while there's still skin on your back. We have to march! Oh, by God, only look at it – listen to it! It's truly excellent.'

There were now not only plenty of excellent things to look at and listen to: drops big as saucers began weirdly to descend, the very air liquefying. The thing awaited so long blew in with uncanny suddenness. The huge wind hit them like a carnival before all the tents were loaded. The old man was everywhere, blowing about sideways, sitting in puddles. He seemed slightly drunk. Everyone seemed slightly drunk. Even the wretched Afra laughed and cried by turn. It had lasted so long, the dry.

But at last they were ready to march, the old man resisting all pleas to ride an ass. 'What, you think I can't keep up? By God, I'll outmarch any one of you. I'll outrun you. Eh? My father, may he enjoy all delights, put me off the ass at three years old, saying, "March, little Bedu," and twice a year since, I've marched. And by God, twice a year I *will* march, until there's earth in my mouth. What? Who'll stop me? Here, give me that little one. His father might have been a Ma'ara, but by God he's not.'

In the carnival spirit of the first day of march, the old man was always humoured, so the little boy was taken off the ass to walk with him.

'Who are you, eh? Mansur, isn't it?'

'Musallem, Great-grandfather.'

'Musallem? By God, yes. That's excellent. It's very excellent,' said the old man with glee. 'Two Musallems on the march. It's as God intended. What, you must be three now, Musallem?'

'Four, Great-grandfather.'

'Better still. Very excellent. Give me your hand, *halaila*. Two Beduin on the march, eh? Two Musallems. By God, His goodness never fails. Always remember it, Musallem. What?'

'Yes, Great-grandfather.'

'Yes. What are you, Musallem, do you know? What people do you spring from?'

'From the Beduin, Great-grandfather. I'm a Bedu.'

'Of course, little Bedu. Of course, *halaila*. What an excellent child! A truly excellent child – the blood of his great-grandfather. But your tribe, Musallem – what has she told you?'

'My father is a Ma'ara, my mother a Wahir.

'And you?'

'I'm from the tents of Wahir, Great-grandfather. As you. We're the same.'

'By God! By God!' the old man said. 'Oh, by God! What excellence. What a manner of speaking the child has. It's a gift of God! Listen to me, Musallem, I'm going to tell you things. If God wills, I'll tell you everything. I'm the oldest and you're the youngest – and what only hasn't happened in between. Ah!'

The child wasn't the youngest, but he kept prudently silent, which was easiest, anyway, for they were going due east and the wind was in his mouth, filling it with sand every time he opened it. The experienced old man kept his head well down, spitting sand from time to time, but he was drunk with the march and with this excellent great-grandchild, and couldn't stop.

'We're of Ishmael, do you know that, Musallem?'

'Ishmael?'

'The free people. They're trying to destroy us, Musallem. They hate freedom. They want us all in the prisons they've made for themselves. They're frightened outside. There are only two kinds of people in the world, *halaila*. There's al Hadar, who've imprisoned themselves in houses, and there's al Badia, that's us, the Beduin. We are free. We trust in God's bounty. What's this, what's this – where are we going?' the old man cried, seeing the column swing right.

'We turn south a little, Grandfather,' Yasir said, walking with them. 'Don't you remember – the officers who tried to stop us before?'

'May their mothers' wombs shrivel. And their wives' and daughters',' he added, recollecting suddenly. It had been touch and go earlier in the year. If they hadn't had fat lambs aplenty, fresh meat to offer as *baksheesh*, they'd have been turned back, or more likely turned *in*, to the police. All had to have papers these days; all had to be numbered, for prison. This time they had nothing to offer: thin sheep, camels barely able to move. By God!

'Ah, Musallem, Musallem, it was once all different,' the old man said. 'It was impossible to count us. Only God could count us. From the desert in the south to the desert in the east, only us. Imagine it! When I was your age, only three – you're three, Musallem?'

'Four, Great-grandfather.'

'Perhaps I was four. There were only us! Anyone wanting to cross the desert – say some pig with his caravan from Damascus to – where do you say, Baghdad, Mosul? Anywhere. He had to ask us. He had to pay us. It was ours. Great tribes of us, *halaila*, in my own lifetime. By God, what battles, what raids we had. What camels there were, what flocks to take, if you dared. Ah, well. By God. It's as He wills. I suppose,' the old man said. 'Though everything's got so hard to understand these days. The prisons have got bigger. How many of us are left? Are you listening to me, Musallem?'

'Yes, Great-grandfather.'

'They're reducing Ishmael. They can't have it that we're free and numbered only by God. They think they can do the work of God. It's the greatest blasphemy, may every one of their faces be blackened! You see how it is, *halaila*. They settle on one patch of land. They grow things in it, they have to stay there to get all the things they've grown, so they build houses, may they all crumble! Well, then, they have to plan what they'll grow to feed all the people and clothe them. There are villages full of them, and if they don't they'll die – if it should only happen! So there they're stuck like prisoners, and they take over more and more of the land so that they can grow and make more things for themselves, and the prison gets bigger and they want us all in it with them. You see how it is, Musallem?'

'Yes, Great-grandfather.'

'And how is it?'

'It's bad.'

'Its worse than bad. It's against God! It's from the devil. And he'll try and trap you, *halaila*, I can tell you. I've seen it all happen. He'll give you seeds and a house to wait in while they grow. And from this comes everything evil. From this comes the whole order of hell. Never plant a seed, *halaila*. Remember, you're of Ishmael. You go where God sends, and eat what He gives. Eh, Musallem?'

'As you, Great-grandfather.'

'Oh, by God! By God!' exclaimed the old man. 'The excellence of this child. Ah, Musallem, there are so many things I have to tell you.'

He told him a good many of them as they went.

They travelled for several hours, first south, but then before dark turning east again. They camped on stony ground, that wouldn't bog, on a hill below which was water. They camped there for ten days, and rested, and the camels were stronger after it, for all around the grass and pasture came up miraculously as it did every year after the rains. The whole thing got even better the further east they went, to their true pastures, which had lain dead all summer. They camped and marched, and camped and marched, ten days here and a couple of weeks there, all of it good, and the old man told Musallem practically everything. He saw that despite the worthless Ma'ara he had had as a father, the boy was of true blood.

Rain fell very steadily everywhere, for these were the first rains, and heavy, and the world was a marvel. It fell in the place they'd left, and the pool at the head of the ravine filled up. But later the level went down, for the upper water soaked away through the porous rock at its rim. Some of it went to feed the surrounding vegetation, which soon became beautifully green again, and some began its annual filtered descent through several hundred metres of rock.

# 5
# All About Jonathan

Motke Bartov came briskly out of the Ussishkin Institute of Natural History, which was situated in Kibbutz Dan, and got into his jeep. He'd slept the night at the kibbutz in order to lose no time in the morning. He had a lot to do today. He opened his briefcase and had a look at his diary before switching on the ignition. Tuesday, June 22, 1965: for the morning, kibbutzim Gei-Harim and Dafna; for the afternoon Mayan Baruch and Kfar Yuval. It was Gei-Harim first. Good. It was a marvellous day, hot but dry as toast, with that smell of mountains in the air. He loved this whole part of the country, but he loved the run to Gei-Harim best.

The fine black tarmac road rose and fell with the hills, swinging and looping below the forests of pine that clad the slope. He turned off at the sign, and coasted down to the kibbutz. He loved this bit too. They'd done an excellent job with it, very pleasing to the eye of a nature lover. Cypress, pine, and eucalyptus gracefully lined the road, screening off the machine sheds, the pickle factory, and the repair plant. Other kibbutzim could learn from this!

Motke left the jeep in the parking lot, and walked with his briefcase towards the school, finding much to commend on the way. There was refinement at Kibbutz Gei-Harim; they'd be keen about his scheme here, no doubt about it.

Numerous kibbutzniks walking in the lanes saluted him. '*Shalom*, Motke!'

'*Shalotn-shalom.*'

'How is nature today?'

'Blossoming.'

He had a word with Esther, the head teacher, while the children assembled in the largest classroom. He found absolutely nothing to criticize about the classroom, either. There was a natural *taste* for nature in this place. The old travel poster that he knew so well was carefully mounted on the wall. He put on his spectacles and noted that the sets of postage stamps, in the fifteen and forty *agorot* denomination, that commemorated the same event, were also there, two whole sheets of them. Between the serrated edges of the stamps, the multiple image of *Gazella smithii*, her beautiful horns black against the skyline, confronted him, taken from General Naftali Mor's famous photograph.

All the children seemed to be in, so he cleared his throat.

'Good morning, dear children,' Motke said.

'Good morning, Motke,' politely responded the children.

'Children, I have news for you.'

Motke told them the news.

The Nature Reserves Authority had decided upon a competition with wonderful prizes. The prizes were two-week holidays, in any part of the country, with extensive trips and excursions each and every day. But no less exciting than the prizes was the competition itself. It was a competition to collect as many as possible of the species of Israel. The prizes would be awarded on an area basis, so that no particular area would be at an advantage through having more species. But first a word as to species.

A species could be anything: it could be a blade of grass or it could be a cow. But a points system had been devised to take into account the relative rarity of some species. So in that part of the competition they would be looking for the less usual things, to get the highest points. But it happened that some people were not so sharp-sighted, and missed things. Very often this kind of person was a dreamer, who while he didn't see what was under his nose, was yet very good at describing what he did see. So here was a wonderful chance for the more poetical kind of person; for the next part of the competition was in a broad sense literary and artistic.

The species had to be both described and illustrated. How described? Described in a scientific sense – this was important – but also in an imaginative way, so that everybody could learn still more about it. For instance, show one person a bean sprouting, and he saw a bean sprouting, but show another and he saw the whole miracle of creation.

In Israel, as the children knew, many species were preserved and it was not permitted to take them. So 'collect' had to be understood in a figurative sense. The collector 'collected' by logging accurately the exact position and time of sighting of the species, giving as much supporting and illustrative detail as possible.

The competition started in the following week, the first of July, to coincide with the beginning of the two-month summer holiday. But it would last a year to complete the round of the seasons. Entries had to be in by July 1 next year, and as soon as possible afterwards the winners would be announced. They would take their prize holidays the following summer.

Motke's sharp eye noted a certain waning of interest at the rather extended period before the prizewinners drew the prizes. So he threw in his last bit of news. At the same time that the winners enjoyed the awards, something yet more interesting would happen. They would also become authors. Yes! A book would be published at that time – this was the reason for the careful timing – containing all the prizewinning entries. It would be illustrated, preferably by the prizewinners, hence the need to try one's hand at illustration, but otherwise by professional artists. The book would be entitled 'The Species of Israel by the Children of Israel' and it would be published not only in Hebrew but also in other languages. A person could thus sit in Gei-Harim, for instance, and know that his work was being studied an over the world. Wasn't this also something?

He saw with relief that it seemed to be something, and ended on that note. 'Children – Esther has the entry forms, The rest is up to you!'

'Stay and have a glass of coffee,' Esther said, as he buckled his briefcase.

'No time, I'm afraid. How are things here?'

'The same. Bangs in the night.'

'Anything recently?'

'A bit of shelling and mortaring, the usual. We had a novelty the other night. Fedayeen ran in and threw incendiaries into the cotton.'

'The children lose sleep, I suppose?'

'And write soulful essays about not hating Arabs. We're a bit strong on that here, you know. It gets samey, though.'

'Well. You can be samey about worse things,' Motke said solemnly. He was never quite sure of Esther's sense of humour. 'How did the talk go?'

'Very nicely. Almost every one of them will enter.'

'You think so?'

'I'm sure of it.'

'Wonderful. So *Shalom*:

'*Shalom-shalom.*'

*Almost* every one, Esther thought. Not quite every one.

Standing in the doorway a bit later, ticking off names, she was able to witness the exactness of her forecast. The children pushed and shoved all around, some taking one entry form, and some taking two for absent friends. Some came back again and remembered others. Jonathan slunk past without taking any forms.

'Jonathan, what about you?' she called after him.

'I took.'

'Did I tick you off?'

'Should I know? All right, I'll take again,' the boy mumbled, seeing her look back through the names, and snatched one from her hand and slouched off.

Esther came from Brixton in South London, and her private opinion was that what this little joker was in urgent need of was a good clip around the bloody ear: a liar, a loafer, a non-joiner. But as a kibbutznik and an educationist of long standing, she fought the reactionary thought down. A kibbutz child who behaved in a manner so markedly unlike that of his peer group must have his problems. This was elementary textbook stuff. She knew what the problems might be. She also knew she wouldn't put it past this child to have read the textbooks himself. Long before any possible problems could have arisen, she thought, the little bugger always had been a liar.

*Highly imaginative*, she corrected herself, walking back to her own apartment.

2

The little bugger tore up his entry form before the school was out of sight, and threw the pieces away, wondering at the same time if he should go home today. He hadn't been home much lately. He was nine years old. He had the same carroty hair as his father. He decided not to go home and went to the pool instead. He knew that his parents didn't like to go to the pool without him. They would wait until he came home. When he didn't come home, they would know where to find him. When they'd found him, he would go somewhere else.

He worked out in his mind how to do this with the maximum offence, and came on it quite easily. Of course.

A natural. He could just see the look on his father's face when he said it. And on his mother's.

He noticed that Dina was already at the pool, with her parents, and gave her a wide berth. Then he thought, why should he avoid Dina? Let her avoid him. He knew that Dina was crazy to dive but too frightened to try. He also knew her parents were eager for her to learn. Jonathan went up the ladder and bounced on the end of the board until he was sure she could see him. Then he did three stunning dives one after the other.

He saw her father pointing out this performance in an approving manner, so he went up the ladder for a fourth time. He didn't quite have time for a fourth dive. Dina scuttled around the pool and threw herself into the water directly in his diving area. She floated past, and while doing so crossed her eyes at him and shoved her belly well up out of the water, at the same time making small wailing noises. The wailing noises weren't loud enough to get to her parents. They were just loud enough to get to Jonathan. Jonathan got them, and he thought what he would like to do most in all the world was to dive head first at Dina's belly, injuring her in some terrible way, perhaps breaking her.

As it was, he timed it to a second, and fell, in a sitting position, exactly beside her, and in the ensuing splash, screened from the eyes of onlookers, pulled her well under. He sat on her while she was under, and got his legs around her neck giving them a good squeeze. He also managed to pull her hair so hard he actually pulled some out. She bit him while he was doing this, but there was no question who got the better of it. The whole thing only took seconds, but he still managed to get in position to help her solicitously to the side, where her father had come running.

'Jonathan, you should be more careful. Are you all right, sweetheart?'

'I tried to avoid her, I tried!' Jonathan said. 'I was already moving, I couldn't stop. Are you all right, Dina?'

He saw with pleasure that she was crying and spewing up water so hard she couldn't speak, so he gave her a good clout on the back to help and put his arm around her, nipping her so savagely in the soft skin of the inner upper arm that he actually felt his fingernails meet.

All this was good, but he saw he'd had the best, so he left Dina to be comforted and took himself off for a bit of underwater work with the brick. The other members of the group came one by one with their parents, but he kept well away from *them*. The whole kibbutz seemed to be at the pool. Presently, keeping his eyes open, he saw his parents were there too. It was too crowded for diving, but he did his special back flip from the side, the one his father had taught him, and in a minute or two found his father beside him in the water.

'We waited for you, *motek*. Where were you?'

'Practising.'

'Is there some problem, Jonathan?'

'No problem.'

'Mummy is very worried. Come and say hello to her.'

He could see his mother was worried. She was looking down at him from the side. 'Later,' he said, 'I have to practise.'

'Leave the practice. Just for a minute. Come and talk.'

He went after the brick without bothering to answer. But he was by no means finished with them, and presently he got out and talked.

'I have to go now,' he said, introducing the talk.

'Go? Already? What is it? What's the matter with you?'

'Sweetheart,' his mother said.

'I wanted to practise before the pool filled up. I left my homework. Now I have to do it. I'm going home.'

'I'll do it with you. Leave it for now. We'll go home together.'

'No, it will be quiet there now. They're all at the pool. I'll have it to myself at *home*,' Jonathan said.

Oo-wah! He got it then, the look he'd worked for, one, two, from both of them. When he saw it on his mother's face he could have bitten his tongue off. He wanted to throw himself at her and kiss her, but he couldn't do that now. It was not only impossible, but in various ways sickening. He opened his mouth to say *Shalom* but was not certain of his voice so he nodded and went. He picked up his sandals, and dried himself in his room. There were four beds in his room, three bedrooms in the house; twelve people in his group altogether. Dina's bed was next to his, and she'd told him. She'd explained the whole thing.

There was a dining-common room, and he went there and looked at the list and saw it was his turn to set for supper anyway:' JONATHAN-DINA'. He'd do it himself, never mind Dina. 'May her womb shrivel,' he said in Arabic. He'd never got the point of the phrase before. It was just something Abdul said. You could say it about any troublesome female, human or animal. He knew now there were many things he hadn't got the point of. He set the tables for supper and did his homework. Later on, the group came back and a bit later his parents called on him. But he saw them first, through the window, and he wasn't there when they looked for him.

'I mean, for Chrissake,' Amos said. 'He's seen it on every side. All of his group have brothers or sisters. I mean, since the motion, what would any of them be doing there if they hadn't?'

He was referring to the housing motion carried in 1963, that in view of the satisfactory financial position, two and a half-room apartments, instead of the normal one and a half-room apartments, would be provided for any parents who wished one child to sleep with them, instead of, as formerly, in the children's houses.

As the new apartments had become available they had been allocated on a seniority basis, which meant that as founding members, Amos and Pnina had been among the first. Jonathan had thus had one of their two and a half rooms for almost two years.

But in those two years any number of children had rotated quietly back to the children's houses as further babies arrived in families. There was nothing abnormal or *undemocratic* about it, for Chrissake, as Amos pointed out. The children were with their peer groups in the children's houses most of the time, anyway; they studied with them, ate with them, had their various group activities with them. It was simply a question of sleeping accommodation. If the natural *background* to the situation had been explained in the proper *place* . . .

'Well,' Esther said, lighting another cigarette, 'it's all a question of the child – what else can I say? We're dealing here with a little – a little fellow who's unusually . . . sensitive.' She was having to choose her words with some care, and felt herself, anyway, obscurely under attack. Behind all this, some localized aggression to do with the biological issue of birds and bees was looming: she could see it from the combative set of his little red beard. The safe thing seemed to be to turn this combativeness into other channels. 'It's a question of *parent-child communication*. It's no criticism,' she said as Amos opened his mouth again.

'Communicate what? It's not for five months yet. There's nothing to *see*. If you could specify the area of criticism that's –'

'No criticism,' Esther said again, 'but simply a question of where, when, and from whom he learns that his way of life – some part of his way of life, is going to be –'

'It's *months* away. If we're going to tackle the specific accommodation issue, which I doubt is the real issue, what was the point –'

'And in this case, apparently through your wife wishing her mother to join her from the States, and quite rightly making early application to Baruch, as secretary of the Accommodation and Catering Committee, and Baruch idly chatting about it with *his* wife' – let him go to Baruch and Sasha if he wanted a fight – 'at a time when Dina happens to be sitting with them doing her homework, he learns about it from Dina,' she said, having to raise her voice above his general expostulations. 'Which is very unfortunate, but leads to a position where all we can do about it is have him sent home, if that's what you really want. Which isn't to say he'd go anyway,' she added.

He was silent.

'Pnina's sick with it,' he said presently.

'I'm sorry.'

'It's two weeks.'

'I'll have a word with him. It's really something for Alizia.' Alizia was the housemother of that particular group. 'Except he isn't getting on with Alizia.'

'He isn't?' he said, a bit eagerly.

'He's not getting on all that well with anybody, is he?'

'Oh. No . . . It's Pnina, you see. Her mother's not coming for four months. His room's waiting there.'

Esther shrugged and knocked off her ash. She knew quite well that his hunch re the birds and the bees had been correct. People thought that because the children grew up so freely here, because they saw nature at work all around them . . . Very little of it counted. Each had still to accommodate to the bizarre fact of his own origin and existence. Most did, without major upsets. Every now and again, one didn't.

But she had no intention of going into that, and she saw she'd successfully knocked the stuffing out of Amos, anyway. So she said, it's a question of patience. You go on demonstrating you care, et cetera, and I'll see what I can do.'

*

Amos didn't feel he'd got very far, and there was also the question of what to tell Pnina, so he took a moody walk. It was a dark night, but there was a pleasant greenish glow in the lanes – they'd restrung the lamps through the trees in 1961. A lot had happened in 1961, and every year since – a result, of course, of the cotton, but even more seminally of the swimming pool.

He skirted the pool and in a melancholy way still got some pleasure out of it. But there were less pleasant memories now. He remembered teaching Jonathan to swim in it. He remembered the occasions when the child had come running on fat legs, and he'd picked him up and bit his bottom. 'Nu, Jonathan?' 'Swim,' Jonathan had said. Well. It was a matter of patience. Things came about. Plenty had come about here.

From the need for the swimming pool had come the cotton; from the economic necessity of servicing their own cotton machinery had come the servicing of everybody else's. They covered all Israel now. Everybody sent the machinery for an annual overhaul. It was a large business. From the skill developed in this business had come all the rest.

There was the factory for the manufacture of bin wheels. In the early years they'd had to buy at great expense numerous wheeled bins in various sizes to accommodate the various types of cotton. One of the members had come upon the notion that what was needed was not more bins but more wheels. He had invented the coupling that enabled two sets of wheels to be adjusted to various distances according to the bin required to go on them.

Then he had invented the new type of bin: pairs of mild steel grids in matched sets. It was a matter of minutes to connect two sides and two ends to make a bin, to go on any two pairs of wheels. They shipped the sets of wheels and grids all over the world now: it was their largest industry.

From the profits of this industry had come the pickling and canning plant, not because of any economic need to pickle or can but merely to resolve the continuing ideological dilemma posed by the Arab and his relations. They'd formed a joint-stock company, in which the kibbutz was one shareholder and the Arab village the other, thus avoiding the iniquity of an employer-employee relationship. The kibbutz provided the plant and did the pickling, canning, and marketing; the Arabs provided the produce from their own and other sources. The Gei-Harim brand of olives, cucumbers, peppers, and other pickles were now on sale in every supermarket in Israel. Accounts were prepared annually and the profits equally distributed. Out of the profits the villagers now had a movie theatre, several trucks, and four young men learning engineering at the Haifa Technion; and the kibbutz had two and a half-room apartments.

Amos brooded over all this and knew it was not in vain, but there was a taste of ashes in his mouth.

3

During the summer holidays a number of *tiyulim*, expeditions and hikes, had been organized for the children, and in view of the competition these were now oriented towards the collection of species. In July they did an exchange with a kibbutz at Shka'im, which though a good way to the south was still in their geographical area so that points could usefully be picked up. There were a lot of points to be picked up there.

Shka'im (the name meant hollows or basins) was in a depression to the east of what was left of the Huleh marshes. This large malarial swamp, avoided by Arabs for centuries, and the grave of numerous enthusiastic but inexperienced Zionists of the preceding one, had been finally drained by the Jewish National Fund in the mid-1950s. A small area of it, zealously sprayed against any malignant species that might yet have designs on Zionists, but still containing some of its original wildlife, had been preserved as a memento of what had been, and also as a nature reserve.

Because of the unusual 'hollows' in which the kibbutz had been situated and its proximity to the Jordan Valley depression, soil and climate were conducive to a subtropical agriculture. The kibbutz had the only banana plantations in the area, was experimenting with pineapples, and did a roaring winter trade to Europe with cut flowers. With subtropical flora went subtropical fauna. The Gei-Harim children organized a committee to ensure that nothing would be missed, but they still didn't know which way to run first with their notebooks.

Two truckloads of them had arrived at Shka'im (and an exchange consignment at Gei-Harim), the idea being for the children to have lunch, supper, and breakfast at the respective kibbutzim, and return the following afternoon. This was what they did, almost all of them.

Jonathan lost interest at a fairly early stage and in the heat of the afternoon wandered off for a sleep in the gloom of the banana plantation. He knew about bananas. Esther had given a talk on the subject. The mother banana annually produced three shoots, two of which were destroyed by injecting paraffin through a hollow needle, and the third left to grow. Jonathan walked through the plantation, kicking at the shoots that had been left to grow. He managed to grind several of them to a pulp, and sat down to examine another more carefully before destroying it.

The shoot was like a long and slender tusk, pale green in colour. Though soft and silky to the touch, it was surprisingly hard when pressed. It ended in a point as sharp as a needle. Jonathan experimentally pricked himself with the point. Then he tried to pull the shoot up. It was tough, unyieldingly attached to the rhizome of its mother. But determined twisting succeeded, and he examined what he had torn away. He saw then why the thing was so hard. The material of which it was composed was very thin, and it was hard when pressed because it was tightly rolled. You had to look hard to see where the roll ended. Jonathan found where it ended, and began to unroll it.

He unrolled and unrolled. The shoot when opened went to a half metre at least, and the inside of it was softer and silkier and of a yet more tender green than the outside. A delicate tracery of veins ran through it, and looking up Jonathan saw that they were the identical veins of the enormous, leathery, bottle-green thing that drooped with fruit above. The whole of that was already there in *this*, cunningly and delicately packed in the slender tusk. The fruit would probably be there too, somewhere. Jonathan tore it up, and kept tearing until the shreds were too small to tear any more. His hands were sticky and the smell of it was there. He rubbed them on the big banana leaves, but the smell was there, too, and stronger, so he rubbed them on his trousers, and stained them, and still had the smell. It was the smell of growing things, and he was sick of all growth. He was sick of the knowledge of what was growing in his mother, and of the grotesque way in which it had got there.

Dina had explained it to him. Dina had been his closest friend. When she'd told him, he'd given her a good beating right away, but although she cried she had been anxious to be believed and she had shown him on herself how it was done. He still hadn't believed her, and she was still anxious, so she'd taken him to watch the animals doing it. He'd seen the animals doing it before. What did it prove, except that they were animals? It was an animal thing to do.

But he knew that it proved it. All of a sudden it illuminated a number of things he'd idly observed.

His hands were still sticky, and he couldn't bear the smell. He knew there would be a standpipe somewhere in the plantation, so he looked about and found one, and washed his hands under the tap. Then he left the tap running and went for a sleep.

He was hungry when he woke up, and knew it must be suppertime, but he didn't fancy rejoining the others. He was sick of them. He didn't want to spend the night at this kibbutz, either. He didn't like the people he knew, and he didn't want to know others. He thought the only person he liked was Abdul, in the olive groves. He liked the way Abdul swore. Abdul had taught him some swear words that nobody else on the kibbutz knew. Jonathan had told Dina some, but not all of them. He was sorry he'd told her any now. He picked a few bananas and ate them, and came to a general kind of decision. He thought that in the future the best thing to do was whatever he wanted to do.

They sent a search party from Shka'im to look for Jonathan in the evening, and they telephoned Gei-Harim to see if he hadn't somehow got back there. He wasn't at Gei-Harim, but Gei-Harim also sent a party down by truck to look for him, and got in touch with the border police. Everybody looked for Jonathan until two o'clock in the morning, when the kibbutz people called off the search and the police alerted the night patrols. Esther was pretty sure he'd sneaked off by himself and fallen asleep somewhere, and that he would show up sharp enough for breakfast.

Jonathan didn't show up for breakfast, and he still hadn't shown up when the party of children returned to Gei-Harim for lunch. About teatime he wandered down from the Arab village where Abdul lived. The kibbutz secretary rang up Shka'im and also the border police to let them know Jonathan had returned, and then tried to find out what had happened to him.

Jonathan wasn't very communicative. He said he'd become detached from the main party at Shka'im while searching for species. He'd been doing this so hard he'd lost himself. He'd gone to sleep somewhere, he didn't know where, and in the morning had managed to get a lift on a truck. It was a truck from an Arab village, and it had fortunately called at Abdul's village. He thought he must have left his notebook on this truck, or maybe it had fallen off, because he didn't have it. They'd given him a nice lunch in the village and he didn't want any tea. He was sorry he'd caused everyone so much trouble. He hadn't known how to get in touch.


4


There was an 'activity' the next morning in the largest classroom, and Esther soon had them describing in poetic terms what they'd seen. She knew the bunch like the back of her hand, and had felt confident enough in advising Motke of success. Several couldn't spare the time to talk and instead hastened to copy into their best books the notes and sketches from their rough ones. Jonathan had unfortunately lost his, of course, and couldn't participate, but he seemed to be listening. He was looking out the window, though, when Esther began listing the things they had seen.

'Jonathan. Join in. We have all these. Tell another.' She'd put two lists on the blackboard, one headed 'Flora' and the other 'Fauna'. There was a good long list of both. Jonathan studied the lists, and he said, 'Oleander.'

'We have oleander. Something else.'

Jonathan thought for a while. 'Yellow oleander,' he said.

Esther had given a talk the previous week on the rare yellow oleander, and she looked at him a bit hard.

'Are you sure, Jonathan?'

'It's in the book I lost.'

'Yes. All right. That's very interesting, Jonathan. Give an example of fauna.'

Jonathan took some time looking at the list again. 'Gazelle,' he said.

'We have gazelle.'

'Some other kind of gazelle, then.'

Esther felt her temper going, but she hung on to it.

'That's *very* interesting, Jonathan,' she said. 'I didn't know we had other kinds. We'd all be interested to know about this one. What kind was it?'

'It's in my book.'

'Maybe you could draw it for us.'

'I don't know,' Jonathan mumbled.

'Try. Here. Take the chalk.'

Jonathan looked a bit blindly around the classroom and went and took the chalk. Even before he'd finished the children burst out laughing. Esther wasn't laughing.

'Do you think that's clever, Jonathan?'

it's the best I can do,' Jonathan said. He was laughing with the rest of them.

Esther felt an overpowering urge to hit him. But she knew that wouldn't be clever, either.

'Are you proud of yourself?' she said.

'Well, it could certainly do with a few finishing touches,' Jonathan said modestly, examining his drawing.

'Those are the exact horns you saw, are they?'

'Who said exact? You said try. In my book it would be exact,' he said, if I had it.'

Esther took the chalk from him, and it broke in her hand.

'That is *Gazella smithii*,' she said.

'What eye?'

'*Smithii*. Smith. *Gazella* Smith.'

'Smith?' Jonathan said.

'Smith. That is the name of the gazelle. As you very well know, it is extinct. It doesn't exist any more. I know that you couldn't have that gazelle in your book, Jonathan.'

'Well,' Jonathan said, 'let's see who's right. One day, maybe, the book will turn up.'

'Jonathan,' Esther said. She tried to control her breathing. 'I would be happy if you would admit that you are not telling the truth.'

'All right,' Jonathan said.

'You admit it?'

'Why not? If it makes you so happy.'

Esther didn't know what to do. She'd been an educationist for a long time. But she thought that people who had been at it even longer would still not know. She said tightly, 'Jonathan, this is an activity. If you don't want to join in, you can go.'

'You want me to go?' Jonathan said, inquiringly.

'I don't care what you do,' Esther said. 'I mean, it's voluntary. If you wish to participate, stay. If you'd sooner go elsewhere, you're at liberty to do that also.

'Well, if you really don't *care*,' Jonathan said politely. 'I would sooner go elsewhere,' and he went.

He went to the olive groves.

It was half past ten and Abdul was having a little snack. He was eating *ful*, black beans in a sharp sauce. He tore off a piece of *pitta* and gave it to Jonathan. Jonathan dipped his *pitta* in the *ful*.

'What's the matter, don't they feed you in that place?'

'We eat well,' Jonathan said.

'I always seem to be giving you meals.'

'I like eating with you.'

'I also like eating with you, *halaila*,' Abdul said, it was only a comment.'

They ate in silence.

'You want olives?'

'I'll take a few olives with you,' Jonathan said.

They sat under the olive trees, and Abdul opened a can.

'They get better,' Jonathan said.

'Of course. It's a good name, the new one.' The new name was Moonstone. It was a pale oval olive, lightly pickled. 'As a matter of fact, a beautiful name. It's beautiful even in both languages,' Abdul said. The one they were talking was Arabic.

'Did you ever hear of a gazelle called Smith?'

'Smith?'

'Yes.'

'No.' Abdul spat out a stone. 'It's an English name,' he said.

'It's also a beautiful name,' Jonathan said.

'Perhaps there is a gazelle of that name in England. Why do you ask?'

'We were discussing gazelles. Esther said this gazelle no longer existed.'

'Then it must be so. She is a very clever woman, Esther. She also has an even temperament, which is rare in women. Her husband is a fortunate man.'

'Her womb should shrivel,' Jonathan said.

'You're still not getting on at school?'

'What is there to get on at?'

'*Halaila*, don't be a fool. Make the best of your opportunities. I'm sixty-six years old, and I know what I'm talking about. God put a good head on your shoulders. For a nine-year-old, it's incredible. Honour Him by using it.'

'For an intelligent person,' Jonathan said, 'you're an even bigger fool. How can a man of sixty-six believe in God?'

'It's hard?'

'Look around you. The whole thing is a scientific process.' Gei-Harim was a secular kibbutz and a very early resolution had been that the scientific basis of the universe should be thoroughly explained to the children.

'Little noodle,' Abdul said, rubbing the carroty head, 'you have still a lot to learn, which He will take into account. But don't continue to say such things or He'll blacken your face.'

'Give a single proof.'

Abdul stood up, chuckling. 'There was once here, many years ago, a young Catholic priest, it's a sect of Christian,' he said. 'This madman talked of nothing day in and day out but proofs. What proofs?' He lit himself a cigarette and looked around at the trees. 'I have work now. Go and make *Shalom* with Esther and learn some more.'

But Jonathan was interested and got up and walked about with him. 'A single piece of evidence,' he said. 'Anything.'

Abdul looked at him tolerantly, and took, the cigarette out of his mouth. 'Over there,' he said, pointing, 'where you see the new olive groves, there used to be another village, populated entirely by imbeciles. When the Zionists first came, the people in that village attacked them and drove them away. They kept driving them away, and the Zionists kept coming back, often in a situation of great danger. To a fool like me, it was clear that it was God's will that they should come back and that He would undoubtedly bring all the Jews back. Those people disagreed. Now they sit in ashes, while olives live where they used to live. *Nu*?'

'*Nu*?'

'God gave the victory.'

'It's a ridiculous simplification,' Jonathan said.

'I expect so,' Abdul said. 'Probably all the Jews sat down in a committee meeting and voted themselves a victory.'

'They fought,' Jonathan said. 'They fought better, that's all.'

'Who knew they were such wonderful fighter before?'

'They always were good fighters,' Jonathan said. 'That isn't the point. You're saying God wanted the others to lose, he wanted them to run from their village.'

'They could have stayed in peace.'

'Why didn't they?'

'They were imbeciles.'

'So who made them imbeciles?'

'They made themselves imbeciles. It's a similar case with you. Were you an imbecile to begin with? He gave you a good brain and all you can think to do with it is prove He doesn't exist. Everything else exists, but He doesn't. Is this sense, *halaila*? Who made all the things that do exist? Who made you?'

'That's another thing,' Jonathan said. 'The way people are made. It's disgusting.'

Abdul looked at him. 'In what way?' he said.

'In every way. If there was a God and he could make everything, wouldn't he have invented a better way than this? Is it a decent way for human beings to be made?'

'How would you sooner they were made?'

'There could be something with blood,' Jonathan said. 'Or chemicals, a scientific process. This is for animals. Should responsible people have to behave like this – the Queen of England, General de Gaulle, parents even?'

Abdul looked at him closely. 'is your mother with child?'

'Yes.'

'Blessed be the Name.'

Jonathan grunted.

Abdul carefully nipped his cigarette and pocketed the unsmoked portion. '*Halaila*,' he said, 'it's plain to me you're mixed up. Which is only to be expected. I often forget how young you are, seeing the head you've got on your shoulders. It's nothing but a miracle. Blood and chemicals! To me, it's another sign of His goodness. I expect it very easily could have been blood and chemicals. You see, bright as you are, there are things you don't know yet. There are things that have appeal only at a certain age. Let me tell you, there is absolutely nothing wrong with the method of making children. Whether children are made or not, it's a pleasant thing to do.'

'Pleasant?' Jonathan said.

'Certainly. It's an excellent thing. Even the Queen of England delights in it.'

'And General de Gaulle?'

'I don't know about General de Gaulle. It's possible. You'll learn. By the look of you, I would say you'll have many opportunities, blessed be the Name. So for the moment try not to be such a fornicating little imbecile. Would it hurt from time to time to praise the Name?'

'It wouldn't hurt,' Jonathan said, it's just an insult to the intelligence.'

'Whose are you insulting, mine or yours?'

'It's just a saying,' Jonathan said.

'Then don't say it to me.'

'Are you angry?'

'Yes, I'm angry. You talk like a parrot. All this sheep's droppings of a scientific process. Things go on by some kind of process, it's obvious.'

'I'm sorry you're angry,' Jonathan said.

'Frig off now. I have things to do. Not everything is known on that kibbutz, you know. Just occasionally they could be wrong.'

'I know it. There was no intention of insulting your intelligence, Abdul.'

'So frig off.'

Jonathan frigged off, but not very far. He didn't speak to anyone at lunch, and afterwards kept to himself at the pool. He thought about a number of things. In bed, he thought of a film they'd once had at the kibbutz. In this film a certain young imbecile had been in the habit of flopping on his knees to pray every ten minutes. Every time he flopped, the members of Jonathan's group flopped too, creasing up so hard that one actually wet himself. The film was to do with a racehorse, and an older imbecile who was mortally ill. The younger one prayed so hard, the horse won a race and the older one recovered. They still joked about it from time to time, and thinking of the group's jokes, and all that he disliked about the group, Jonathan thought it would be a fine idea to say a prayer himself. He couldn't bother getting out of bed to say it, so he said it there.

He'd never said one before, and he couldn't think of what to say. He experimentally tried Abdul's formula, 'Praise the Name', but it seemed to lack body. So he tried a few employed by the young imbecile in the film. 'God bless my mother and father,' Jonathan said. 'God bless Abdul. God bless the kibbutz. God bless Israel.' He thought of having Dina blessed, but then he thought he wouldn't. He had her womb shrivelled instead. Just as he was going off to sleep, he recalled what had brought all this to mind, and added another prayer. 'God bless Smith,' Jonathan said.

Three young women were pregnant on the kibbutz, so a rabbi came up by bus from Kiryat Shemona the following week, and married them. There was no secular marriage in Israel, and the kibbutz accepted the rabbi's regular visits as a necessary joke. The rabbi knew all about this, but he was an optimistic and tolerant man and he regarded his visits as in a sense of a missionary nature. He knew that the kibbutz kitchens were not kosher, so he never ate anything or so much as touched a plate. But glass was a material that ordinary washing could restore to a state of ritual purity, so he usually took a glass of wine with them. Last year he had been doing so when a young boy had come up to ask him why he blessed the wine.

'Jews do so, *motek*,' the rabbi had replied. 'We always make the blessing before drinking.'

'For whose benefit?'

The rabbi looked at his carroty-haired interrogator with some interest.

'For everybody's benefit. It reminds us that God made the wine.'

'Not this wine, he didn't. They made it at Zichron. I was there and saw them.'

'So where did the grapes come from?'

'Kibbutz Ha Carmel. I was there, too.'

'*Motek*, let me tell you, if all the kibbutzniks in the world sat together, they couldn't make so much as a single grape.'

'What makes you so certain?'

'It's a scientific fact. It's not possible to do it. I'll tell you another. Have you got chickens here?'

'No chickens.'

'Well, I suppose you know what an egg looks like. Could anything be more common? Yet the cleverest scientists in the world couldn't put one together again if it broke.'

'With glue they couldn't?'

'The shell, yes. The inside, no. It's a scientific impossibility to reconstitute a broken egg, never mind make a new one. Yet God makes millions, billions, every day. This is why we make the blessings, to remind us of things that become so ordinary.'

'It's part of the scientific process, I suppose.'

'Naturally. Do you suppose God would be unscientific?'

The bus had hooted then, so the rabbi had had to hurry.

He looked for the boy this time, but couldn't find him. He drank his glass of wine, refused biscuits and cake, and took a solitary stroll around the kibbutz until it was time for the bus to go. When well out of sight of the festivities, he was suddenly aware that the boy was with him.

'*Shalom*, rabbi.'

'*Shalom, motek*.'

'I'll walk with you a few steps.'

'With pleasure. Did you find ways yet to put together a broken egg?' the rabbi asked playfully,

'Have you any more blessings?'

'What?'

'I need a few blessings,' the boy said urgently.

The rabbi changed his spectacles and looked at him. 'What blessings do you want?' he said.

'What have you got?'

'In the prayer book you'll find everything.'

'There is no prayer book here.'

The rabbi made haste to find his own. 'Here. Take it. Keep it, *motek*.' No prayer book! 'What particular *kind* of blessing do you require?'

'Would there be anything special for a gazelle?'

'A gazelle?'

'The animal. It has horns. A gazelle.'

The rabbi blinked. He couldn't recall being asked such a question before. 'Would it be the first time you saw the animal?' he said.

'Who said I saw it? What difference, anyway?'

'There is a difference. For instance, for gazelles in general, there's one blessing. You could use that in praise of the various orders of creation. For the first sighting of the animal in a particular season, there's another. You might use the form, "who has brought us to this day when . . ." et cetera. On the other hand, for the first sight of a kind you've never seen before, you might prefer to use that special one for strange forms – we can even use it for dwarfs or hunchbacks – "who variest the forms of His creatures." There's a number, you see. It's hard to advise without knowing more.'

'They're all here, though?'

'Every one. Let me show you.'

The rabbi riffled through the pages with practised ease and turned up the Blessings for Special Occasions.

Jonathan skimmed through it rapidly. There seemed to be some useful stuff here. There seemed to be plenty of body.

'So why the special interest in gazelles?'

'It's a nice animal.'

'A beautiful animal. As a matter of fact Israel was often referred to symbolically as a gazelle.'

'I thought it was a lion.'

'The lion of Judah – it's a narrower idea, a kingly one, The gazelle represented Israel as a people. Let me see if you know how this people got its name Israel.'

'Who doesn't know it? From Jacob, Jacob killed an angel so they changed his name to Israel. I never got the point of it.'

'He never killed it, God forbid! He wrestled with the angel. If you like, it was a test for Jacob, and he passed the test, so his name was changed to Is-ra-El, which means "he that prevails with God" or "who is a champion for God." It symbolizes the purpose of the Jew, *motek* – also your own purpose.'

'Yes, well, I have to go now,' Jonathan said. 'Thanks for the book.'

The rabbi saw that enthusiasm had impelled him to run where even the angel might have feared to tread.

'Walk with me to the bus,' he said, 'unless you want to get back to the party.'

'I'll walk,' Jonathan said.

'It's a fine kibbutz.'

'It's all right.'

'I remember it as a heap of stones.'

'Now it's a heap of imbeciles.'

The rabbi looked at him. 'How old are you, *motek*?'

'Nine.'

'Have you many friends?'

'Abdul in the olive groves is my friend.'

'Abdul told you everyone here was an imbecile?'

'Of course not. He talks the way you talk. He says God is on the side of the Jews.'

'Say rather the reverse proposition. Still, he seems a well-meaning man. All the same, I wouldn't talk so much to Abdul, *motek*. In this world there are basically two kinds of people, Jacob and Ishmael.'

'Everyone knows there are more. There are hundreds of kinds.'

'I said *basically*. If I wanted to be clever I could say the two kinds were men and women. *Nu*? But in a broader way, it's also true. Jacob is for settlement, society, and the moral law which regulates them. Ishmael is the wild man who acts as the mood takes him. Figuratively, we can say Ishmael made the heap of stones and Jacob the kibbutz.'

'Why only figuratively? I can tell you that's exactly what happened.'

'In this case, yes. I'm aware of it,' the rabbi said. It was a warm day, but he felt suddenly warmer and fanned himself. 'It's a mistake to be too clever, *motek*. We shouldn't try to be too clever. I was talking, of course, in a broad sense. It's why we need so many blessings. Who else has so many? Wouldn't it be enough to bless the Creation as a whole? For us, not. We're students of these things, of every aspect of the creation. If you want, we're the *scientists* of it,' the rabbi said triumphantly.

'The bus driver is waving,' Jonathan said.

'I can see. Is there some other question I can answer?'

'No. It was very interesting,' Jonathan said.

'I'm glad. Remember, *motek*, you're of Jacob.'

'I mean about the gazelles,' Jonathan said.

'Also good.'

'You would say "who variest the forms of his creatures" for a new one, if I should happen to see one?'

'Or "who has brought us to this day." Either is suitable.'

'Maybe use both?'

'It can do no harm.'

'Well, thanks for the advice.'

'A pleasure, *motek*.'

Jonathan went back to the silent children's house and studied the blessings. There was certainly plenty of body, but for the time being he thought he'd stick to the old favourites. In bed at night, he said, 'God bless Smith,' and he said it early. He had to be up early,

## 5

He was afraid it was not early enough, because outside it was not so dark. On the other side of Dina he could see Allon sleeping. Allon had a wristwatch on. He went and had a look at it. Not yet four. It was all right. There and back by breakfast. He slipped into his shirt and shorts and carried his sandals outside, and padded in bare feet through the kibbutz. With the buildings well behind him, he put his sandals on and ran down to the lower ground, past the fishponds. It was a long way and it took him a quarter of an hour, running fast. He was out of breath at the bottom, and he wasn't sure where the military units were, so he took it easy going through the citrus, sniffing for cigarette smoke.

He picked his way slowly through the grapefruits and came out to the lemons. Beyond the lemons he could see the cotton fields and the burned patches in the middle, and beyond them the rock at the head of the ravine. He'd already worked out that he was going to have to crawl flat through the cotton. There was bound to be someone watching from the citrus.

'Hey!' somebody said from the citrus, just as he went flat.

Jonathan remained flat, in case the 'hey' was not for him.

'You in the cotton. Stand up. Come here.'

Jonathan stood up and went back.

A young man with a heavy machine gun was sitting in the irrigation pit of a lemon tree. He had a steel helmet on and was chewing gum.

'Where do you think you're going?'

'For a walk,' Jonathan said.

'On your face?'

'I was looking for species. We've got a nature competition.'

'So what are you going to find in the cotton?'

'Who knows? It's why you've got to look so close.'

'All right, I'm going to report you. You know that, don't you? What's your name?'

'Allon,' Jonathan said.

'How many times have you been told, Allon, that you're not to come down here?'

'I don't know.'

'There's fedayeen out there, waiting to blow your head off. They're sitting on the other side of the ravine. They could even be in the cotton.'

'So what are you supposed to be doing letting them get in the cotton?'

The young man stopped chewing for a moment. Then he got out a notebook. 'Allon what?' he said.

'Avny.'

'Okay, Allon Avny, I hope you're a good little scrubber. I'll personally see to it you get some experience during your holiday. Now stay away from here.'

'And you try and stay awake. I watched you for a good ten minutes. I flapped up and down in the cotton to see if you'd ever come to. I'll be interested in your report,' Jonathan said.

'Beat it,' the soldier said.

Jonathan beat it, back through the citrus, and wondered what to do. It was getting lighter. He could go around the long way, beyond their land, as he'd done accidentally the first time, and work back again. But it would take time.

He couldn't even remember the spot exactly. It would need looking for. He remembered the kind of droppings, though. If the droppings were still there, and he could find them immediately . . .

Jonathan added up the time it would take. If everything worked right, he could make it for breakfast. If not, no amount of lying would get him out of it. The soldier hadn't been able to see him in the dark. But he'd make his report, and if he weren't there it would be obvious, never mind about Allon. It might stop him ever trying again.

Jonathan weighed all this while still moving, and kept moving. He spotted the military on the other side of the grapefruits. There were two groups with tanks and mortars. He knew there should be another group somewhere, so he went carefully, and spotted that one too. This took time, and when he was past, he ran, hard.

The ground was rocky beyond their land, and not easy to run on. Jonathan also knew that the fedayeen had come in this way a few nights before, so he kept up a rhythmic chant of 'Praise the Name' as he ran. As Abdul and the rabbi seemed both to agree, a prayer could never do a person any harm.

He arrived at the far end of the ravine, and started working his way back. He spotted one or two familiar spots and looked around, but he knew they weren't right. There was no doubt whatever when he came to the right one: he knew it immediately and in a couple of minutes had found the droppings.

'Praise the Name,' Jonathan said, and got down on his hands and knees and followed them. He saw the trail went up over the boulders that lined the ravine at this point, and presumably went down again over the other side. He didn't know what to do about it. The ravine was narrow here, and the fedayeen might use it. It was madness even to get his head up over the boulders. He could easily be spotted from the other side.

He raised himself a little at a time and tried to find some gap in the boulders to look through. There was no gap. So he got his eyes slowly up to the level of the boulders and carefully scanned the other side. Then he got himself up. He moved very slowly to attract no attention and lay down on a boulder and tried to see below. A lot of tumbled rock jutted out below. He saw that the furthest one was large and flat, and he thought that if he could snake his way down to it, he would have a fine view of everything below.

He debated with himself about this, and knew it was still madness. But he knew that it always would be madness, and that there was no other way to find out.

Jonathan began snaking his way down, terribly slowly, keeping his eyes on the other side. The sun raised itself suddenly on the other side, half blinding him. But he got to the rock without mishap and lay flat on it and looked down into the ravine. He was still half blinded by the sun and at first couldn't see anything. Then he saw there were trees and bushes growing out from the walls, and that not much of the ravine was to be seen anyway. It was still grey and dark down there. But gradually his eyes adjusted, and through the trees and bushes he suddenly saw what else was there. 'Who has brought us to this day,' Jonathan said. 'Who variest the forms of his creatures.' He was still saying it when something ricocheted hard immediately below him, and a fragment of rock splintered off and spun in the air.

He got his head down immediately, and put his hands over it, as if it could possibly help. It had come from the other side, and even in his panic it occurred to him that from the other side he was now in full sunlight and that a stairway of rocks lay between him and safety and that he was not going to make it for breakfast.

# 6
## All About Musallem

The first hint of trouble came at Post No. 6 on the oil pipeline. Since time out of mind they'd sold them lambs there; they were always keen for fresh meat at Post No. 6. In a good year they bought rugs, too, and saddlecloths and various other things. The men took the articles home on leave to Damascus, or from wherever else God had sent them. At Post No. 6 now there were soldiers, and officers in shining boots, and a landing strip. There was also frozen meat delivered by transport plane from Damascus. No lambs, or anything else, would be required this year, the Beduin were informed.

The old man actually saw the accursed machine landing and its cargo unloaded, and for some minutes was speechless with rage. When able, he pleaded powerfully with God for the wombs of the mothers and wives and daughters of all at Post No. 6 to be shrivelled, and the men themselves to have their faces painfully blackened after first being rendered leprous and impotent.

He tried arguing with the officials and was directed to a provisions officer. A provisions officer at Post No. 6! The provisions officer was also the political officer, and he ordered the old man to take his people immediately out of the area, which was a military area, and showed him on a map a line, directing him to stay well to the east of it. The old man couldn't understand the map, but the officer read out the positions on it. With incredulity and horror, the old man heard that their old pool was now a blockhouse and an artillery post.

'But we'll perish!' he told the officer. 'I am eighty-six years old and every year of my life I've used that pool. We've just come from the east. We always come from there for the summer. We need water.'

'In villages you'll find water. Go and settle in villages, as the revolution demands. Think of your children growing up in ignorance. Don't you want them to be liberated?'

The old man had tried to plead further, but the officer had asked to see his papers, so that was the end of it. A couple of soldiers accompanied them out of the area. The soldiers left when they camped for the night, so an hour later they folded the tents and moved back to the west – well away from the pipeline, though.

Cursing continuously, the old man drew on his memory for other watering places. They decided in the end to make for Barata, where there was also a pool. The old man couldn't remember the officer saying there was any particular installation there, although it was still in the forbidden zone. It was a good ten kilometres to the east of their former pool, and not so reliable. It was also a Ma'ara pool, and the misbegotten swine would probably charge them for using it. Still, most of the Ma'ara had settled now in villages, as indeed had many of the Wahir – a depleted band! – so for some weeks at least there would be water for all. Disputes would certainly arise, but there was no way out.

'Ah, Musallem,' the old man said. 'Ishmael is being reduced. Every year the renegades are leaving us, and I suppose you can't blame them. But why is He doing this to us? What can be the intention?'

'Perhaps to test us,' the boy said, knowing the expected response.

'We must stand up to it, then.'

'As you've always done, Great-grandfather.'

'It's well said, you excellent child. As God's my guide, you're my true heir, *halaila*. I'll disinherit those renegades.'

'Don't think of such a thing!'

'We'll see. I'll go to the Sha'aria court in Kuneitra. I'll find some God-fearing man there who'll tell me the position. There are laws about these things, you see. We can't disinherit as we want. You're eight now, Musallem?'

'Nine, Great-grandfather.'

'Only a few more years. If I'm only preserved until you're old enough, it's all I ask.'

'Don't say such things. He'll preserve you until a hundred and twenty.'

'It can't be so, *halaila*. I'm in low spirits.'

'Then I'll give you a verse.'

He declaimed a couple, and the old man cheered up a bit. The boy always cheered him up, and the old man loved him.

The expected disputes soon developed at Barata. The Ma'ara, who had the right, insisted that the Wahir deplete their flocks: the water wouldn't last. It was a bad time to sell because others had similar problems, and the swine in the villages took advantage. Prices were low, very low. They sold a few animals every week, even had to sell good breeding females, but as the water went down the Ma'ara insisted that they sell still more, and charged them the same for the reduced supplies of water they took.

Everything that they bought went up in price, and everything that they sold went down. Even the good rugs and the blankets that the women had made went for practically nothing. Everywhere now the swine had the upper hand, for the Beduin were in no position to hold on to their stocks. The Ma'ara, taking payment for their water, managed to hold on to most of theirs, and also to their rugs and blankets, seeing themselves in a stronger and even a strengthening position. So there was bad feeling.

There was bad feeling among the Wahir themselves. Those who'd left to settle in villages came to visit, and wanted a careful accounting of the flocks they'd left with the tribe. They paid for the herding and the grazing of the flocks, and violent quarrels broke out when they heard the poor prices that had been fetched. There were accusations that families were being defrauded of their inheritance, that fortunes must have been made and hidden away; that it was unlawful, anyway, to sell breeding stock without permission. In vain, the position was explained to them. The old man ended up cursing everyone equally.

'Musallem, Musallem, you see what happens when people leave the old ways? The devil takes hold. It's owning a pinhead of land that does it. It makes them selfish. Not content with leaving the old traditions, they want to destroy them as well, which means destroying us.'

'Don't the Ma'ara also want to destroy us?'

'What traditions have the Ma'ara got? They were always cunning rogues. But with them at least it's not a question of wanting to destroy us, but of bettering themselves at our expense. They've no sense of evil. They never had. They don't believe in djinns.'

'They don't?'

'They do not. Musallem, be guided always by what you see here. Never plant a seed.'

Many people, at this season, were indicating to Musallem in which ways he should be guided. His mother, who had married again, had come up from the village, where she was settled.

'*Halaila*, there's a warm bed for you when it's cold, and nice drinks when it's hot. A person doesn't have to work all hours herding sheep. You pay someone else to do it, and meanwhile do more interesting things. The boys play football in the village, *halaila*. They go to school and learn useful things. Everybody's proud of them and they don't have to run when they see a policeman. The time's gone now for tramping about in this way. You're young and don't realize, but I've lived both ways and I know which is best. Don't listen to people who know only one way. Come home with me, *halaila*.

'I'll think about it,' Musallem said.

But in the tents of the Ma'ara he received different guidance. He learned to smoke cigarettes there, and he often sat and smoked with his cousins. He learned many new things about his father.

'Did anybody ever see two faces more alike? The boy's the image of him.'

Nobody had ever told Musallem this, and he was interested.

'Why did he run with the sheep?' he said.

'Who run with a sheep? The sheep was his own. Why should he run with it? It's Wahir lies, little fool. The Wahir are made of dung and can't think for themselves. Wouldn't we have heard if he'd run somewhere? He paid good money for your mother, and he took his inheritance with him. They only say this to avoid their obligations. We got nothing back of what he took.'

Musallem knew there were two views with regard to this inheritance, which would be his own, anyway, so he wisely refrained from comment. He said, 'So what do you think happened to him?'

'He lost a sheep in the ravine and went after it.'

'That was dangerous.'

'Of course, but not for the reason you think. There are no djinns there.'

Again Musallem refused comment. 'What other dangers?'

'Wild animals, perhaps. Wolves have been heard there.'

'Why would he go if he knew it?'

'He was a Ma'ara and did what he wanted. This is how

we are. It's how you are, as anybody can see. Come and join us, as you're entitled, through your father, Musallem. Protect your inheritance while you've still got it.'

'My great-grandfather has promised me a bigger inheritance. He'll make me his heir.'

This caused some amusement. 'Let the old fool try! There are too many before you, Musallem. They'd certainly contest it. But even if he could, what would you get? There'll be nothing to get by that time. How long can the Wahir go on like this?'

'How long can anybody go on? My mother says we're finished. She wants me to go and live in the village.'

'There's nothing wrong with that, if it's what you want. Only the best will survive here, anyway. But we are the best, Musallem. There'll always be plenty for us. In a bad season, it's possible to join the fedayeen. Even boys can join, for special missions. They take us willingly, knowing we're not afraid. They pay good money for the simplest work.'

'What work?'

'Against the Jews. They give you a gun and ammunition, which you can sometimes sell, also bombs. Several of our young men are with the fedayeen this season, it's useful. You get your food, keep, good pay, and all they do, they take you to the stolen land and send you in to kill a few Jews. Every time you kill one, you're paid more. What can be wrong with that?'

'What stolen land?'

The Ma'ara were astonished at the ignorance that the Wahir had kept the boy in, and they laughed a good deal at his quaint ways.

'Over to the west, on the other side of the ravine. The Jews are supposed to have kicked the al Hadar off the land there and stolen it from them. The government pays the fedayeen to go in and reduce them, and meanwhile they're planning a campaign to finish them off. Why do you think they've cleared everyone out of the area? What do you think all these guns and soldiers are for? When they've finished with their revolution, they'll go down with an army and take the land back.'

'Did the Jews steal it?'

'Who knows? It's a branch of the al Hadar, anyway. It's for certain a strange people. They break their mouths when they try to speak Arabic. The women walk about with nothing on and offer themselves to anyone. They offer themselves to the fedayeen.'

'Can it be?'

'Ask any of the fedayeen. They go in and kill a few men, and when the rest run the women gladly offer themselves.'

'It's shameful.'

'Yes, it's shameful, but what of it? For us it's only a question of business. Everything's as God sends. If it's not this business, there'll be other business. We're in a good position. But the Wahir are certainly doomed. Think about it, Musallem.'

'I will,' Musallem said.

There was a lot to think about. He thought about what his mother had told him. He liked the idea of the football and the drinks, but not the school and the friendly policemen. He also didn't like the idea of living in one place, which seemed, as his great-grandfather said, in some way sinful and gross. How much better to live in a tent, which you took down and set up wherever you wanted! How very much better to live in his great-grandfather's tent, which, though now tattered, was still the airy three-pole tent of a sheikh, a thing of grace! He'd seen the hovels they inhabited in villages when he'd gone with the men to sell sheep.

Still, it was to be thought about.

But he also thought about the inheritance, and on a day in June went with his great-grandfather to the town of Kuneitra. The old man was secretive about the trip, and they went alone, riding donkeys in the heat, and taking a few sheep to sell. They got better prices for the sheep in Kuneitra than in the villages, which cheered the old man. But when he came out of the Sha'aria court a few hours later, he wasn't so cheerful.

'It didn't go well, Great-grandfather?'

It hadn't. Although the old man had outlived several sons and daughters, there were still several left. Also, because of his patriarchal role, it seemed that he had complicated responsibilities towards still further members of his seed.

'You're allowed a larger share, *halaila*, by reason of your mother's children by the al Hadar, whom one can count when it comes to assessing, but needn't when it comes to sharing. It's in my discretion, that man of God said. But it's nothing like what I want you to have. It's not a fraction.'

'Have I asked you for any? I pray you'll live to a hundred and twenty.'

'I know you do, Musallem. I know it, *halaila*. And I'm by no means finished yet. I'll take another opinion. There must be other opinions in view of the circumstances with the renegades. If they can turn tradition upside down, then so can I, and the devil take the lot of them. All the same, I'm grieved.'

He bought some hashish in the town out of the money they'd got for the sheep, and smoked a bit on the way back. And that night he smoked some more in the tent, asking Musallem to sit with him so that he could turn away visitors on the pretext of illness. Musallem didn't mind. He loved the tent at all times, but particularly at night. There was something proper and right in the tough black cloth and the long strips that were sewn in in the traditional Wahir patterns. There were three spacious divisions in the oblong structure, separated by full-length cloth walls, one for the women, which included the kitchen, one for the men, and the central one, which was the reception and guest area. They were lying in this one, on sheepskins laid over saddles, and the four oil lamps, suspended from the poles and beams, pleasantly lit up the rugs and the familiar brass and copper objects. There were some widows and other female dependents in the next room, talking softly, and a pleasant smell wafted from that kitchen quarter, and also from the hashish and the little fire that smouldered in the middle.

'I think I will take coffee, *halaila*.'

Musallem got up and added a little fuel from the bag of dried camel dung that lay nearby and blew up the fire with the bellows. Then he poured a few beans in the pan and roasted them. While they roasted, he pounded a bit of *hel* in the mortar, and then he shook the roasted beans into the mortar, and pounded them, too, and transferred the whole lot back to the pan for a minute, and kept the grains moving, while he boiled a drop of water. He shook the coffee into a copper jug and poured in the water and let it boil over three times, and stood the jug near the fire to retain the heat, while the old man drank a few small cups. His great-grandfather didn't say anything, and Musallem said nothing either.

'What is it?' the old man said.

'Was my father such a rogue?'

'He wasn't a rogue. He was a Ma'ara.'

'Yes.'

The old man looked at him.

'What is it?' he said.

'Why should he have run with the sheep?'

'I don't think he did. I will take one more cup.'

Musallem poured him a cup and watched him sip the bitter black liquid.

'It was a question of your mother,' the old man said. 'The rain had started and it was time to go. She didn't want to go. It was a question of telling her something that would enable her to go. Does it answer the question?'

'I'm happy he wasn't a rogue.'

'It does you credit.'

'What happened to the sheep?'

'It ran into the ravine. Perhaps he went after it.'

'He shouldn't have done it'

'Of course not.'

'The Ma'ara say there are no djinns there.'

'Your father also said so.'

'They say wolves might have killed him.'

'There are no wolves there in summer.'

Musallem thought about this.

'They also say I look like him.'

'You do,' the old man said. 'It signifies nothing. I myself resemble a Rashid, through my grandmother. What we are depends on what tradition we accept. Don't be afraid, Musallem. You're a Wahir and no Ma'ara. In this season, the Ma'ara prosper and we can't tell why He allows it. But one day you will also prosper. I'm going to fight for it.'

'Are the Ma'ara such good fighters?'

'They take chances that reasonable people don't. Their motive is usually greed. Sixty years ago they were almost wiped out through entering a blood feud which was none of their concern, in the hope of gain. They learned nothing from that disaster. They have a basic cunning which in a favourable season will bring them profit, but in the end will destroy them. It's blasphemous to predict, but we can safely say that one day the Ma'ara will take one chance too many.'

'Is it wrong to take chances?'

'It depends on the motive. The Prophet himself calls on us to take them in certain cases. Men risked their lives in the wars against unbelievers.'

'For what motive?'

To uphold what was right, what else? To establish the truth of their beliefs.'

'We can take chances to establish the truth?'

'We've got to. It's a precept. A proper order of things has got to be fought for,' the old man said, 'which I most certainly intend to do. I'm by no means satisfied that this *kadi* today understood the rights of the matter, learned as he is. There's often another interpretation of these laws. It can't be right to distribute a traditional inheritance to those whose only wish is to destroy the tradition. Don't worry about it, Musallem. I'm not dead yet.'

'I don't worry, Great-grandfather.'

'You're tired, *halaila*. Go to bed.'

'If there's nothing more you want.'

'How long since you gave me a kiss?'

'Who counts?'

'I count. How long have I got to count till?'

'Until a hundred and twenty,' Musallem said, and gave him one, and went off to bed to wonder about those aspects of the truth and of chance-taking that so lately had come to interest him.


2

These were boring days at Barata. Owing to the disputes, there were times when he couldn't visit the Ma'ara, and when everyone of the Wahir was in a despondent mood. The times of watering had to be carefully regulated. People couldn't wander as they wished for fear of running into army or police patrols, with perhaps some political official. It was not as it had been at the old pool. Nothing was as it used to be.

Among all the Beduin at the pool there were doubts as to how long the traditional life could continue, and not a few came to a decision to leave it – for the time being, at any rate. The days were dull, but the nights were some-times enlivened by fire, from the north and the south of them – all directed towards the west, towards the stolen land. There was a good deal of enthusiasm for these night displays, and Musallem was disappointed when there were none.

His great-grandfather was apathetic about the whole business. 'It's no concern of ours.'

'But shameful things are happening there.'

'Shameful things are happening everywhere.'

'You said yourself we must fight for what's right!'

'I intend to. Never fear, Musallem."

The boy knew that his great-grandfather was a very old man now, and that his mind had become very fixed, so he didn't argue with him. But some new ideas had come to his mind lately, and he put them to his cousins, on the oocasions when he could visit the Ma'ara.

'If there are no djinns in the ravine, how could a person die there?'

'From wolves, as you've been told.'

'There are no wolves in summer.'

'Who's proved it? He could also fall. The walls are like precipices.'

'But if he was very careful.'

'Who knows?'

'Could he be seen by other people?'

'What other people?'

'The people from the other side.'

'The Jews?' Again the Ma'ara had to laugh at the quaintness. 'The Jews are sheep. The fedayeen have driven them off.'

'Five years ago they hadn't driven them off.'

'Then not. But they'd never have attacked a Ma'ara. They'd have been mad to. Also, what would they want of him?'

'Would they attack one now?'

There aren't any now. The fedayeen have driven them off.'

'So what are the guns firing at?'

'Only listen to the child! It's a Ma'ara's quick wits. All the same, *halaila*, there are things you don't understand. When a government sets up huge guns, in tremendous fortresses, it costs a fortune in money. You don't suppose they'll leave them there to rot? They have to shoot off the guns. It keeps the soldiers busy. Also these guns fire enormous distances. They seek out the Jews wherever they are. Of course, they creep back from time to time. It's why there's still work for the fedayeen. But they creep in fear of their lives. They know what is coming.'

'They wouldn't go near the ravine, then?'

'Certainly not.'

'And even if they did, they'd run if they saw a Bedu?'

'Like lightning.'

'Yes. It's as I thought,' Musallem said.

But he did nothing quickly, very conscious these days of his mixed blood. Only the Ma'ara acted quickly, and it got them into trouble. The Wahir thought about things, but were often left behind. On the other hand, his great-grandfather said it was not wrong to take a chance in the interest of truth. There were several aspects of the truth that Musallem was interested in.

But mainly he was bored.

He was very bored when the disputes raged, and thought it might be better to play football and have drinks. But the disputes didn't always rage. In the early part of July there were no disputes. Musallem asked his great-grandfather if he could spend a night with the Ma'ara.

'For what reason?'

'There's some interesting argument there about an inheritance from my grandfather Ma'ara.'

'What is it to you?'

'Who knows?'

The old man looked at him for a long time, and then he kissed him. 'Musallem, I'm getting old. You do right to protect yourself in these evil days. It convinces me more than ever that you're my true successor. We'll go again to Kuneitra. The thing's getting urgent. The whole world is going mad. It horrifies me.'

'Should I go, then?'

'Of course go. Say little, but listen carefully.'

Musallem went. He went in the late afternoon, in the direction of the Ma'ara tents, but then turned west. He'd made careful inquiries, and he took a full water bottle with him, and a goat's cheese wrapped in a *pitta*. He'd heard what the fortresses looked like, massive bunkers dug out of the rock, with guns disguised by nets to look like other rock. They weren't easy to spot, but he kept his eyes open and spotted them, and kept well clear. He also kept clear of their old pool, knowing that it, too, was a fortress, and turned some distance to the north of it. The ground was much higher here, and he had to climb the last stretch.

The sun was setting as he came to the edge of the ravine. It was setting on a fantastic spectacle.

Musallem saw the stolen land.

He'd never seen it before. From their old pool, the opposite wall of the ravine was higher and nothing could be seen beyond it. Now, as far as he could see, everything was green. The hills were green. The valleys were green. The great plain between the hills was a vast checkerboard of green. There were forests of trees, and crops growing, and cattle at pasture. The thing was like a glimpse of Paradise. It was no wonder the Jews had stolen it.

Musallem had drawn in his breath, and for a minute or two actually stopped breathing. But now, lying down on his belly, he gazed below and took in more carefully the astounding world that was spread there. It wasn't a thing he could have imagined. It was unbelievable that underneath the real world this other world was going on.

Slowly, he became aware of details still less explicable. There were roads, a whole network of roads. There was traffic on the roads. There were machines in the fields. Groups of buildings stood here and there on the checkerboard. There were people outside the buildings, and there were people in the fields. The people didn't seem to be creeping about. He wondered if they were fedayeen. But even from here he could see they weren't. They weren't Beduin. They weren't Arabs at all. It was a different race of people, with bare legs. It must be the Jews. Musallem tried to work it out. If they were Jews, what were they doing here? If they were here, why weren't they creeping?

There was too much to take in. He couldn't make sense of it. He tried to see the women who went with nothing on, but the light was going and he couldn't.

But he spent such a long time looking that he forgot why he was here. When it came to him, with a start, he realized he was not in a good position, anyway. From this high perch, jutting out over the ravine, there was nothing to be seen directly below. He could see the opposite wall and a tumble of rock that went down in a series of steps, but it was soon lost in bushes. He saw he was going to have to shift his position. He didn't fancy doing it in the failing light. He might wander by accident too near a fortress or into a band of fedayeen.

Musallem saw that the wise thing was to stay where he was until the sun came up again, so he found himself a sheltered spot in the rocks, and had a drink, and some of his *pitta* and goat's cheese. He listened intently in the silence for any sounds that might indicate the presence of djinns or wolves. But there were no sounds like that. There were some other sounds that he couldn't place. They were distant whinnying sounds, and he thought that in the calm air they might be drifting up from unknown species of cattle in the stolen land.

For some hours in the dark, he watched the stolen land. Lights had sprung up all over it, little clusters and networks
of them, some greenish and some orange, glittering and sparkling like patterns of stars, but more beautiful than stars. By night as by day: a jewel.

He was up early, before it was light. He wasn't of age, and therefore not obliged to make the dawn observance. He thought he would make it, all the same. The dawn observance was a useful insurance in all circumstances. He watched for the last star to go, and poured water from his. bottle, and rubbed his hands with it, and his face, and his feet. He poured more and sucked it into his nostrils, and put his wet fingers in his ears. Then he poured a third time, and spread wet hands on his head.

Musallem cleared the ground of sharp stones, and keeping the brightening area of sky to his left, faced south to Mecca, and went into the remembered movements, He stood upright and bowed, with his hands on his knees. Then he knelt and touched the earth with his head. Then he knelt upwards, and held his arms out, palms upwards, and ran into a difficulty. He couldn't remember the prayer. All he could remember was the introduction to prayer in general. He decided to repeat this a few times.

*'In the name of God, the Compassionate, the Merciful.*
*Praise be to God, Lord of the world!*
*The Compassionate, the Merciful!*
*King on the Day of Reckoning!'*

He knew the Compassionate, the Merciful, would make allowances, particularly since he was not obliged to say it at all. One way or the other, it ought to have the effect of drawing the attention of the Merciful, the Compassionate, to him, which would be a useful effect, for with the sky to the east now brightening rapidly he suddenly saw that an exceptionally weird cap of mist sat on top of the ravine, like a cork, sealing and protecting it. He wondered uneasily if this matter did not require more thought, a good deal more.

A small dawn breeze dislodged this cap, which began to break up. As it did so, a smell came up out of the ravine. Musallem sniffed it, and knew it, but he couldn't say what it was. There were familiar elements, of bodies, of burning; a camp smell. But it was sour and musky. It was *old*, Musallem thought, and he didn't like it. He thought that he'd wait for the sun to come up, and then either reconnoitre for a better position, or go away. Not everything had to be done at once. He'd found out how to get here. Yes, he thought, that was the thing – leave all decisions until the sun was up, and meanwhile eat something.

He did this, eating another portion of his *pitta* and cheese, and drinking sparingly, while watching the sky take on light. It did this not gradually, but in sharp, perceptible stages, as the sun mounted distant obstacles. The familiar mauve aura was suddenly there, above the hills to the east, where it had not been a second ago. Just as abruptly, and with an almost throbbing rhythm, the semicircle enlarged, became red, pink, flame, steady as the beating of a heart, as the still-unseen thing mounted its familiar route. Musallem had seen it most days of his life, and he finished eating, paying no particular attention. He thought he wouldn't mind a cigarette. He should have thought to bring a cigarette. He could see it would be some minutes yet before the sun appeared. It seemed a useful opportunity to relieve himself.

He did so, not watching the oncoming sun, but squatting in the direction of the stolen land, now returning to visibility again. Banks of mist drifted across it, but there were glimpses in between, and as he watched, they turned deep pink. He saw the sudden lightening of colour, to rose, to apricot, and knew the sun was about to come up behind him. In the same moment he was aware of something else. There had been a movement on the opposite wall of the ravine.

Musallem abruptly ceased relieving himself.

He didn't know where the movement had come from. He simply knew there'd been one. Presently there was another. This time he saw it. A reddish object raised itself above the line of rock. It was a human head. A body followed it, and mounted the rock, and remained crouched there, very still, peering intently at him.

Musallem knew that he couldn't be seen. The light was coming from behind, directed on to the other bank. At any moment now, the sun would come up, putting the matter still less in doubt. It would blind the person on the other bank. Musallem was glad about this. He could see now that the person was a boy, about his own size; not an Arab boy. It must be a Jew. The Jew was below him, in an exposed position – almost near enough, Musallem thought with exhilaration, to spit on. Not quite that near, but not more than a hundred metres away.

Musallem waited for the marvellous moment when the sun would come up, and when it did, he completed what he had to do and adjusted his clothing, and, selecting several sharp stones, stood up. He knew he was still in excellent cover, and he almost laughed aloud at the way the other boy, who had now commenced crawling down the tumble of rock steps, kept his eyes intently on him – not for a moment aware that he was there!

Musallem thought it was time to let him know he was there. He aimed carefully and threw the stone as hard as he could. It missed, hitting the rock immediately below and spinning off into the ravine. But the effect was practically as good as a hit, and Musallem nearly fell over, laughing. The Jew dropped as if paralysed and covered his head with his hands Musallem let him wait there a little bit. He saw that to go back to safety the Jew was going to have to turn around and crawl back up. He could either do it slowly, on his face, or faster by raising himself. Either way, Musallem knew he was not going to miss all the time.

He thought he would let the Jew make the first movement. He would let him get his head up. He waited for this good and expected moment, but when it came unfortunately missed again. What happened after that was not so expected. The Jew sprang to his feet and stood upright, and he had a stone in each hand.

'Throw once more, and you'll get it back!' he shouted, 'I can see you!'

Musallem knew the Jew couldn't see him. On the other hand, who knew what a Jew could see? There was something still more puzzling here. The Jew had called to him in Arabic. Musallem didn't say anything, turning this over in his mind.

But as the Jew turned slowly away, he felt humiliation, and knew he couldn't let him get away like this, so he threw. Immediately the Jew threw back. Musallem's stone didn't hit, and the Jew's didn't. But it smashed hard against rock, a mere handsbreadth from his ear, and Musallem realized a couple of things in the same moment. One was that whether the Jew could see him or not, he'd seen where his stone had come from and therefore knew roughly where he was. The other was that the Jew had probably worked this out for himself slightly before he had. Another thought occurred a moment later while he stood in shock. The Jew had a better aim.

Musallem remained quite still and thought about this. He knew that the Jew couldn't go up again backwards. At some stage he was going to have to turn around. When he did, he could change his own position and try again. While he thought this, the Jew called out again.

'Why do you throw stones at me? Are you mad?'

Musallem didn't say anything.

They watched each other for a while. Musallem knew the Jew couldn't see him. It was very *improbable* that the Jew could see him. His face was now in full sun and bright red. But the eyes weren't blinking. Musallem knew he could put it to the test by moving and seeing if the Jew's eyes moved. But he might make a noise, so he thought it best to let the Jew move first. Again the Jew puzzled him.

'All right,' he called. 'Don't talk. But also don't throw. It's a warning. We don't want to shoot you. One more move, and the soldiers will have to. They have their orders. I'm going to turn around now and go back. The first time you throw, you're a dead man!'

Musallem remained absolutely dead still. Soldiers? What soldiers? The Jew was lying, of course. It was a near certainty he was lying. A *near* certainty. But Musallem remembered, all of a sudden, that his father hadn't returned from this place. Could it possibly be . . .? Anyway, what soldiers? The Jews didn't have any soldiers. They also couldn't talk Arabic, as everybody knew. Was it possible that this Jew wasn't a Jew, was in some way . . . Only the fedayeen had soldiers at present in the stolen land.

Musallem kept his voice very gruff.

'What soldiers?' he said.

'Soldiers. You know what soldiers are. Men with guns. There's a patrol of them just behind these rocks.'

'Fedayeen?' Musallem said.

There was no answer for a moment, and then he saw that the other boy was smiling in a relaxed manner and tossing the stone from one hand to the other. 'What do you expect?' he said.

Musallem relaxed.

'I didn't know,' he said.

'There's a lot you don't know. What's your business here?'

'Nothing. I'm just – here,' Musallem said.

'It's God's grace you were spotted early. If it wasn't that I saw myself you were only a boy, unarmed, your face would be blackened. It's all right!' he called behind him. 'I think it's just the one boy. I'm talking with him. Tell the truth now – did more come with you? If so, I can promise nothing. We have a way with spies.'

'I'm alone. I swear it. There are no spies!' Musallem said.

'So what are you doing here?'

Musallem licked his lips.

'I wanted to see the ravine. My father went down in it five years ago, and he never came back.'

'Oh. Did he?' the other boy said thoughtfully. He didn't say anything for a while, looking down into the ravine. Then he said, 'So what do you want with it?'

'Only to see what's there.'

'So what is there?'

'I don't know. I can't see.'

'You've not been spying to see what we've got there?'

'I swear by the Name!'

'Don't take it so lightly, or He'll certainly blacken your face,' the other boy said, shaming him. 'Anyway, what did a young imbecile like you plan to do – climb down there?'

'Maybe. I didn't know it was secret. I'm not such an imbecile,' Musallem said, stung, and taking courage, 'I'm a very good climber. Also, I'm very careful. Maybe if I'd gone down with my father, if I'd been old enough, he wouldn't have been lost.'

The other boy looked at him for quite a long time.

'I don't know if you're to be trusted,' he said.

'I swear I am. I swear it!'

'We'll see. Wait there!' he called behind him. 'I'm going to show this young imbecile something. Don't move, but keep us covered.' He turned back to Musallem again. 'Move two hundred metres to your right,' he said. 'I can see there's a position which will give you a view down into the ravine. I'll keep pace with you on this side. Now move.'

Musallem moved. He moved quickly. He knew the safest course was to wait until he was behind a rock and then run as if the devil was behind him, back to camp. He didn't do this. He was in a state of some confusion, but also in one of intense excitement. He couldn't remember anything more exciting happening to him in his whole life. Who was this boy? What was he? He knew that boys worked with the fedayeen. He'd never heard they could order fedayeen about.

He found the position in just a few minutes, and saw that the other boy was already there, on the opposite bank.

'There are some rocks below you. Go down to the third one.'

Musallem thought about this.

'Carry on! If we wanted to shoot, couldn't we do it from here? Prove yourself.'

Musallem went down, very carefully.

'Now lie down. Look below you.'

Musallem thought about this, too, just as carefully, but again he did it, calling silently upon the Name as he did so. He had to look twice. 'In the name of the Compassionate,' he said. 'In the name of the Merciful.'

'And that's nothing,' the boy said. 'It's to show only a small part, to involve you. Speak one word of this to anyone, and you have no tongue left to speak. Do you swear?'

'I swear!' Musallem said. 'I swear by everything.'

'Here's the next thing. Look back to where you first saw me. If you're such a good climber, is it possible to get down from there? It's just to test you.'

Musallem peered. 'I can see it's possible to halfway,' he said. 'After that, you can't see.'

The boy grunted.

'Who tells you you're such a good climber?'

'Everybody knows.'

'What's your name, Bedu?'

'Musallem.'

The boy was silent for some time.

'Musallem, I think I will trust you,' he said. 'Do you want to go down into that ravine with me?'

'Yes,' Musallem said.

'Be here at this time tomorrow – earlier, before the sun is up. Remember about your tongue, if you wish to keep it. We have ways of knowing.'

'It's not necessary to say that,' Musallem said, with dignity.

'It's always necessary to say it. There have been cases. And there have been missing tongues,' the boy said.

'What shall I call you?'

'We're not allowed to give names. You know who I am, don't you?'

'Yes. No,' Musallem said.

'Exactly. That's the way to keep it, for the time being. I'm taking a big risk already in trusting you. But nothing like the one you'd be taking,' the boy said rapidly, 'if you said anything.'

'Believe me!' Musallem said.

'I will. Be here tomorrow. Move now.'

'Go with God,' Musallem said, and went.

Jonathan went too. He went fast. He almost killed himself laughing as he went. He felt marvellously exhilarated. Incredibly, the alarm clock was only just going off as he crept back in. Even more incredibly, he saw Allon in the bathroom, under the shower. Whoever knew Allon to get up so early? Everything was going his way. He rapidly stripped to his underpants and managed to get back to bed in time to be yawning awake with the rest of them.

'Allon is up early,' he said, sleepily pointing to the empty bed. 'Who ever knew Allon to be up so early before?'

# 7
# All About Smith

For a number of years there had been two main seasonal problems in the ravine. In winter the problem had been food, and in summer water. In the first year after the disaster both had been problems. But since then solutions had evolved. Winter was still certainly dangerous. Water stood deep in the ravine then, and the gazelles had to scramble on slippery ledges for their food, for that was the only way to get it. There had been accidents, and deaths. But in summer now the problem was time.

Time was a terrible problem.

The gazelles watered and fed in the dark. But in a short summer night there wasn't much darkness. When the shelling and mortaring had first begun above, even this short period had been disrupted, for the gazelles had been too frightened to move. Experience had shown that it was quite safe to move during these periods. Even during the day it was safe to move if shelling or mortaring began above, for the people there were too busy with each other to worry them in the ravine. But old habits died hard, and by day the gazelles remained in cover.

In cover they had multiplied. It was because of the multiplication that time had come to be the problem. It took time for so many gazelles to be watered. Because of the numbers, the operation had to be conducted in an orderly manner; so quite often now it was light before all the gazelles had finished and returned.

With numbers growing so rapidly, it was obvious the problem would get worse. But as yet there was no sign of a solution, although Hamud constantly looked for one. What he mainly feared was that owing to lack of sleep he might not notice the sign when it came. He hardly had time to sleep at all. The only way to find more time would be to abbreviate his prayers still further, and this he knew he couldn't do. As it was he prayed only four times a day, and even so couldn't perform the movements required for the prayers. This was because he could barely move at all.

It took him an hour to get to the pool these days: an hour there, an hour back. It took him an hour and a half to get to the growing area: three hours. For five hours a day he was simply walking. Every other minute of the day he could similarly account for.

Under his summer schedule, Hamud rose at six in the afternoon, when the mother gazelle woke him. He would go and open the gazelles' enclosure, and leave her there while he went to the pool. When he'd got there he would whistle, and the mother gazelle would bring the herd. By the time they arrived, Hamud would have laboriously climbed to the ledge, and have knocked out the bung for the first filling of the pool.

It took a couple of hours to water the herd, and then the gazelles browsed until two hours before dawn, when he watered them again. Then the mother gazelle took the herd back, and an hour later Hamud rejoined them. He counted the herd and sealed up the enclosure again. After this, he was free to start the day's work.

He washed and prayed and ate, and then attended to the conies. Then he went to the growing area. It was always the middle of the morning before he got there, and always the middle of the afternoon before he got back. He prayed, ate, and attended to the conies again, and slept. About three hours later the mother gazelle woke him, and he got up again, and the cycle recommenced.

It was paradoxically because of the size of the herd that very little of Hamud's daily labour concerned them: for such numbers there was not much that he could do.

The herd numbered 209 at the moment. Next year, he expected it would number 350, and the one after 600. The year after that, Hamud thought, numbers would go easily over a thousand. It was beyond the capacity of any individual to cope with such numbers, of course, so God would certainly send a sign. It was simply a question of remaining alert enough to spot it when it came.

Remaining alert, under present circumstances, was by no means easy. Hamud tried. He had cut all inessentials from his life. These days he grew only alfalfa, barley, and onions in the growing area, and he mainly lived on the barley and onions. Sometimes he ate a cony or two and had a bowl of soup; but he had rather gone off conies. However, he drank a good deal of gazelle milk and made quite a lot of cheese, for he was conscious of the need to keep himself in good shape – which indeed he was, in marvelous shape for a man with a broken back who only slept three hours out of the twenty-four. The prevailing state of his health was indeed a continuing marvel to him, and a further sign of God's grace. The slightest slip, the smallest ailment, could incapacitate him completely. But he knew God wouldn't allow it. He hadn't at the time of the disaster.

God had put it into the mind of the intelligent creature to bite through her halter and come and drag him off the rock at the time of the disaster. He had also made the water rise rapidly at the same time, so that his servant Hamud could be half dragged and half floated back. Hamud had known, as he went through the water, that God was washing him clean of all blemish after the final test; and since then there had been no more tests – only the continuing one of having to proceed with his schedule while bent double.

Hamud had spent that first winter on the floor of the ledge, barely able to crawl. It had been cold, and he hadn't been able to make a fire, so that he had curled up, and this was the way his spine had set. He had lived mainly in the conies' cave, for that was where their food was stored, and he knew he had to keep the conies going. There was no bread, and he couldn't get at the onions, stored higher, so to stay alive he'd had to eat the conies raw. This was what had rather put him off conies.

His only coherent recollection of the early days was of drinking the gazelle's milk direct from the udder, and noticing that the other gazelles were with her, and realizing that she had released them, and that they followed her. They still followed her. Each new gazelle followed her. It was the provision made by God so that his servant Hamud could continue to superintend the herd.

Four times a day Hamud thanked God for the general perfection of arrangements, and also the larger one, the continuing wonder of the dream. But apart from the larger area of wonder, there were some smaller ones. In particular, Hamud wondered about the water. He had noticed something strange about the water. For the past few years he had drained the cistern every winter so that there would be fresh water next season. In earlier years the water had taken weeks to drain. This winter, it had drained in days.

Hamud was aware that something was going on at the pool above. He was no longer able to climb up to see, but it was his impression that someone had put a gun in it. Ear-splitting blasts came from that general area, never when he was in the vicinity, so he was unable to locate it precisely. He wondered what intention lay behind this curious development. He was pretty sure he hadn't willed it himself, although if it had appeared in the dream, it obviously had a part to play in it. He had a shrewd idea of what this part might be.

It was already apparent that in a few years the herd

would be not only too large for any individual to manage, but also too large to continue in the ravine. In this Hamud saw a strong indication that God would provide help with the management and take the herd from the ravine.

Hamud wondered where He would take it. He would obviously not take it to the east, for the Beduin there would eat it. He would probably take it to the west. He recalled his father's story of the miracle that had happened there previously when God had cleared the land so that the Beduin could freely roam. In Hamud's own lifetime there had been a general move afoot to stop the Beduin roaming anywhere, so he didn't think they'd get the chance to roam in the west. He knew that the revolution intended taking over the land, however. He remembered what the lawyer from Horns had had to say on the subject. The lawyer had said that the revolution would put up large guns and blow the Jews out of the stolen land, and then send an army to take it back.

Hamud wondered what the revolution would do with the land when it had got it. He didn't think it would give the land to the Palestinians. Hamud had met a couple of Palestinians who passed through Kufr Kassem. They hadn't seemed to agree that Palestine was a part of Syria. No, he didn't think the revolution would give it to them. It was after all the holy land, the land of Abraham and the prophets Moses and Jesus. It was true God had given it to the Jews, but then they had done wrong and He had turned them out. Perhaps the Palestinians had also done wrong and been turned out.

Hamud had been toying with an interesting theory.

Was it possible that God didn't want people in the holy land any more?

Was it possible that he wanted gazelles instead?

Under this interpretation, the revolution might have come about so that it could blow the people out of the land, and Hamud have been placed in the ravine so that he could lead the gazelles into it. It seemed logical. It seemed very logical. If correct, then the gun placed in his pool was not an irrelevance but a practical and essential part of the dream. What wasn't entirely clear to Hamud was how he was going to get up to the top of the ravine himself. But he knew it was useless to speculate. When a thing became necessary, God sent a sign.

2

Apart from taking the bung out twice a night, there was not much that Hamud had to do for the gazelles these days. The numbers were too large for him to feed or to halter, so he didn't have the close relationships that he'd had with the original few. He knew them all, though.

Since he was up all night, either watering or guarding them, he had ample time for study, and he had made some interesting observations. The females were quicker to come to him than the males; and the males were, conversely, quicker to take alarm than the females. This led him to some general conclusions. In a situation where they might be hunted, the females would suffer the heaviest losses. He thought this was probably why God made so many of them. After several years, Hamud was able to plot the breeding pattern pretty exactly, and he knew that twice as many females were produced as males. It was because of this that he could calculate with some confidence the general sort of total to be expected in any particular year.

For his own interest he'd calculated a few totals. In ten years, for instance, barring accidents, numbers ought to be running in the region of 55,800. Ten years after, with a normal death rate, it should be in the order of 16,740,000. A head of gazelle of that nature, he thought, ought to spread out rather well in the holy land, giving it a distinctive and beautiful identity that was probably unobtainable with Jews, or Beduin, or indeed people of any kind.

He didn't expect to see such fine things himself. He knew his own function was essentially interim, but he was very glad now that he knew what it was. It wasn't given to many to know their true purpose in the world. The number of one-eyed, one-eared, broken-backed shepherds with no roofs to their mouths who knew why they were born could probably be counted on the fingers of one hand. All this was a matter for blessing and celebration, and Hamud did so fairly continuously. He knew that his task was to build up and protect the herd, and he was doing it to the best of his ability.

He couldn't any longer provide summer quarters on the bed of the ravine, for winter floods broke down whatever he built. But he had made a very fine enclosure on the ledge. He had to extend it every year, but it was easily done: a mere matter of removing an end wall and extending the sides.

The enclosure was made of rock, well camouflaged with branches and foliage, with a strong wooden door, hinged into sockets. It was roofed with skins, and those parts of the wall exposed to the weather were lined with more skins. Because of winter gales, the roof needed tying down with ropes, and the ropes were also made out of skins.

It was for the skins that Hamud needed the conies.

Most of his work in the growing area was on behalf of the conies: an endless succession of sowing, cultivating, harvesting, and storing their food, and later on feeding it to them and watering them, with all the subsequent labour of slaughtering and skinning.

The conies no longer sickened and died in captivity, and he no longer had to keep them in separate cubicles. But he kept the sexes separated so that the breeding programme should accord with his schedule. He superintended the breeding pretty closely. It took five conies to make a metre-length of rope, and ten of them to make a square metre of lining. All this called for a good head of conies, and in the mating and littering seasons, Hamud was run off his feet. But he was kept busy by the conies in all seasons. In the present one he was harvesting and re-sowing (he cut the alfalfa every two weeks and re-sowed every other year), and he was thinking of all that lay before him when he lowered himself from the cistern one morning and shuffled after the last of the gazelles back down the ravine. The sun was up, as it usually was these days, so he hurried. But in hurrying, his dragging feet produced a curious effect on the stones, as if of an echo or a voice. Hamud stopped, but the effect didn't.

Hamud listened, with his head on one side. It was quite definitely an echo or a voice. It was of the small, still type mentioned by the prophets Moses and Samuel. Hamud felt his heart racing, and he said, 'Lord, here am I,' as the men of God had said before him, and waited, listening hard.

'Move two hundred metres to the right,' the voice said. He thought this was what it said. It was so small he couldn't be sure. A small breeze was blowing through the ravine, and he couldn't hear any more. He wondered if he'd even heard that. Two hundred metres to the right? The ravine wasn't two hundred metres wide. At this point it was barely twenty. Still, he moved in the direction indicated, and waited patiently for further instructions. None came.

Hamud knew he was in a bit of a muddle these days, owing to lack of sleep. There was often a singing in his ears, and he sometimes saw or heard things that turned out not to be there. Could it be that he had sought so hard for a sign that he'd imagined one?

In a standing position, Hamud couldn't see upwards, so he lay down. Through the vegetation he quite distinctly saw something moving. It stopped and gestured. The voice and echo resumed, and Hamud was aware there were two of them. He was also aware, with disappointment, that it was not the voice of God. It was the voice of children.

He couldn't pick out any further words, but after a few minutes the exceptional nature of what was happening dawned on him. Children at the ravine? Talking to each other across the ravine? It was not normal. It was highly abnormal. So was the hair on the head of the child he could see. It was red.

There was undoubtedly a sign of some kind here. It was possibly a warning sign. Try as he might, he could only pick out one other word. He thought it was 'tomorrow.' Tomorrow? What tomorrow? He thought about it for some time and then realized the children had gone, and scrambled to his feet and went home.

He counted the gazelles and locked them up, and decided not to bother about eating or work. He said his prayers and went to bed. What was needed here was a good sleep. A considerable degree of alertness seemed to be called for.

Hamud slept all day, and when he woke up he was very alert. The gazelle had wakened him for the sunset watering. Hamud said his prayers and set off for the pool. He gave the gazelles a good watering and let them browse for a bit. But he didn't water them a second time. He called them back with him to the enclosure and sealed them up. Then he picked up some bread and onions and his water bottle, and also a couple of slings and his knife, and made his way back down the ravine.

He spent some time selecting a spot which allowed a view of both banks. Then he built a low barricade for concealment, and behind it a pattern of stones for his back, and lay down. It was his normal posture when predators had to be disposed of. There was nothing wrong with his single eye, and his aim and strength were both exceptional. Suitably deployed, Hamud was still a match for predators.

He knew there was still some time before dawn so he had a small meal. He felt very rested and fit, brain in excellent condition, wits well about him. If signs were to be given, he was in good shape to receive them.

Since waking, he had worked continuously on the problem of the children, and he knew for certain that he hadn't willed them. If children appeared, they were either a sign or an intrusion. Either way, any attempt to approach the gazelles would make them immediate subjects for disposal. He was perfectly clear about that.

Mist covered the ravine at night at this season of the year, and observing its imminent dispersal, Hamud saw it was time to complete his meal. He had a drink, saw that his slings and stones were comfortably to hand, and went very still.

As the sky lightened, Hamud lay like a stone in the ravine.

Although he could neither see nor hear them, he knew to a second when they began coming down. From each side of the ravine there was the small clink of falling stones. He felt his back hairs bristling, not unpleasantly. It had been some time since he'd been called upon to dispose of predators. Presently he heard them. They seemed to be guiding each other. After a few minutes, Hamud qualified this. One apparently knew the way down. He appeared to be testing the other.

Hamud picked up his sling in some alarm. How could he know the way down? Hamud had been in the ravine for eight years now. In that time only one person had come down, and he hadn't gone back up again. How was it possible for this child to know? Hamud narrowed his eye in some puzzlement. A sign of some kind was certainly in the making here.

He let them get to the bottom. The one from the east bank had first to negotiate the ledge. The child from the west gave him detailed instructions about this also.

Hamud's alarm increased. He saw that he must not act rashly. He knew he must act in some way. He wondered which way he ought to act. He let them come well into view. He let them come far too close for comfort, awaiting some manifestation which would advise him how to act. None came, so at five metres he yelled, 'Stop!'

Both stopped dead. Then the dark-haired one turned and ran. Hamud sent a stone whistling like a bullet above his head and called him back. The boy came back. The redhead had stood gazing in the general direction of Hamud, thunderstruck. Hamud wasn't sure if the boy could see him. It was still grey in the ravine, and lying on his back among the stones, he was well camouflaged: he had scarcely moved when he fired. Hamud saw that this was the one he had to deal with, so he fitted another stone in his sling and waved it to let the boy see. 'What do you want?' he said.

The boy didn't answer, but the one who had returned, after a good look at Hamud, seemed to have taken courage. He said to the redhead. 'Don't you know him?'

The redhead took his time answering. He said, 'Yes.'

'You know me?' Hamud said, astonished.

This time the boy merely nodded.

'Who told you?'

'You know,' the boy said.

Hamud felt his back hairs bristle horizontally out from his head. He said, 'You've been *sent*?' He knew that his speech was not clear, and he saw that the dark-haired boy hadn't understood it at all. But the redhead evidently did, for he nodded firmly.

'*Who* sent you?' Hamud said, as clearly as he could.

'Who sends people here?' the boy said.

Hamud began to tremble.

'Why are you lying on your back?' the boy said.

'Forgive me, forgive me,' Hamud said, and he got up and very slowly bent forward, as he hadn't done even in his prayers, and touched his head against the ground. When he raised himself, he saw that the mouth of the dark-haired boy had dropped wide open, and that the other one was watching him rather closely. Hamud got tremblingly to his feet.

'Blessed be he who comes in the name of God,' he said.

'Amen,' the redhead said.

The other one still had his mouth open.

'Tell me what to do,' Hamud said.

He saw again that his speech wasn't clear, for the dark-haired one said, 'What does he say?' But again the other one understood, for he nodded again, this time with complete confidence, although his reply when it came was not direct.

'Where are the gazelles?' he said.

Hamud's heart gave a great leap.

'You have been sent to take the gazelles?' he said.

'What does he say?'

'There is a gazelle here called Smith,' the redhead said.

'Smith?' Hamud said.

'Smith. That is the name of the gazelle.'

'Blessed be the Name!' Hamud said fervently. He hadn't realized the gazelle had a name. He knew which gazelle was meant. Of course it would have a name – known to God, and this messenger! Smith. An exceptionally beautiful name.

'Where – are – the – gazelles?' the messenger was saying, very slowly and clearly.

Hamud realized he had delayed replying too long and that the messenger was looking at him as if he were an imbecile. He didn't want to be taken for an imbecile. He didn't know whether it was proper to take the messenger by the hand. He put out his hand to see, and the messenger took it. Hamud kissed the hand, and noticed the dark-haired boy's mouth drop open again. Weak with relief and joy, and also weeping a little, Hamud leaned on the messenger as he led him to the enclosure. He tried to talk as they went. He tried to tell him everything of his problems.

'Speak slower,' the messenger said, as they'd often said in Kufr Kassem. It had been so long ago he'd forgotten. Hamud began to speak slower. He spoke so slowly that by the time they got to the enclosure he saw that even the dark-haired one could understand him. Hamud opened the enclosure.

'In the name of the Compassionate!' the dark-haired one said.

In the name of the Merciful!' the messenger said.

The gazelles took immediate alarm, but Hamud called the mother gazelle, not whistling, but for the first time using her name. 'Smith,' he called. Smith came to him, somewhat uncertainly. 'Come, Smith,' he said, and went with her among the herd, quietening them. The boys followed him, exclaiming freely.

'But how did they all get here?' the dark-haired one said.

'Never mind!' the messenger said.

'But there are hundreds of them.'

'Two hundred and nine,' Hamud said. 'And next year, three hundred and fifty, and the year after six hundred, God willing it's the large head of females, you see.'

'But there are more males,' the dark-haired one said.

'They're females,' the messenger told him.

'It's the male with the larger horn.'

'The female, imbecile. Blessed be the Name.

Hamud heard all this and rejoiced.

'Who told you females have larger horns?' the dark-haired one said.

'You ask too many questions.'

'How do you know the gazelle is called Smith, anyway?'

'You talk too much altogether.'

Hamud indignantly agreed. 'Who is this imbecile?' he said.

'It's a young Bedu of the name Musallem. You don't have to worry about him,' the messenger said.

'Am I permitted to know – your name?'

'No.'

'Forgive me,' Hamud said, apologetically.

'You can state your own.'

'Hamud.'

'Correct,' the messenger said. 'Well, Hamud, this is only a brief inspection. Tell me what you want, and I'll see what can be done.'

Hamud began to tell him, very carefully. He knew he had to speak slowly. He said he needed help with the watering. He was not complaining, he said. God knew that he never complained. He was a faithful servant. But if God thought he had done well he would be glad of help.

'What would be best at the moment?'

At the moment, Hamud said, the best would be if he could get a proper sleep in. What he would like to do was sleep all night, Hamud said, or all morning, or all afternoon. He didn't mind much when it was, just so that he could get it in. He thought that if he could get in, say, five uninterrupted hours, he would be able to continue with his duties without strain. Of course this referred to the present. God knew of the special arrangements that would be required for the future.

The messenger said God knew all about the future arrangements; but he was thoughtful as to Hamud's ideas for the present. He said, 'You want someone to do the watering for you?'

Hamud said that would be a blessing.

'What if it was only one watering?'

Hamud said that in that case it would be best if it were the first watering, at sunset. The only time he had to sleep was in the afternoon, and there wasn't much of it left these days; only three hours. If someone could do this watering for him, then he could get in another two hours' sleep, which would bring him up to the five, which would be a blessing.

The messenger said he couldn't promise anything, but it was probable that help would be given. He said it would very likely be on an irregular basis, so that Hamud shouldn't learn to rely on it. But now he had to go.

Hamud would have liked to bow down again, but there was no time. As it was, he only managed to get another kiss at the hand.

But he bowed down and prayed after the messenger had gone.

'The old man's mad' Musallem said.

'Not as mad as you think.'

'He bowed down to you. He kissed your hand.'

'You get it sometimes. It's a lonely post there.'

'You mean he's one of the fedayeen?'

'Not so many questions.'

'But what's he doing there?'

'Stores,' Jonathan said.

'Stores?'

'Listen, Bedu. It's just possible I can put in a word for you. Would you be willing to help with the watering?'

'Join the fedayeen?'

'On a part-time basis.'

'For what payment?'

'There's no payment.'

'Everybody knows there's payment.'

'For the trial period?' Jonathan said. He smiled. 'There's so much you don't know, Bedu, it's hardly possible to talk to you. Anyway, there's such a thing as doing a job for the honour of it, you know. Right this minute, you can forget the whole thing.'

'Listen, I'll do it,' Musallem said. 'I'd like to do it.'

'Just supposing it were possible, when could you do it?'

'I'll find out. I'll come and tell you.'

'Make it tomorrow, same time. If I'm not here, come the next day. I'll do the same if you're not here. On no account go into the ravine without me. Understand?'

'Well, there's a whole lot I don't understand,' Musallem confessed.

'Very good,' Jonathan said, and nodded approvingly. 'That's the way to keep it. I don't have to mention what would happen to you if you should speak a word about any of this. We have people everywhere, you know. We even have them with the Beduin.'

'I know. My cousins are in the fedayeen. I often talk with them. They've told me all kinds of things,' Musallem said proudly.

'Oh. Have they?' Jonathan said, frowning. 'Well, don't believe them. They're known liars.'

'I know it. They told me a pack of lies about the stolen land.'

'About what land?'

'The stolen land.'

'Ah . . . H'm, did they?' Jonathan said. 'Well, it's what I would expect. Those who *know* don't talk. They just carry out instructions. As they will in your case, the first time you open your mouth.'

'Until tomorrow, then,' Musallem said.

'People have to know where they stand. It's only fair.'

'Until tomorrow, then,' Musallem said.

'Go with God,' Jonathan said. He quite liked the phrase. He'd almost given himself away with it the previous day. 'Where did you pick up that Beduin saying?' Abdul had said. 'Oh, somewhere,' Jonathan had said.


3


The messenger and Musallem commenced watering the gazelles at the end of July. Hamud got some wonderful sleeps in, and felt as fit as a fiddle. Often he didn't take his full sleep in order to have the privilege of chatting with the messenger. But in the first week there was a disturbing chat that warned him not to chat too freely. This chat was with Musallem.

Musallem said, 'Did you ever see my father here?'

'Your father?'

'He lost a sheep and came down for it.'

Hamud felt a shiver go up his spine. 'No, I never saw him,' he said.

'They say he came, five years ago. What can have happened to him?'

'What do they say happened?'

'They say wolves or djinns got him.'

'That's probably what happened,' Hamud said.

'Have you seen djinns here?'

'You don't see them.'

'Why haven't they got you, then?'

'You don't understand,' Hamud said, and looked at the messenger. He found that the messenger was looking back at him. 'You don't understand,' he said again.

The next day he tried to climb up to see if anything was left of Musallem's father, but he couldn't. He didn't think anything was left. He had lain in a place where there was a runoff of water, and bones had been washed down. He thought practically all of him must have been washed down now. He wondered if he should ask advice of the messenger, but the messenger said nothing to him about it, so he didn't. He was worried by the messenger. The messenger wouldn't tell him anything of the future, and steered him away from the subject, so that he knew he was still not allowed to know it.

For the first time in his eight years in the ravine, Hamud began to feel discouraged, and he did't know why.

# 8
# All About The Game

At the Beduin camp, as at Kibbutz Gei-Harim, the arrangements called for a good deal of invention. This was easily
within the capacity of both boys, but occasionally led to
difficulties, so that sometimes only one of them was able
to water the gazelles.

Quite early on, they knew where they were with regard
to each other, but it took a week or two of cautious
sparring to establish the facts. By that time they were sure
of each other, anyway, so it didn't matter. It was Musallem
who broached the subject. They were having a smoke at
the time, with cigarettes provided by him, which he
thought probably gave him the right.

'What makes you such a big liar?' he said.

Jonathan drew in some smoke and let it out.

'What do you think?' he said.

'Answering one question with another is just a clever
trick. I saw that with you a long time ago.'

'Not so clever. Only clever enough to fix you.'

'It didn't fix me. I could fix you a lot easier. I could tell
Hamud.'

'Tell him what?'

'What you are.'

'What am I?'

'You do it again. What good is it? Why keep on lying
when you know I know you're lying?'

'Well, I'll tell you,' Jonathan said, eating an olive from

the bag that he had provided. 'You go and tell Hamud. See if he believes you.'

'He's mad.'

'Of course.'

Musallem pondered this, and saw that once more he was a second late. He said, 'I could fix you, anyway I *do* know some fedayeen. I could get them to fix you any time you came here.'

'Why should you want to?'

'I don't want to. I just mention it. I don't like being called an imbecile every minute.'

Jonathan had another olive, and Musallem had one.

'Musallem, you're not an imbecile,' Jonathan said, 'I just had to say that.'

'Why did you?'

'You could have fixed me. It's true what you say.'

'I won't fix you.'

'I know it. You're not an imbecile.'

'What's your name?'

'Jonathan.'

'How is it you talk Arabic?'

'I've always talked it. I have a friend in an Arab village. He's my best friend.'

'In the stolen land?'

'It isn't stolen. There's a lot you don't know, Musallem, even though you're not an imbecile. Next time I'll tell you. But wake Hamud now,' he said, looking at his watch. The watch was a present from his parents to mark his return home. He wasn't home much, but it was established that it *was* his home. It was also established that he could sleep in the children's house, when he liked, among his friends. When he wasn't in the children's house, the friends assumed he was at home, and when he wasn't at home, his parents assumed he was with the friends.

It was a satisfactory arrangement, on the whole.

*

Musallem heard about the stolen land, and Jonathan heard about the Beduin, but they found it hard to explain the virtues of either way of life. Jonathan said society and settlement were best, and Musallem that the wandering life was; but neither was really interested, and anyway they preferred the secret way of the ravine, which seemed to have a bit of both.

Quite early, they'd taken to bringing each other presents. Musallem had brought cigarettes, and Jonathan olives, but then the shower of stolen goods from the kibbutz – chocolate and biscuits and bottle drinks – began to shame Musallem, whose own tattered home provided little to steal. He brought a bit of hashish once, but this was for Hamud, and though much appreciated by him, didn't seem to count. So he brooded about it, and planned the thing, and one day brought a hand grenade.

'What is it?' Jonathan said.

'What do you think? It's from the fedayeen – my cousins in the Ma'ara. It needed courage to take it, also to climb down with it,' he said proudly.

'Courage? It needed an imbecile.'

Musallem felt himself shrivel at this reception of his gift, and was aware in the same moment that it was indeed foolish. So he smiled unpleasantly and said, 'Maybe you're afraid?'

'What afraid? What good is the thing, imbecile?'

'Call me that once more and I'll show you.'

'What would you show?'

'Try me.'

'You'd never dare.'

'See if you dare. Say it.'

Jonathan licked his lips but he didn't say it, and Musallem, warming to this unexpected and salving development, smiled again. 'Coward,' he said.

Jonathan saw the way the development was going, and

also that Musallem was offended, so he said, 'All right, you're not an imbecile.'

'Because you don't dare call me one.'

'It's not a matter of daring.'

'So what is it a matter of? Coward?'

Jonathan saw he was going to have to settle this, so he shrugged, and said, 'All right, you are one.'

'Catch,' Musallem said, and lightly tossed the grenade, and was glad to see Jonathan almost going into a fit trying to catch it. He managed to hang on to it, trembling, and when he could speak, which wasn't for some moments, said quietly, 'You really are mad.'

'But brave. Will you throw it back?'

'To an imbecile who can't catch?'

'You have four seconds to run. You'll be safe.'

'And the gazelles?'

Musallem laughed. 'You're not only a liar and a coward, but also a fraud. You're not worried about the gazelles, or about me. You're just worried for yourself. Stop worrying, and keep the grenade,' Musallem said. 'Also stay a coward.'

Jonathan had been looking at the grenade, and now noticed a couple of things about it that he should have noticed earlier. One was that the pin was in, and the other that the striker arm was therefore 'safe'. So he tossed it in the air a couple of times, and handed it delicately back to Musallem. 'Take your gift, hero,' he said. 'And next time you want to be brave, try pulling the pin out.'

Musallem had reached for the gift, but he didn't take it. 'You want me to pull it out?' he said.

'If you want to be a brave imbecile.'

'All right,' Musallem said, and pulled it out.

Jonathan gripped the grenade hard to keep the striker arm down. 'Put it back,' he said.

'If you give me the grenade.'

'We'll both go up, you fool.'

'Not if you hold it properly. I expect you will. Keep it, then,' Musallem said, and sat down and lit a cigarette.

Jonathan kept both hands around the grenade, and didn't know what to do with it. He stood and looked at Musallem.

'You know what you look like?' Musallem said comfortably. 'You look like a big imbecile. That's what you look like.'

'There are accidents with these things!'

'You're scared?'

'Of course I'm scared. Give me the pin.'

'I'll give you a puff. You want a puff?'

'I want the pin.'

'I'll give you a puff,' Musallem said, and got up and gave him one. He left the cigarette in Jonathan's mouth, and watched the smoke go in his eyes. He left it in for some time before taking it out. 'A really big imbecile,' he said. 'That's what you look like.'

'Say what you want me to do,' Jonathan said.

'Well, you can admit you're the imbecile, not me.'

'Okay, I admit it.'

'I didn't hear you.'

'I'm the imbecile, not you.'

'Also a coward.'

'Also a coward.'

'And you'll never take back what you just admitted.'

'I'll never take back what I just admitted.'

'Because however you twist it, it's true. You're the one that's afraid now, not me. Also to put yourself in that position calls for a special kind of imbecile. I have the pin and you have the grenade, and there's nothing you can do about it.'

'You want me to say all that?' Jonathan said.

'No. You don't have to say it,' Musallem said, fairly. it's obvious. I'm just pointing it out so you won't be able to twist it later.'

'So put the pin back.'

'I told you,' Musallem said. 'I'll put it back when you give me the grenade.'

'How can I give it to you?' Jonathan said. His hands were sweating around it. 'I've got my thumb on the striker arm.'

'So I'll put mine on it. Unless you don't trust me. Don't you trust me?'

'I trust you,' Jonathan said, gritting his teeth. 'Only my hands are sweating. I'll drop the thing.'

'Oh no you won't,' Musallem said, smiling. 'That's one thing I'm certain of. You see how much I trust you?'

'Musallem, it's dangerous,' Jonathan said. 'A pin you can put back in. But if the arm goes up it starts the fuse, and you can't stop it. Just put the pin back, and we'll forget it. I said what you wanted me to say.'

'I don't know if you believed it.'

'I believed it.'

'So trust me and that will show you believe it.'

'All right,' Jonathan said, and gritted his teeth again. 'But if you hold it wrongly, we both go up. Get a move on before there's more sweat.'

'Right away,' Musallem said, and nipped the cigarette and put the end in his pocket and blew on both hands and rubbed them. 'And just to show you, I'll take it with *one* hand.'

Jonathan didn't argue with him. He kept his teeth tight shut and offered the grenade with both hands. He saw that Musallem's thumb was firmly on the striker arm before he started sliding his own off. Musallem nonchalantly held up the grenade with one hand, and put the pin in with the other, and offered the safe grenade to Jonathan.

Jonathan looked at him, and turned his back and climbed up to the ledge, and knocked out the bung and refilled the pool. He didn't come down again when he'd done this. He sat on his haunches and watched the gazelles drinking.

It was a light night, plenty of stars about, and much reflected moonshine. In the silvery gloaming he could see Musallem moving and hear him chuckling. He seemed to be working hard at the chuckles. Presently he sat down and relit the bit of cigarette.

'You want a smoke?' he called.

Jonathan didn't answer.

'You're not a coward,' Musallem called.

Jonathan saw the pool was emptying again, so he knocked the bung out and allowed it to refill.

'I'm the imbecile,' Musallem said. 'I got excited.'

Jonathan sat on his haunches and whistled softly to himself.

He didn't let Musallem know when it was his turn. He completed the whole thing and secured the bung assembly.

Musallem saw what he was doing and came up to the ledge, 'What's the matter, what about me?' he said.

'Go away,' Jonathan said. 'Don't come back.'

'Look, I'm sorry,' Musallem said, and put his hand on Jonathan's shoulder. Jonathan gave him a good nudge, and Musallem went backwards off the ledge. Jonathan saw the whole thing happen in a sort of slow motion, every nerve suddenly aware what might, what he already knew *would*, occur. In the slow motion, legs wide apart, Musallem went endlessly off the ledge, arms open to arrest his fall. He arrested it on a boulder, and slid down the other side, and the thing he had been carrying, either in his hand or in some part of his clothing, hit the slope and tumbled down to the brink of the pool, and in the same endless moment, Jonathan saw that the pin was half out of it and that the striker arm was at an angle, and his heart gave a single thump and seemed to congeal.

Musallem was looking up at him, mouth open.

'Keep down,' Jonathan said, and was aware he was whispering, as if anything else might set it off.

'What?'

'The grenade.'

'Where?'

'On the other side. You can't see it. Don't move.'

Musallem was moving, mouth still open, on hands and knees, around the boulder. Jonathan seemed paralysed. But he knew too many seconds had passed for the thing to go off if it was set to go. The harder he looked at it, the less he could see. He thought that if the pin was half out and the arm only half up, there must be some tiny gap in the fuse train. The slightest touch would close it.

'Musallem, stay where you are!'

'Can you see it?'

'Listen – the pin is half out. It's not quite out. The arm is stuck. If you touch it, it will go off.'

They looked at each other.

'If I throw it in the pool?' Musallem said.

'There's not enough water in the pool. Wait a minute, I'll put more water there. Stay still. Don't move.'

Jonathan turned and, still keeping his eye on the grenade, loosened the bung assembly again. He released a little water at a time, watching to see that no pebbles were washed down and that nothing splashed the thing lying at the brink. While he did this he worked out what would be the best. The gazelles had left the pool and the nearest were browsing several metres away. Once the pool was full, the blast would be muffled. Musallem could throw the grenade and have four seconds to get back behind the boulder. At the same moment Jonathan would jump there himself. Yes, this seemed the best. He was concentrating so hard on controlling the water and working out the plan that he didn't, right away, see what was happening with the gazelles. When he did, he shoved the bung in again, immediately. The gazelles were coming back to the water.

'Musallem, chase them away!'

'What?'

'The gazelles. Don't let them get near it.'

'Eh?'

'Oh, God!' Jonathan said, and bent and picked up stones and began throwing them.

Musallem stood up to see what was happening, and began throwing stones himself. The gazelles scattered and ran, and a couple ran around the other side of the pool, and one fell in, and the female with him waited to see which way he'd come out. Jonathan saw which way he would come out, and shouted, 'Musallem, stop! Don't throw. It's there.'

'Where?'

Just then the male came out, and its front legs crossed the grenade, and the hind ones gave it a good kick, and Musallem saw where. The grenade was kicked some way from the pool to a position below where Jonathan watched from the ledge. They both saw, and quite distinctly heard, the pin fall out and the arm spring fully open.

'All right,' Musallem said.

'Get down, leave it!' Jonathan shouted, and, too shocked to jump, got down himself in the furthest corner of the ledge, and waited with his hands over his head. He counted the massive hammer blows of his heart as he waited, and he counted quite a few. He counted altogether too many, and got his head slowly up, and looked over. He saw Musallem also down with his hands over his head. He couldn't see the grenade.

'Where is it?'

Musallem slowly raised his head.

'In the pool.'

'What?'

'I thought it would blow up. Upwards,' Musallem said.

They both looked at the pool. Jonathan saw Musallem was shaking. Then he saw he was sobbing. He came groggily down from the ledge and sat beside him. They looked dazedly at the pool.

'It was a dud,' Jonathan said.

'What?'

Jonathan had used the Hebrew word and couldn't think of the Arabic. 'It didn't go off,' he said.

'God didn't allow.'

'It would have killed you.'

'Yes.' He was still trembling. Jonathan put his arm around his shoulder, and they sat for a while without saying anything. Then Jonathan said, 'Musallem, you go now. *I'll* wake Hamud.'

'I'll wait a while. I'll wait for you.'

Jonathan went and woke Hamud, and the boys left.

Before they parted, Jonathan put his arm again on Musallem's shoulder. 'Musallem, we are brothers.'

'God saved us both.'

Jonathan watched Musallem climbing, but Musallem, still shaken, didn't look back.

In bed in his parents' apartment, Jonathan thought it over, and he knew the thing was a dud. There'd been a few duds among the incendiaries thrown by the fedayeen. The explanation didn't seem to conflict with the one offered by Musallem. He knew which one was more attractive. When he looked back on it later, Jonathan knew that was when The Game started.


2

In The Game there were no unanswerable questions. The same answer went for all questions. He played it mainly in the ravine, but it could be played anywhere. He sometimes played it in the kibbutz, although he didn't tell anyone: it gave better value if you didn't.

They had another 'activity' in the largest classroom: a

vote had to be taken on the best specimens grown in the children's garden. Jonathan had grown carrots, which seemed to him a useful species, and he brought in three fine ones. But the vote went to Allon, who had brought in a rose. There was no love lost between Jonathan and Allon (who had a fair idea who had given his name to the military, although he'd not been punished, and the matter had never been cleared up), so Jonathan didn't vote for him. But when Esther pointed out a few interesting facts about the rose, including the one that it was quite new, he became interested.

'How do you mean new?'

'It's a new introduction.'

'Who introduced it?'

Esther thought someone should go and get Avner, who was the expert on roses. Avner was a corresponding member of the three great rose societies of the world, and very expert indeed. He was a cheerful and humorous man, and he came willingly to give the children the benefit of his knowledge. He confirmed that the rose was a new intro-duction. He said a breeder in Canada called Mr Eddie had introduced it, and that it was called Ardelle and had seventy-two petals.

'You know it for a fact?' Jonathan said, fascinated.

'You want to count?' Avner said humorously.

'Roses have *got* to have seventy-two petals?'

'Not at all,' Avner said, chuckling. '*This* one has. You can see the size of it. It's a fine reliable cream, and every one has seventy-two petals.'

'Why?' Jonathan said.

Avner chuckled some more and started explaining why, but the explanation got difficult and he transferred it to the blackboard. Even on the blackboard it was difficult. Ardelle was a cross between Peace and Mrs C. Lamplough. Mrs C. Lamplough was a cross between Frau Karl Druschki and Crimson Victory; and Peace between Joanna

Hill and a seedling that was a cross between Charles P. Kilham and Rosa Foetida. Avner went on to tell all the facts about Charles P. Kilham and Mrs Lamplough, and presently ran out of blackboard. Jonathan followed closely, but he still couldn't follow how Eddie the Canadian had got a cream rose with seventy-two petals out of red, orange, and yellow ones which had less.

Avner began to explain about chromosomes, and he rubbed out half the blackboard to show how they worked. Then he had to rub the other half out, and the children got a bit lost, and so did Avner. When he left he wasn't so cheerful and it had been established that he wasn't quite sure why Ardelle had seventy-two petals, or was cream in colour, or even smelled the way it did.

But Hamud, when the question of this wonder rose was put to him later in the evening, was quite sure.

'Because God made it so,' he said.

Hamud was a bit miserable about this, because the messenger had been throwing a few such simple problems at him lately, as though he were still under test; but Jonathan was delighted. It struck him as the best game he'd ever heard of, and one at which you could get really unbeatable, particularly with people who didn't know you were playing it. It seemed to shed light, too, on the activities of the Queen of England, and General de Gaulle, and parents.

By late October, Musallem had left, and it was no longer necessary to water the gazelles; there was plenty of water in the ravine. Jonathan was depressed about this, but around the same time a new fact of life appeared in the kibbutz, which helped. They'd asked him if he preferred a brother or a sister, and he'd said a brother. But it was a sister. A short list of names had been prepared for either eventuality and because he was disappointed, they let Jonathan pick.

But the one he picked wasn't on the list.

'Yael – a gazelle. Lovely. What put that in your mind?'

'Who knows?' Jonathan said.

Numbers were rising on the kibbutz. With Yael, that autumn of 1965, they went to nearly 350.

He hadn't been seeing much of Abdul in the olive groves lately, but he saw a bit more of him in the winter. Abdul's 'Praise the Name' and other blessings began to grate on him, and so did his illustrations of God's will. It was a game, and there was too much magic in it for regular play. It answered for seventy-two-petalled roses and similar wonders, but what was wonderful about the kibbutz?

Abdul got to be a bit of a bore, so Jonathan dropped him.

Between rains, he managed to visit the ravine. Hamud was much encouraged by the visits, for the messenger, on his own, was a good deal more communicative about God's will. Emboldened by it, Hamud raised a matter that had been troubling him. Was it God's will that Musallem should know what happened to his father?

'What did happen?' the messenger said, adding quickly, 'As far as you know?'

Hamud understood the qualification, for there was a lot he didn't know about the incident – including the meaning – which the messenger obviously would.

So he told all he knew, and Jonathan's stomach turned over as he listened, although he didn't show it.

At the end, he said God didn't want Musallem to know, and Hamud was very glad to hear it, because he wasn't eager to tell him. He was so glad that he told the messenger all about his ear, too, and showed it to him. The ear, though somewhat shrivelled by regular pickling in grape vinegar, was still in good condition, and Hamud kept it in a box. He asked the messenger if he had done right to keep it, and the messenger said he had, and after a little reflection favoured him with the meaning.

If the ear hadn't been only half on, he said, Musallem's father wouldn't have been able to bite it all off. In that moment, holding Hamud firmly by the ear, he might have killed him. As a further consequence, if Musallem's father hadn't been killed, Musallem himself wouldn't have been driven to look for him, and hence would not have come to the ravine. All these events derived from the state of Hamud's ear, which in turn derived from the attack by the wolves, which had obviously been sent.

Hamud was lost in wonder at this interpretation, which lasted him the rest of the winter.

Jonathan liked it too. The Game always worked well in the ravine. But it wasn't the fine opportunities for play that he mainly missed. Remembering the grenade, the cigarettes, the shared secrets, he hankered badly for Musallem that winter. Who else was there to talk to? Abdul was a dead loss, and Dina, who hovered again, seemed merely silly after the rich company of the ravine. All through the winter he hankered for Musallem, and looked forward to April, when he would return.

3

But Musallem didn't return in April, and he hadn't returned by early May. Jonathan had a fair idea why he hadn't returned, but it didn't help. The shelling had increased, and so had the fedayeen attacks. Who knew where the Beduin were now?

It was no longer easy for Jonathan himself to get to the ravine. Security around the kibbutz had increased, and there was the further complication of his sister Yael – now, after her first weeks in the baby house, installed in his old room in his parents' apartment. This one was easier to deal with. Jonathan had a few tantrums that spring.

His parents discussed the tantrums with Esther, and Alizia, and the kibbutz secretary, and anybody who would listen, and they decided in the end that Jonathan was a sensitive type who might suffer irreparable damage if denied the parental home, while baby Yael was that angelic type who was quite pleased to be in anyone's home. The upshot was that Yael returned to the baby house, and Jonathan to his old room, so all he had to worry about was security. But he worried about that. He kept his visits to the ravine to two, or at the most three, times a week, and tried to vary his route each time. He knew he had only to be caught once.

In the ravine the situation was so fantastic he had little time to brood over Musallem. He knew what a crop of new lambs looked like. He'd never imagined what so many gazelles could look like. It took a couple of weeks for the gazelles to become accustomed to him, but he never became accustomed to them.

Hamud said the forecast was accurate: a shade over 140 new gazelles had been born, bringing the number to around 350. To Jonathan, it seemed like as many thousands. In the enclosure, in the narrow ravine, around the pool, the forest of horns jostled everywhere. Looking down at them from the cistern, or wandering among them, touching, stroking, as they drank and browsed, he marvelled at the incredible sight. It wouldn't have surprised him if dragons or angels began to multiply here.

In the kibbutz, looking at the famous photographs of the extinct animal, on the poster and on the stamps, he held his secret knowledge to himself. But he wished there was someone he could talk to about it. There was only one person he could talk to, and he wondered when he would come. He knew he would come. Jonathan knew that he himself, whatever the circumstances, would come, at least once, if only to say he wouldn't be able to come again. Presently Musauem did come.

He came in the middle of May, and he came fifteen kilometres. It had taken him a day and a night, hiding much of the time, because of the military activity at the other side. He stayed in the ravine for three days, and Jonathan saw him on two of them. Musallem said he was supposed to be visiting his cousins at the Ma'ara camp. He was supposed to be visiting them for a week. He said he didn't know when he could come again. It was all a matter of how long he could keep up the story of the Ma'ara inheritance. He wasn't worried that people would find out there was nothing in it. The tribes were far apart now and had no contact. But it upset his great-grandfather.

Musallem came in the middle of May, and again in July, and in September; and in September he said he wouldn't be able to come again. They'd told each other many things during these visits. Musallem had told of all the military activity on the other side, the positions of the guns and of the army camps; and Jonathan had told the military positions around the kibbutz. They'd sworn each other to secrecy about these matters, as about the gazelles. They'd taken a good many oaths of one kind or another, owing to the occasion when God had made them brothers. When Musallem came the last time, he said he'd like all these oaths, together with their brotherhood, sealed in blood, and in the ravine it didn't seem a mad idea to Jonathan, so they did it, wrist to wrist. Musallem was staying the night in the ravine, so it was Jonathan who left first; and this time it was Musallem who looked after him, and Jonathan who didn't look back.

4

Knowing Musallem wouldn't return, knowing it would probably be just as difficult next year, gave Jonathan a sick feeling that he carried around with him. It wasn't so bad in the ravine, where magic work was to be done. But in the stupid world of every day it was terrible. The familiar round of nonsense continued. Not content with winning the prize for his seventy-two-petalled rose, Allon picked one up from *The Species of Israel* too – the only winner from the kibbutz. Let him have it! Jonathan thought grimly. There was a species he didn't know about, that none of them knew about.

In the ravine, Hamud was also troublesome. In the early part of the summer, when Jonathan had arrived irregularly and unexpectedly, he had willingly snatched a couple of hours' sleep among the rocks while the messenger watered the herd. But after Musallem went, he took to staying awake and plying the messenger with questions regarding God's intentions. Jonathan told him to mind his own business. But as the weeks went by and the rainy season approached, when he knew he wouldn't have seen Musallem anyway, he paid more attention.

Hamud said he had to know what to do. Next April there would be 600 gazelles. How could he manage 600? God must have some plan for the management of the 600. Was the time yet nigh for them to enter the holy land, and if so, how?

Jonathan said it wasn't nigh yet, but he'd let Hamud know about it. And after thinking it over, in bed in the kibbutz, and bearing in mind what 350 gazelles were like, and trying to imagine what 600 would be, he thought that even though he didn't know what would happen, the time must be pretty nigh for something.

So he told Hamud this, and when Hamuo asked how he would know when it was nigh, he said that there would undoubtedly be a good deal of confusion, and that this would be a sign. Hamud was glad about this because he'd wondered what type of sign would be offered. At the end of October, when rain clouds were already about, he asked a further question. He asked if, when the time had come, the messenger would be there. The messenger said he would.

Jonathan certainly hoped so. He could see that spring might be rather chaotic in the ravine.

# 9
# All About The Species of Israel

At the offices of the Nature Reserves Authority, spring was also rather chaotic. To get *The Species of Israel* out by July 1, Motke had to have it printed and bound by early June. Because of colour plates, and a bottleneck at the binder's, this meant printing had to start in March. But March had come and gone and printing had still not started.

'You are trying to drive me mad,' Motke told the man at the printer's. The man had just told him he was a bit doubtful about April also. 'You think because we've got so far we can't take it away from you.'

'You can't,' the man agreed, 'but even if you could what good would it do you? Everybody has the same problems. Go and argue with the army.'

Motke put the phone down and took a pill. He hated office work. It was bad for his digestion and his blood pressure. He hated it, anyway. He wished the army would call him up. They'd called General Mor up a couple of times. They'd called half the staff up. They'd called the printers up, too. Motke envied them the fresh air.

He went in and told Mor about it.

'So when does he say they can start?'

'Maybe the end of the month, but more likely May.'

'What do the binders say?'

'I haven't asked the binders. Naftali, why can't I go in the army? Why can't I go to the Wadi Parek?'

'You're needed here, Motke, contain yourself,' the general said. 'When the situation eases you'll go to the wadi, I promise.'

'How long?'

'By May it will be quiet. The thing is a storm in a teacup. Probably by then the bottleneck at the bindery will be straightened out, too. You'll get the book out on time. If not, we'll circularize the booksellers – what of it? The delay is understandable.'

'It isn't the booksellers. It's the kibbutzim. They've all ordered several copies. It's terrible to arouse interest and then let them down.'

The general grunted. 'The kibbutzim have other problems,' he said.

At Gei-Harim they had a variety, the most urgent being the cotton. They sowed the cotton every year when the soil temperature stabilized at sixteen degrees Centigrade. The soil temperature had hit sixteen degrees some time ago, but no sowing had as yet taken place. This was because whenever a tractor ventured out it was shelled. For the unseen Syrian gunners the target was so close that shells had to be flung almost vertically in the air to fall on the cotton fields below – now a desert of craters. The citrus groves had taken a plastering too, and even the kibbutz itself. All the kibbutzim in the area had taken a plastering of late

Officials of one kind or another had come up and given them lectures, and the consensus was that it was simply spring high spirits, and that the thing would die down. Russian arms had piled into Syria, and they were trying them out. Also the Mixed Armistice Commission on Border Cultivation had recently got itself deadlocked and the Syrians were jittery. The last thing to do was to build adequate shelters – funds readily provided – and offer no provocation. Air reconnaissance showed the difficulty of hitting back. The unseen guns were beyond the ridge, deeply embedded in rock and concrete. Counterfire had little effect on them. On the other hand, no other response could at the moment be considered, for it would be rated escalation. If a kibbutz came under any special attack, then it should dig trenches connecting the various parts, so that some kind of normal life could continue even if work could not.

Several of the kibbutzim came under steady attack, so they dug trenches, but at Gei-Halim they couldn't bring themselves to do it. The lawns, the shrubs, The shaded walks, tended with such devotion for years – dig them up? Already they had the inconvenience of army units dug in on their land. To prevent the fedayeen from running in while they were in the shelter, the army had drawn a tight ring around the kibbutz and had sealed off a large area adjoining the ravine.

Jonathan didn't know which was worse, the fedayeen or the army. Lying didn't work this time. Nothing worked this time. That April, thinking of the 250 new gazelles coming quietly into the world below, of Hamud, and Musallem, and The Game, Jonathan went frantic. But he didn't get off the kibbutz.

Also that April the policy of sitting it out while the Syrians had high spirits took a tumble. The incident began at kibbutz Ha'on, some kilometres to the south of Gei-Harim. Adversely affected by the recession that was then taking an economic toll of the country, the kibbutz urgently needed to get its beetroots sown. Plot 52, a rather exposed position, was the beetroot field, and when shelling twice prevented work, the D4 Caterpillar tractors in use were called in, and an armoured tractor sent out. This tractor was also shelled, but without damage, which annoyed the Syrians.

They called up heavy artillery from the rear, and also

tanks to operate from other positions. Those in a village called Khirbet Tawafik, nicely placed on the ridge, seemed to be doing best, when the Israelis suddenly got their range and knocked one of them out, incidentally setting fire to several village houses. This annoyed the Syrians even more, and they intensified the attack. The tractor on Plot 52, under fire from several quarters, was hit in the engine and stopped. This annoyed the kibbutzniks, who became obstinate. They got the tractor back, and sent another one out. Everybody kept on shelling each other, and the tractor kept on sowing beetroot.

About midday the UN managed to get a ceasefire, but an hour later, driven witless by the spectacle of the tractor still going doggedly up and down Plot 52, the Syrians opened up on it again. This was when Israel decided enough was enough, and sent aeroplanes in to stop them. The aeroplanes put twelve artillery positions out of action. While they were doing it, Syrian MiG-21s came up to intercept. Within a matter of minutes, three of them were shot down.

During the lull that followed, Damascus radio announced that several Israeli planes had been shot down while attempting to raid Damascus, and appeared to believe it. But within a couple of hours, realizing whose planes had been shot down, and how, a further punitive shelling was authorized. Four kibbutzim came immediately under very heavy bombardment. (In one of them, Gadot, two hundred shells were counted and no single house left undamaged.)

Israeli planes went in again to silence the positions.

While doing it, they were again intercepted by MiG-21s.

Again three of them were shot down – in twenty-five seconds.

The kibbutzniks were relieved about this, and they hoped the high spirits might stop now.

2

Fifteen kilometres away on the ridge, Musallem saw the
planes shot down in the afternoon. Two of them seemed
to explode simultaneously in a single enormous fireball,
halting the harangue that had been going on for half an
hour on the ground. Everyone watched, open-mouthed, as
a third plane suddenly blossomed and disintegrated. The
officer who had been conducting the harangue, rightly
more expert at politics, which was his job, than at aircraft
identification, shook his fist in the air and led his men in
three hearty cheers. 'So it will be for all of them!' he said.
'This is the way to deal with the Zionist gangsters. It
emphasizes again what I've been trying to get into your
thick heads – only when the revolution mobilizes all its
resources can it begin to cope with the problems of the
day.'

It was after four o'clock now, and it would be dark in
an hour or so. Musallem saw, with sluggish indifference,
that they would get nowhere this time, although his great-
uncle Mansur continued to interject a word of pleading
whenever the officer drew breath.

'But your soldiers must eat, Effendi –'

'Not Effendi, imbecile. Call me brother!'

'Brother. With respect. It's fresh meat. There may be
difficulties with your other meat supplies. We keep off the
roads. We're in nobody's way . . .'

Musallem felt sick, listening to him, and he thought he'd
probably arrived at a decision now, but again couldn't be
sure. Dozens of times in the past few months he'd arrived
at a decision, and changed it again only hours later. During
the winter, he had lost a goatskin in a mud pool, and after
diving for it a few times had found it. The skin was heavy
and waterlogged, not sinking, not floating. He felt like that
skin. He had thought he would postpone a decision until

he had talked with Jonathan but now he knew he would not be seeing Jonathan.

In the end the officer began striking Mansur with his stick.

That's all. It's enough! You'll be shot if you're found within five kilometres of here after dark. Understand, imbecile? Shot, all of you,' the officer cried, punctuating his words with the stick.

'Effendi, we have to live!' Mansur shouted, through crossed, protective hands.

'Not Effendi, you scum. I'm your brother!'

'But we'll perish, brother, if we go back to the east!' Mansur shouted, desperation drawing rhetoric from him. 'It's the same as shooting us now. Shoot us, then, and have done with it.'

It looked for a moment as if the officer, in his excitement, might. But he turned on his heel, detailing soldiers to see them out of the area.

The soldiers, enthused by the air battle, were rather more sympathetic. 'Stay near one of the villages. Nobody will chase you away if you're careful. There are great things doing, and you'll get your share.'

'It's pasture and water we want. They'll bleed us dry in the villages. We can't pay for these things.'

'Soon there'll be pasture and water in plenty. Have patience.'

The soldiers left them when they pitched for the night outside a village. But this time they didn't fold the tents and move. They'd seen what was happening in the area. Everywhere there were guns and tanks and transports of troops. Jeeps shuttled about the tracks, the whole length of the ridge. There were no loopholes to the west now.

Since his great-grandfather's death, Musallem was only one of six children in the tent, for his great-uncle Mansur was now the sheikh. He wasn't treated unkindly. Everybody had known the special relationship between him and the old man, even though it had caused unpleasant suspicion in the past. But all that was over now, for he'd got nothing much in the way of an inheritance: there was nothing much to be got. They were a raggle-taggle bunch now, less than fifty heads including the women; and all the women old enough to speak said they would sooner live in villages. Musallem thought he would himself, but he wasn't certain. He wasn't certain of anything these days.

He wondered where the Ma'ara were. He hadn't seen them all winter. He thought it possible that in the present difficulties the women had gone to the villages while the men had joined the fedayeen, It was the sort of solution the resilient Ma'ara might think of. Musallem wondered what the solution was for him. He wished he could talk about it to somebody, to Jonathan, or his great-grand-father. It was only lately that he wanted to talk of such things with the old man. There were many things he wanted to talk about with him now.

It had happened in January, in a grey drizzly period that had continued for a week. The old man had gone out to relieve himself and had slipped in the wet. Musallem had helped him in, and it had seemed nothing, but then a couple of days later he had fallen down in the tent for no reason. Musallem had told one of the women, and she had pursed her lips. 'Ah. It's his brain, then.'

'His brain? It's his foot. He slips.'

'It's the brain. I've known it before. It's started to go now.'

'Why should it go? What do you mean?'

'It happens with old people who have nothing else the matter with them. The brain suddenly goes and it affects everything else. It's that that's making him fall over. Don't let him go near the fire.'

'What?' Musallem said, horrified but at the same time excited.

'Keep a sharp watch on him. Can he do everything for himself still?'

'What do you mean?'

'Never mind, then. Let me know the first time you see something wrong.'

That very night there was something wrong. With fascination Musallem saw the old man's eyes suddenly turn up and his mouth fan open in a black circle. The arm on which he was leaning fell off the rug-covered saddle, and his head dropped softly on to it. Scarcely able to believe it, Musallem wondered at first if the old man had merely dropped off to sleep. But he wasn't asleep, for the eyes were half open. Musallem shouted out in alarm to the next compartment, and the women ran in.

'It's as I thought. Yes, it's as I thought.'

They kept him on his rug after that, and wouldn't let him get up. The old man protested at first, but soon gave up. This frightened Musallem, for he'd expected to hear the sharp edge of his tongue. But he realized suddenly how frail the old man had become, how shrunken away inside his clothes. Musallem had noticed that he ate little lately: cups of coffee, bits of *pitta*. He seemed incapable of bothering with anything else. The women asked Mansur, who was eldest, if he thought a sheep ought to be slaughtered, and Mansur thought about it moodily for a while and said he supposed so. But after a few mouthfuls of the meat the old man couldn't eat any more, although he drank the soup; and again Musallem was frightened, for he had not even asked who had killed a sheep.

Everything happened quickly after that – in a matter of days. Lying on his rug, sometimes with his hand in Musallem's, the old man fainted often, and Musallem learned to recognize the signs, a slight lifting of the eyebrow almost in enquiry, as though he were trying to understand something, and then the eyes turning up and the mouth a circle. He was increasingly more confused

*when he came to but also in some way gayer and younger.*
One morning he suddenly burst out with a little verse from
his boyhood that nobody had heard before, and was
childishly pleased when the boy repeated it back to him,
chuckling and kneading Musallem's hand. 'By God, yes.
By God, exactly. Excellent Excellent.' But then he began
to frighten Musallem again by asking if he remembered
how they had played as children, and soon had forgotten
Musallem's name und was calling him by other names.
Musallem wanted to leave, but the old man grew queru-
lous when he removed his hand.

Before the end, Musallem almost hated him, and wished
he would die more quickly. He understood now what the
woman had meant when she inquired if he could still do
everything for himself, for he couldn't. The women came
in from time to time and cleaned him up, but he still stank
horribly. All of him seemed to stink. His breath stank. The
papery clawlike hand, scrabbling at Musallem's, stank.

But towards the end, after several faints, he sank into a
coma, and everybody gathered to watch him. For a few
hours the breath sighed and gurgled in his throat, becoming slower and more irregular, and then slower still, until
Musallem, watching him, had the powerful impression
that the old man was plodding on some last, final march,
over exhausting ground, with camp almost in sight, and
between the laboured gurgles, painfully held his own
breath, waiting for the next. And then there was not a
next. They waited for it, but it didn't come. One of the
women bent over with a mirror to see if there was any
breath, and in the same moment the old man's eyes
suddenly flicked open, wider than anybody remembered,
and they were surprisingly young and keen, with a pleased
look, as if camp had been reached and it was excellent,
very excellent indeed.

The traditional wailing began then, and the men prayed,
and Musallem mumbled with them, although he didn't

know the prayer. He couldn't take his eyes off the old man's eyes, sparkling in the lamplight: he was aware that he was in the presence of the uncanny, and that the spirit of his great-grandfather was there in the tent with them, regarding the stinking old bundle that he had left on the rug. He had a feeling also that he had been betrayed and left, that this person, closest of any in the world to him, had slipped away easily, at the end without regard for him, for what would happen to him, and this was the thought that suddenly stunned him.

He didn't cry. He was known for his control. He felt simply bewildered. He didn't know what to do next, where he would sleep. He slept in the women's compartment, and everyone was kind to him. The ground was still muddy outside, so they waited two days until it dried before burying the old man. He stayed on his rug meanwhile, with another thrown over his face. After he was buried, the rugs were carefully washed, and when his great-uncle Mansur and his family took over the tent, the rugs were placed in their customary positions. But Musallem never stepped on the rugs again.

For weeks afterwards, although he performed all his usual tasks, and was certain nobody could tell any difference in him, he wasn't sure of himself, not even sure who he was. Sometimes he went off by himself – although he had always done this and was certain nobody noticed anything special in it – and thought about himself and what he had previously thought himself to be. He was overwhelmed by the richness and wholeness of the relationship that had ended, although he hadn't been aware of it at the time. When he thought over it, he saw many puzzles in it. He'd always accepted that the love the old man bore him was far greater than that which he returned. He had thought he hadn't really loved the old man at all, that he'd in some way constandy deceived him, bided his time with him, for some subtle reason that he had never troubled to analyse but which had seemed to spring from his mixed blood and the thought that he was 'different' and that in the course of time he would make some decision for himself. But it seemed to him now that he had been the one deceived. Now that he was not there, he savoured to the full the flavour of the old man. In going, he seemed to have taken a vital part of Musallem's identity.

They were good to him in the tent, but they were empty people after his great-grandfather, and he couldn't find himself in them. He wondered if he could find himself anywhere in his mother, and if he could love her. For he saw now that he had loved the old man, without knowing it. But how could he go to his mother? He had an urge to be true to the old man's memory, and he had wanted him to stay with the tribe. Sometimes Musallem came to one decision, and sometimes he came to another. He felt directionless, heavy and waterlogged, like the goatskin in the pool. The world had changed, and he couldn't understand it, although he was eleven years old.

A few days later the guns began booming again. They'd stopped after the air battle, and nobody knew why. But once started, they kept on. After a while, trouble developed in the village, where the women had been going twice a day with their water jars. The villagers wanted to buy sheep cheaply, and when the Beduin refused, they told them to go elsewhere for their water or they'd set the dogs on them. The situation was unpleasant, but it didn't last long, because soon the army came and told everyone to go. They told the villagers, too, which delighted the Beduin. The frantic villagers, not used to having to pack their goods and move, had to hire the Beduin's camels and donkeys, and the Beduin were richly repaid for the former insults and the extortion that had been practised on them. Nobody knew where they were going, and the officer in charge had no clear information.

'You'll get directions on the road east. Everybody is being cleared – all the villages around here. Probably you'll be given housing or tents in other villages.'

'What for? Why? What's happening?'

'The revolution is in danger. The people's war is near.'

'What is it to us?'

'Move. Move now.'

As the people moved out, some of the revolution's sappers moved in. They sowed mines. They sowed them the whole length of the Golan Heights. A lot of revolutionary activity had been going on lately.


3

It had been going on in Moscow and Damascus and Cairo, where the loss of the six MiG-21s had caused considerable upheavals. On paper a MiG-21 was not supposed to be shot down by a Mirage 3, which it easily outflew and outmaneuvred. The MiG-21 was a very advanced aeroplane, so the revolution only let the most advanced people fly it: dedicated members of the ruling Ba'ath party. Less dedicated people might take it into their heads to fly it to some other country, which would be very glad of it. There weren't many dedicated pilots in the Ba'ath party, and less still after April, which caused panic in the government, and put the revolution in danger.

In Moscow, they didn't like to see the revolution in danger, so they produced official information that Israel was about to make war on Syria, and said that everyone had better rally around the flag. The effect of this was to drive the Syrians into hysteria, causing them to invoke their military pact with Egypt and call on Cairo to mobilize.

The call was unwelcome in Cairo, where they weren't ready for a war, and anyway quite liked the situation as it was. Israel's economic depression had caused a good deal of pleasure there, drawing remarks from Colonel Nasser on 'the economics of Cohen'. A bit of judicious Syrian shelling, to keep the tourists away and the farmers in the shelters, was obviously just the thing to keep Cohen's economy going in the right direction.

But Damascus was past worrying about economics, Cohen's or anyone else's. Its radio pointed out that the Arab revolution was being threatened and that those who claimed to defend it had better get their armies out, as Syria's was.

It certainly was. A slow but systematic shelling of border kibbutzim began. One day it was the turn of Tel Katzir, which was meticulously bombarded at the rate of one 120mm shell per minute; the next of Kibbutz Gonen.

The Israelis cautiously observed what was going on and did not return the fire. Instead they invited the Russian ambassador to tour the country for himself to see that no preparations for war were going on. The ambassador said he wasn't a military man himself, and declined the invitation. So on May 11, under pressure from the kibbutzim, the prime minister warned Syria not to shell too hard because 'in view of fourteen incidents in the past month we may have to adopt measures no less drastic than those of April 7.' April 7 was when Israeli planes had silenced the guns and shot down the MiGs. This speech was at once triumphantly denounced by Moscow as 'insolent' and sabre-rattling, and just as immediately by Damascus, on its Cairo wavelength.

Five days later, the goaded Nasser reluctantly put an army into Sinai.

Damascus at once pointed out that a UN observer force stood between this army and its enemy, stopping it from the useful type of work that the Syrian army was doing.

Two days later, Nassar told the UN to go.

The day after, it did.

The day after that, Israel mobilized.

That was May 19, and on Plot 52 at Kibbutz Ha'on, the beetroots had made six weeks' excellent growth.

4

In the middle of May, Motke gathered from the talk that was coming at him from the telephone that the fellow at the printer's was building up new excuses. He told him what he thought of him. He said that March had been the date promised, and then April. Now it was halfway through May and still nothing had been started. What was going on?

The man told him to look at the newspapers to see what was going on, and Motke asked him if they had stopped work entirely. No, the man said, they were working as hard as they could on orders that had waited even longer than Motke's.

'In that case,' Motke said quietly, 'just listen.' He told the man a large number of children was involved in the project, and that it was easier to lose their interest than to gain it. He said he knew all about the other orders, and he understood that the printer didn't want to disappoint them, and also that he would probably have to wait just as long with any other printer. But this was something he'd find out for himself, because if the printer failed him now it was the last order he would ever get from Motke's organization, and there would be plenty to get – this was only the first of a series, books, pamphlets, everything, not one of which would the printer get a smell of. It was true perhaps the printer didn't need the orders now, but there would come a time when he did. So what he wanted him to do, Motke said, was to put aside some of the other orders, and give him a genuine date, which must be absolutely no later than the first week of June. This was all he wanted, Motke said, no jokes, no advice, just the date.

The man didn't say anything, He put the phone down on a bare desk, which Motke could hear resonating with the distant thunder of somebody else's order, and presently picked it up again, clearing his throat. 'June the fourth,' he said.

Motke was startled out of his wits. It had only been temper talking, not sense. 'Is that definite?' he said.

'Quite definite. I've altered the schedule.'

That's a Sunday,' Motke said, gleefully noting it in his diary.

'Sunday. Which means we'll have to complete the make-ready by Friday, before Shabbat. First thing Sunday morning, seven o'clock, we'll run. You'd better be here for last-minute difficulties. Two large orders postponed from esteemed clients,' he said bitterly, 'who deserve better from me. I hope you're satisfied.'

'Sunday, seven a.m. I'll be there,' Motke said expressing no opinion.

He was more than satisfied. He'd begun to stop believing in the thing. Only three weeks now . . . This way, he could still wrestle a few hundred from the binder's and get them to the kibbutzim on the promised date. He felt suddenly better, though still not good. There was a *khamsin* on, and the air-conditioners were not functioning properly. Even this early in the morning he was running with sweat. He felt slightly nauseated and took a drink of water, and went in to tell Mor about it. He found Mor wasn't in yet. In the large office, the secretaries were gathered around the radio. 'Egypt has called the army up,' one of them said.

'So they'll send it home again,' Motke said, irritated. But he had another twinge of nausea, and went to his own room and sat down, mopping his brow. It wasn't the Egyptians and it wasn't the *khamsin*. It was just the office.

He hated the sight of it. He decided he'd definitely ask Mor for a week off, the minute he came in. It wasn't right to keep a man, all his life used to fresh air, cooped up in an office. What use was he in an office? He never knew where anything was, had no system.

He looked blindly at the open mail on his desk, and saw the top letter was in German, another enquiry for *Gazella smithii*. The letter seemed to mock him, and he had a sudden desire to tear it up and set fire to it, to all the mail, to the whole office. But he carefully copied out the address of the zoo and put it in his out tray for the standard reply, and took the letter to the file. The last inquiry for *Gazella smithii* was number 133, so he marked this one 134. The offers seemed to have stabilized at 25,000 dollars. Madmen!

On his way back to the desk he realized he'd broken the system again. He'd filed a letter himself, Mor had told him a dozen times, make use of the secretaries, have system. Had he ever claimed to have a system? But he read quietly through the rest of the mail after that, without jumping about, composing in his mind at the same time the brief but decisive interview that would take place the minute Mor shoved his nose in the door. He was doing this when the phone rang It was Mrs Mor, to say the general wouldn't be in.

'Is something wrong?' Motke said.

'Not with him,' the general's wife said. 'You know.'

'Oh,' Motke said. Mor had rejoined the reserves again.

'He said to stick it out, Motke, and he'll soon be back.'

'All right,' Motke said, dully.

He stuck it out for the best part of two weeks. The news was terrible so he stopped listening to it. He didn't like weekends since his wife had died and almost looked forward to going to the office again, to see a face. But once there he couldn't stand that, either. At the end of May he was suddenly sick in the washroom at the office. He sat down on the lavatory seat afterwards, with his eyes streaming, and dabbed the cold sweat off his head. He was ill. He should be in bed.

It was lunchtime, so he left a note for his secretary and went home. There he slept like a baby for hours and awoke refreshed. It was night when he awoke and cooler, so he made himself a cup of coffee, and took a little stroll. The minute he was in the fresh air and walking the length of Achad Ha'am Street, he felt fine, limbs moving smoothly, like old times. He had a marvellous idea. He was in charge of the office now, and nothing was doing in it. Almost all the wardens had been called up. The Nature Reserves Authority was in business to look after reserves. In practical terms he *was* the Authority. Why shouldn't he reassign himself to go and look after a reserve?

Motke began to whistle quite cheerfully. He covered the length of Achad Ha'am and turned back. There was a wall calendar in the kitchen, and he had a look at it over another cup of coffee. Tomorrow was the twenty-ninth. He had to be back very early on the fourth – better the third. The best part of six days lay ahead of him, useful, healthful days in one of the reserves.

He put a can of beans on the stove and some bread to toast under the grill, and bustled about rooting out his kit.

He was out at the crack of dawn, refuelled and bought provisions at Beersheba, and by breakfast time was nicely installed in the Wadi Parek, sun hot and dry on his back. The marvellous neutral smell of baking rock was everywhere from the day before, and already the air was heating up again; he could feel it smarting in his nostrils. Good clean stuff; it scoured you out, unlike that lowering muck in Tel-Aviv that kept a person feeling so lousy.

Motke always ate well in the desert, and he fried himself four eggs with sausages and bread, and washed it down with two cups of coffee; his biggest meal for ages. He was taking a little walk an hour later when he realized he shouldn't have eaten so much all of a sudden. He felt sick again. He rested and it passed off, but he knew he still wasn't himself. But with him there was nothing that a few days in the desert wouldn't cure; and all around his eager eye noted things that needed setting to rights. The young fellow they had here must have his mind on other things. Floods had brought down boulders to the wadi bed that could dam it for next winter, reducing the useful length of the waterway and hence the vegetation further down. There were also a couple of birds not yet reported, which Motke saw must have been here for three or four weeks now. He had an eye for these things. You couldn't learn it in ten minutes. It took a lifetime to learn it. When you'd learned it, they made you go and sit in an office.

However, he had no occasion to complain now. He was in the place he best liked to be, and numerous interesting species were in it with him. He had an unsettled feeling, though, as if something important were about to happen. He'd had it once before here, ten years ago . . . He remembered coming on the thing at dusk and peering at it. He knew it was probably the letter from the German zoo that had brought it to mind. Idiots. Did they think you could breed them – an export trade, 25,000 dollars a head, forty for a million dollars? At the same time, he recalled that an Eggptian army had run about in Sinai at that period, too, disturbing the wildlife . . .

It would do no harm to build a little hide.

He built one, and watched carefully from it; at dawn and at dusk.

After two days he was practically himself again, and on the third day, Wednesday, was in absolutely top form. He was walking around after breakfast then, when without warning a stream of vomit shot out of his mouth. When he stopped vomiting he began to tremble and his teeth rattled. Right away, he knew the reason for the off-colour weeks, and also for the unsettled feeling of the last two days. He also knew that he had nothing with him to deal with it. Every year in early summer his wife had seen to it that he took the pills. The year she had died he had been so mixed up he'd forgotten to take them, and after that had never taken them again. He'd thought the malaria must have finished with him, had gone out of his blood. He saw now that it hadn't, and realized he was in for a rough time.

He managed to get back to the tent, but his legs were shaking so much he had little control of them. He remembered to look at his watch when he crept into his bag, and when it was finished he saw the attack had lasted four hours, which was about par for the course. The bag was wringing wet and he turned it inside out and put it in the sun. He felt strange and lightheaded, and also dehydrated from the heavy sweating. He took a drink of water and in a dazed kind of way wondered what to do. He could get to a doctor in Beersheba in a couple of hours, but there was no telling when the next attack would come. He thought that if he was going to do it he'd better do it immediately.

Waves of nausea were still sweeping weakly over him, but he got into the jeep. He was on rocky ground. His vision was so blurred he had to drive with his eyelashes almost brushing the windshield in an effort to see. He was casually sick again, over the wheel and over his knees, as he did this, but he kept on, very slowly, until he felt his hands shaking and his knees knocking again; then he pulled up. Not this time. He tried to turn the jeep around, but he couldn't manage it, his foot jumping dangerously on and off the pedals, so he left it there. He fell out of the jeep. He knew he shouldn't lie in the sun, so he crawled under the car, and shook and threw himself about there, banging his head and bloodying his nose.

It was a bad one this time. He saw that after the years of dormancy it was very bad. He thought he'd better pass it in the tent, even without drugs, and give up the Beer-sheba idea. When the shaking was over, he got back in the jeep and returned to the tent. He left the sleeping bag inside out, and got in it as it was. In the next couple of days, all of it was going to get drenched, so what was the difference?

In the middle of the night, in a clear moment, he had an idea. Beduin were wandering in the area. It wasn't such a wonderful plan to leave things standing about while he was disabled. He opened the jeep's hood and removed the rotor arm. This he wrapped in a plastic bag, together with his keys and his wallet and his watch, and dug a hole under the sleeping bag, and buried everything there. He turned the sleeping bag inside out again, or inside in, or whichever way it wasn't before, rather past caring now, and got back in it.

He drank a good deal of water, and he ate a bit from time to time, ravenous hunger coming on him, and just as suddenly departing the moment he swallowed anything. As to the rest, he wasn't certain. He thought he must have slept, but it was hard to tell which was dream and which was delirium. He was mainly conscious of trembling with the cold, although he knew the temperature was that of a bake-house. Sweat ran more or less constantly out of him, and he clutched himself tightly and tried to grip his teeth to prevent them from rattling. He was an old hand at this, though, and in the relatively clearer moments, knew the thing was taking its expected, if unduly violent, course.

He knew it was over, suddenly, at night-time. The tense unease was no longer there. He felt merely limp, burned out, weak as a kitten. He knew he'd just surfaced from a good sleep. He let the shreds of sleep waft away, blinking in the dark, then he wriggled his way out of the bag and reeled about for a bit, light as air.

He lit the lamp and poured water in the bucket and washed himself all over. He had to sit down for a good part of this. Then he put his clothes on and felt better. He had a mad yearning for a bowl of chicken soup. He had a packet of soup with him, so he made one, and found it stayed down, and had another. After this he felt able to cope with the issues of the day.

He dug up his watch and had a look at it. It said ten to nine. He realized that the thing must have stopped and have started again when he picked it up. It was an automatic date watch that his wife had bought him on their fortieth. He could see from the position of the stars outside that it was nothing like nine o'clock. It was more like two o'clock in the morning. The question was, which morning? He had a look at the watch again. The figure in the date slot showed 2: the second of June. That was evidently when it had stopped.

Motke sat and worked all this out rather slowly. The watch had a reserve of power of two days. If it had stopped on June 2, he must have taken it off on May 31. He thought about this, and realized he was right. May 31 had been a Wednesday, and that was when he'd been taken ill. So today must be Friday: or rather, the day when the watch had stopped had been Friday. This still seemed to leave open the central question. How long had it been stopped?

Motke knew that in the early years the attacks used to last about four days. But that was in the Huleh, where they had a young husky kind of malaria that had killed plenty of people. This was just an old used-up bug that had lingered around for years and sneaked up on him when he wasn't looking. He didn't feel he'd been in his bag four days. Still, he couldn't tell. If he had, he thought, then the watch had been stopped two days, and it was now the fourth of June. June 4 was Sunday.

Oh my God, Motke thought, and started throwing things together, his kit and his bag. Sunday: they were printing *The Species of Israel* on Sunday. He got the tent down, and threw it in the jeep, and put the rotor arm back in, and was on his way.

He knew it wasn't Sunday. How could it be Sunday? Still, it might be Sunday. He was still a little shaky and had to concentrate hard on his driving. When he hit the main road, an hour later, he saw with enormous satisfaction that a lot of traffic was going his way, ice cream vans and cars and little trucks: people were coming home, late, from the weekend. It wasn't Sunday, then. It was Saturday! Tomorrow must be Sunday, the first day of the working week. He was still in time. Running in through Tel-Aviv, he saw the time on the clocks, a quarter to five, and put his watch right.

It was five o'clock and already quite light when he parked outside his flat. He thought he would grab an hour or so's sleep. He left everything in the jeep and went up and got into bed, setting the alarm clock for a quarter to seven. He was still dazed when it went off and couldn't get up immediately. When he did, there was no time for coffee. He washed at the sink brushed his teeth, and got moving.

He noticed something odd in the street.

There was hardly any traffic.

Was today Saturday, then, not Sunday? He was still half asleep. He couldn't work it out at all. He concentrated on getting to the printer's.

The printer's was in a busy section. There was no traffic there, either.

What the hell, Motke wondered, was going on? It *must* be Saturday, then. Tomorrow was Sunday. He was a day early. The front door of the printer's was closed, but he saw a side door open, down an alley, and he went in it.

The big press room was totally deserted; but on the presses he could see *The Species of Israel*. He could see a pile of sheets already printed. Already printed? How could they be printed? They weren't going to be printed until tomorrow. Which meant it must already be tomorrow. That was to say, if they were already printed, after tomorrow. Motke had a faint notion that everything was getting just that little bit beyond him, and that the truth of the matter probably was that he wasn't here at all, but in his bag, in the Wadi Parek, soundly sleeping. He looked for somewhere to sit, and was still looking when a little old man with a broom came suspiciously into the room.

'Can I help you?' he said.

'I don't know. I'm not sure. I couldn't say at all,' Motke said. 'I was asleep. I woke up. It was Friday. That is, Saturday. Now, I suppose Sunday. Maybe you can help.'

'Eh?' the old man said

'What day is it today?' Motke said simply.

'What day is it? It's Wednesday.'

'Wednesday?' Motke said, and found a chair just in time. 'Wednesday? Where is everybody, then?'

'Where are they? They're at the war.'

'What war?' Motke said. 'You mean – it actually started?'

'Started?' the old man said. 'It's practically finished. We have taken Sinai. We are sitting on the Suez. We have taken Jerusalem. We have got the Wall. It's all ours.'

'What?' Motke said. 'What? What?'

'Yes.'

'No!'

'I'm telling you.'

'Oh,' Motke said, and held his heart. Then he held his head. To have slept through a war – such a war! He felt like Rip van Winkle.

'You want a drink of water?'

'Yes. You mean – Jerusalem?'

'Jerusalem. It's ours. All of it.'

'Oh,' Motke said again. 'And it's all over now?' he said a moment later.

'Not yet,' the old man said, over his shoulder as he went for the water. 'Those dogs on the Golan Heights are giving it to the kibbutzim. Day after day they've been giving it. Let them wait! Tomorrow is our day.'

Waiting for the water, Motke's stupefied gaze fell on the presses, and on the sheets that had already come off them. He could read the title page, *The Species of Israel by The Children of Israel*, and a throatv chuckle issued from him, not so much from his throat as from his entire being. Even if fast asleep and dreaming, he thought, this was a moment he had better remember. Among the many notable species listed in the work, there was one that had been somehow overlooked, except on the title page.

## 10
# All About War and Peace

On the Syrian Heights they were certainly giving it to the kibbutzim. Day after day they gave it to them. The shells rained down like hail, nonstop. Under cover of the bombardment, the revolution came down to take back the stolen land, because the hour of destiny had struck. Damascus radio said it had struck. It said this on Tuesday, because the issue wasn't quite certain on Monday. But on Tuesday, Cairo passed the nod that the Zionist gangsters were as good as finished, and that it was right that brothers should act together. A nod was as good as a wink so the revolution came down very strong. It came down on three selected weak points, Tel Dan, Kibbutz Dan, and Tel Katzir, all of which had received an extra good plastering for the occasion.

A strange thing happened again, though.

Despite the plastering, and the weakness of the points, the gangsters there started jumping out of holes in the ground and throwing bombs. There was obviously no sense in endangering good equipment, so the revolution turned around and went back again. It did it in much better style this time, and even faster, for the equipment was all brand new and Russian and had a good turn of speed.

When the revolution's army got back it let the people in Damascus know what had happened, and they fully approved of the strategic withdrawal, and ordered the gunners on the heights to lay it on a bit thicker.

They laid it on very thick for the rest of Tuesday and all Wednesday. But the ice cream vans and the little trucks and cars that had taken all the gangsters to Sinai were on the way back then. The aeroplanes that had been busy there had also just about finished.

Around the time Motke was learning what he'd slept through, they were all going at a fair clip in the general direction of the revolution.

At Gei-Harim they'd finally had to dig the trenches. The myrtle and the hibiscus and the virgin's bower had been torn up, and the fine lawns excavated. The trenches crisscrossed the kibbutz, and proved the only way to get about, under the further protection of steel helmets, in the constant rain of shrapnel. All the men of the kibbutz had shared the digging of the trenches, and then the young ones had left to join the army, leaving the older ones to guard the women and children. The women and children had filled sandbags from the spoil of the trenches, and stacked them around the buildings. They managed it just in time, and after that went to the shelters.

They were there day and night, and they were very frightened, for they knew they were on their own, the army and the air force being occupied hundreds of miles away. They were frightened by the noise, anyway, for even in the shelters the incessant whine and crash of shells was deafening. The babies cried and the teachers tried to get the children to sing songs. But they didn't sing very hard, for a lot of them were sobbing with fear.

The older men, who remained on lookout above, were not very calm either. They could see the hail of fire coming down and they knew the intention of the powerful army behind it: it had promised pillage, rapine, and 'a lake of blood'. At Gei-Harim radio reception from Damascus was rather better than from Israeli stations, and Damascus had already announced that, owing to destiny, the creation of this lake had commenced, with Syrian units sweeping through Lower Galilee. It seemed likely. It was hard to think anything could withstand such deadly and concentrated power.

From the upper ground at Gei-Harim, the men saw the formidable Syrian tank columns and the motorized battalions descending to attack Kibbutz Dan, and they licked dry lips and looked at each other, wondering how they would behave when their turn came.

But that was on the Tuesday, and the Syrian army didn't come down again. Apart from the three abortive attacks on the kibbutzim, it didn't come down at all. For by the Wednesday, the revolution had formed a fair idea of what was going on in Sinai and the principle under which their fraternal revolutionary Colonel Nasser had advised them to join in – one down, all down – and they reappraised the situation to produce a dynamic but thoroughly practical new conception of the theory of warfare. An army was only potent if kept in being. The thing to do with this one was to keep it well behind the fortifications, until destiny should call again. The fortifications were several kilometres deep, the spaces in between well strewn with mines. Nobody was going to get through; but in case anyone should try, a few precautions would not come amiss.

The political and provisions officers saw to it that there was food in the fortresses so that the soldiers would have enough to eat, and then they locked them in so that they would have to fight. The officers went about doing this, and then they established themselves in the various headquarters well behind the fortresses and kept a keen eye on things. That was on Wednesday, and on Thursday the gangsters tore into them.

*

They did it fast, for time was short. For the first two days of the Six-Day War, the Russians had believed the Egyptian claims and had steadily blocked all attempts to get a ceasefire. But when they got the point, at about the same time that the Syrians got it, they moved very rapidly.

The people in the ice cream vans weren't keen on a ceasefire until they had destroyed the Syrian power. So they tore in, not only in ice cream vans, but with all the armour that could slog its way back several hundred miles across two deserts: tanks, half tracks, troop transports, jeeps. The aircraft went in, too, and the mountains turned red and white and yellow in the middle of the night, and the noise that had been before was a whisper to what it was now.

This was on the fourth day of the Six-Day War, and for the following two days and nights, a prevision of hell was observable on the Heights of Golan.

Those locked in the bunkers roasted in them, and had later to be removed with shovels.

The Israelis had no time to capture documents and had no plans of the minefields. There was no time, either, to send in sappers, or to employ flails to touch off the mines. There was not even time, in the headlong rush, to call for volunteers, and there was also no need. The young men tore in their vehicles through the minefields, and those in front were disintegrated, and could see, before they were killed, the leaders of other columns being disintegrated. Several scores of them went this way. Firing their guns, many other young men swarmed into the muzzles of bigger guns, to die that way.

This was the kind of war it was, quite a large war, but compressed, like many novel things, into miniaturized form, and it created a new reality in the area.

For six days, following an old tradition, this labour continued, and on the seventh ceased.

2

At Gei-Harim they didn't know whether to laugh or cry, and most people did both, although some did only the latter, all night, by themselves; for those who'd shared the nights with them were lying about in pieces somewhere. Those bodies that were returnable were buried on the kibbutz and trees were planted around and about. Amos, that originator of the swimming pool and progenitor of industries, was one of these. The rabbi came up again from Kiryat Shemona and did the job, and he showed Jonathan that other Blessing for Special Occasions that, as the son, he had to recite over the grave. It was the *Kaddish*, the exceedingly antique Jewish prayer for the dead that so curiously blesses life and doesn't mention death.

Jonathan read out the prayer, and they filled Amos in, and the rabbi moved on to the next job. The rabbi wanted to say something to Jonathan, but he couldn't think of anything, so he rubbed the carroty head, and kissed it, and rubbed it again, making a little painful buzzing noise through his beard.

Jonathan's mother hadn't gone to the funeral, and when he went home he found that she was in bed, with the door locked. He asked if there was anything she wanted, and after a while she said in a low voice, 'Yes.' It sounded weirdly as if she were laughing. He waited a bit longer but she only blew her nose and presently said wearily, 'Go and see Yael. I haven't seen her today.'

He went to the baby house and saw his little sister, and played with her for a bit.

He knew that he should feel something about all this, but he didn't.

They were dazed all of that week. People wandered about in the middle of the night, and drank coffee at all times. It was hard to believe that there was no longer the threat of the Syrian guns, almost harder to look at the towering rocks and realize that men had stormed up them, had hurled themselves into annihilating fire and minefields;

that they were safe now, the whole country, the people, because the young men had grasped the nettle. Nobody had wanted it. They had all been frightened of it. It had been willed on them by fantasists to the north and the south who had played with fire and seen their shadows grow wonderfully big in its glow.

Now the victory was incredible to the victors.

All week there were soldiers about, still coming down from the plateau, and much equipment, and transporters lugging wrecks and military booty. Young soldiers lay about in groups everywhere, or sat hugging their knees. Lines of trucks were pulled up at the sides of roads. A bit of sporadic firing was still going on here and there as bands of irregulars were flushed out, and quite early in the week, movement was noticed in the ravine, and it was decided to flush that out too

Jonathan heard about it, and he knew that now he must tell somebody, and quickly.

He told Esther, the schoolteacher, and she told the local commander. They both thought it a crazy story, but they'd heard crazier, so they thought they had better try and tell Motke, which they did, on the telephone. Motke couldn't hear very well, but he got the basic point, which was as believable as most others at the time, and he thought he had better tell Mor, which was less easy because he was sitting on the banks of the Suez Canal.

But helicopters were running there and back across Sinai. Everybody was running everywhere, some in small circles, of bewilderment, relief, disbelief, grief. This was the aftermath of victory in the gangster state, and although people ran none danced.

3

Motke and Mor made several passes along the length of the ravine, and in a couple of places were able to hover between the walls. They watched, through glasses, and saw very clearly. They couldn't speak above the clatter of the rotor, but they had nothing of an informative nature to communicate, and hands did just as well.

Mor had brought three bottles of Very Special Fine Old stuff from his travels in Egypt's land, and when they landed he gave the kibbutz a couple, and he and Motke sat with the other in the dining hall. 'Motke, *le'chayim,*' the general said, clinking his glass. '*Le'-chayim,* Naftali,' Motke said. He thought the general looked very slightly deranged, and he put it down to lack of sleep. But he felt a little bit that way himself, and sleep was not a thing he had lately lacked. He thought of telling the general about his Rip van Winkle experience, but he still didn't know if it was a very good joke or not. While he was pondering the matter, the general refilled for them both.

'*Le'chayim,* Motke.'

'*Le'chayim.*'

'So explain it.'

The general did not explain what he wished explained, *Gazella smithii* or other mysteries, but Motke thought all were comprised.

'It's a miracle,' he said.

'A miracle, you say?'

'What else?'

'How tall is a person?'

'Which person?'

'How tall am I?'

'I would put you at going on two metres – over one ninety. You are a big person.'

'Exactly. A big person. Of exactly one ninety. Yet I've

seen bigger, Motke, much bigger. We must drink a special *le'chayim* to a specially big person. Toast him, Motke.'

'*Le'chayim*,' Motke said affably, noting that he had been refilled once more.

'*Le' chayim.*'

'So who is he?' Motke said, on drinking.

'I don't know,' the general said. 'But he partook of the miracle. Motke, I have seen sights that are nothing short of marvels. Marvellous things, I tell you! For instance, one day I had to execute a pincer movement on a wide vector, splitting the forces under my command. In such a movement, it's essential that each arm should be able to rely on the other, so although speed was important, there were other considerations, the need to maintain our joint strength. It was an operation of complexity and extreme difficulty, Motke, with the enemy ably defending himself while dug in, and we had to go through him, and were mauled, and ourselves inflicted an enormous destruction. We met minefields, and although they slowed us, for the reason mentioned earlier I had to order that flails should be employed in the leading columns. We were going on that occasion for twenty hours, so naturally it was necessary to stop for refuelling, which we did, between minefields. On these occasions people fall out of the tanks and drop instantly asleep for a few minutes. But it was impossible that I should do so; so to stay awake I had scalding coffee prepared, and I also took a closer look at something that had puzzled me. Attached to the flail of a leading tank I saw a palm tree, a most unusual thing in such a desert. And Motke, do you know, on close inspection, it was not a palm tree. It was the colour and consistency of a palm tree, but it was a different species entirely, it was a man. That person was all of *four* metres tall, Motke – imagine it, more than twice my height – even without his head. He didn't have a head. It must have been all flailed off. As a matter of fact, it took a keen eye to identify to which part of the created order it belonged at all, but it was undoubt-edly *Homo sapiens*, I would say Egyptian, and it partook of the miracle. This was the biggest man I ever saw, twice as big as any I saw, so it's only right to give him a double *Le' chayim. Le'chayim*, Motke.'

'Naftali,' Motke said. 'Naftali.'

'You won't drink to miracles and wonders?'

'I won't drink "To life" in this case. It's a mockery.'

'Motke,' the general said wearily, 'you've no head for system, and never had. Miracles of this kind have a system like anything else. Someone has to lose. It's not enough to be a hero, although strictly speaking this tall fellow wasn't one. I remember in my younger days there was a little English verse that defined a hero as one who kept his head when all around had fled. The fact of the matter is, this chap didn't. He certainly didn't have it when I saw him. All the same, I insist you do the largest man I ever saw the honour of giving him a special *Le'chayim*, after which you can explain how you find yourself mocked by miracles.'

'It's a blasphemous toast, Naftali. I won't praise life for this terrible death.'

'Well,' the general said, absently pouring himself another, 'it's something I've been doing a good deal lately. I can't number the *Kaddishim*, Motke, or the letters of consolation. I suppose with this gazelle it's a different order of miracle. You can tell me tomorrow, I couldn't follow tonight. To tell the truth, Motke, I'm tired, They tire a man out, miracles.'

4

Jonathan, when he went in to tell them in the morning, had made his mind up how he was going to do it. But on entering the room he found not only General Mor and Motke, as expected, but also Esther, and the secretary of the kibbutz, and the local commander, and his deputy, and two men who turned out to be wardens of the Nature Reserves Authority, and the sight of so many responsible faces threw him a bit. It didn't make him change his mind, though.

He knew what they would think of the story, and how he might think of it himself sometime in the future. But he didn't think of it in that way now. This was the one thing he was sure about. He wasn't sure about anything else.

He wasn't sure what he felt about his father's death, or the war, or any of the bedlam that had been going on lately. All these things seemed to be aspects of the workaday world, but gone topsy-turvy; but the topsy-turviness, like the previous untopsy-turviness, did not as yet seem to have reached any important part of him. The important part was still involved with The Game, and he had the desolating awareness that The Game was nearly over now. But it wasn't over yet. While it was on, the rules were on.

Jonathan told the story strictly according to the rules.

General Mor and Motke were not themselves after disposing of the Old stuff the night before, and they heard him out in silence. Because they didn't interrupt, nobody else did. But when the story was finished, the general found that everybody was looking at him. He held the top of his head, as though to establish something about it, and while doing this, thought what was the best thing to do in the circumstances. He had fallen into the habit lately of recapping complicated reports to be sure he'd got everything right, so this was what he did.

He said he understood a certain shepherd had left his people and his land in the east to travel to the ravine in the west. There God had told him that his function was to raise up a chosen species called Smith to inhabit the holy land. Various miracles had enabled the race of Smith to multiply, and most of the events in surrounding areas had been designed with this end in view. The shepherd had interceded with God to bring a good many of them about, but others God had brought about himself, including the recent war.

'Is that it?' the general said.

'Yes, that's it,' Jonathan said.

'Well, you can go and have a walk now, Jonathan. Don't walk too far. I'll call you.'

'Is that lad a bit touched?' he said seriously, when Jonathan had gone.

'He's a bit awkward,' Esther said. 'He always has been.'

'Awkward?' the general said. 'It's lunacy – unless . . . This isn't a religious kibbutz, is it?'

'It certainly isn't,' the kibbutz secretary said.

'Or *anti*-religious?'

'Not that, either. It has nothing to do with us.'

'It's the son of Amos,' Motke said. 'Of the cotton. The one that was killed.'

'Oh. Ah. H'm.'

'It's not that, either,' Esther said, divining the grounds of this explanation. 'I don't know what it is. I never have,' she said a bit helplessly. 'It's just him. He makes things up.'

'He didn't make the gazelles up. They're there.'

'That's true,' Esther said. 'And it's probably the only thing that is. About the rest – if you want my advice, leave it absolutely alone. He'll have answers for everything you can think of, and for quite a few you can't. If you just want to get the gazelles – ask him how.'

'All right,' the general said, after a pause. 'Get him.'

'Now, Jonathan,' he said in a brisk and friendly manner, when this had been effected, 'you know what we are all here for, don't you? We have to get all those gazelles up out of the ravine.'

'Into the holy land,' Jonathan said, nodding.

'That's right. You said there was an enclosure there.'

'That was last year. This year I don't know. There are six hundred gazelles now'

'Who told you?'

'God,' Jonathan said.

'Did he?' the general said, and groped for a while.

While he was groping, Jonathan added that God had also told him that by 1975 there would be 55,800 gazelles, and by 1985 about seventeen million.

'I think it was the enclosure, Naftali,' Motke said uncertainly, in the pause that followed.

'Yes, it was,' the general said, it was the enclosure. You see, Jonathan, the problem is to get these gazelles together in one place. While there are still only six hundred of them,' he said, it's a question of how to do it. How would you do it?'

'I'd tell Hamud,' Jonathan said, 'and he'd tell Smith.'

'And what,' the general said, essaying a little joke, 'if Smith won't listen?'

'She will. God appointed her to.'

'All right. Very good,' the general said, belatedly recognizing that strategy had to be adjusted to the enemy's. 'So let's consider. Hamud tells Smith, and Smith does what? Suppose Smith brings all the gazelles up here. You know how a gazelle behaves, Jonathan, when it sees strange people. It jumps about and runs. This is how God made it.'

'Of course,' Jonathan said.

'Which is no good either for the gazelles or us. What we want, until there are seventeen million of them, is to get them in an orderly way into nature reserves. So the question arises, how? In general it's best to take a few at a time, in such a way that the others won't jump about and run away. What I have in mind is to get them into the enclosure. I expect God also has it in mind – wouldn't you say?'

'I can't say what God has in mind,' Jonathan said

seriously. He saw the general had picked up the rules quite quickly, which made him suspicious.

'But He gave us brains to interpret – eh?'

'I'd have to discuss it with Hamud,' Jonathan said.

'I want you to. But first we should also have plans. You think it would be difficult to get them in the enclosure.'

'I don't know,' Jonathan said. 'In winter it would be easy. They like it because it's waterproof and windproof – the rock is of a good quality. God sent it down from the kibbutz. Also it's well lined with skins. But in summer I don't know.'

'He has been skinning them?' Motke said, with alarm.

'Not the gazelles. The conies.'

'The fellow also traps conies?'

'He doesn't trap them. He breeds them.'

'You can't,' Motke said. 'It's impossible to breed conies.'

'If God allows?' Jonathan said, with a smile. 'Hamud breeds thousands of conies. He breeds them in caves.'

Motke was more outraged by this statement than by anything he had heard so far. He was an expert on conies, and he knew you couldn't breed them. He opened his mouth to say so again, but instead said, 'So how are thousands fed in caves?'

'With alfalfa.'

'What alfalfa?'

'The alfalfa he grows, on the farm.'

'What do you mean, farm? What are you talking about?'

'A place where things grow. A farm. He has one.'

'In the ravine?'

'That's right,' Jonathan said patiently. 'Where he lives. With the gazelles and the conies.'

Motke's face turned purple and strange things started coming out of it. 'You terrible little liar!' he said. 'You bad, bad liar, you should be ashamed! How could things grow? Where would he obtain them to grow? How would he cultivate?'

'With swords,' Jonathan said, 'which he beat into ploughshares. The plants were saved for him by God, and he selected and grew them. If there's something more he wants, he asks and is given. At one time he grew many things – radishes, onions, grapes even. Now he hasn't the time.'

'No, well he wouldn't have,' the general said, with a frown at Motke. 'So we'll leave all that and stick to the enclosure. If it should turn out he can't get them in there, where else would be suitable? Water, now. I daresay God will have put a spring down there in the ravine for him, won't He?'

'No, there's no spring,' Jonathan said. 'He made a cistern.'

'The genius made a cistern – for six hundred gazelles?' Motke burst out, enraged, before he could be stopped.

'Hamud didn't. God made it. Out of a mountain,' Jonathan said.

'So it will be a fine one,' the general said, determinedly. 'And there will be a way to enclose it, I expect.'

'Well,' Jonathan said, 'I also thought of it. The difficulty would be if the operation of taking only a few at a time goes on too long. I suppose it would, with six hundred gazelles. It's drying up, you see, the cistern. Though I suppose that could be helped by putting more water on top. It comes from on top,' he said. 'There was a pool there. Only the Syrians put a gun in it, and it's been growing less. That was when God started the war so that the gazelles could come into the land.'

'God didn't start the war, Jonathan,' the general said, in a pleasant manner. He hadn't meant to say anything. He had meant to leave this lunacy totally alone. But something seemed to rise quite suddenly in his chest, suffocating him, at the same time producing a pinkish haze before his eyes which had the additional effect of making him bunch and unbunch his large hands below the level of the table. It didn't affect the warm smile that was fixed quite firmly to his face. 'God wouldn't do a thing like that, Jonathan. I am sure you know quite well how the war started. It started because they attacked us for years and we got fed up and hit back. That's how it started.'

'Well, in a general way, I agree,' Jonathan said.

'I'm glad about that,' the general said, a little breathlessly. 'But it wasn't all that general, you know. There were some quite specific things – complicated socio-political things that I expect you don't know about yet.'

'Yes he does,' Esther said. 'He knows all about them.'

But the general couldn't stop now. The thing had gone a bit higher up, to the level of his voice box, altering it slightly. 'Even military things,' he said, 'which are still more complicated. The MiGs, for instance, which we didn't want to shoot down, but which we had to. Which is quite a difficult thing to do, anyway. It's difficult for a Mirage to shoot down a MiG, Jonathan.'

'Not if God allows,' Jonathan said.

'No. Of course. You're right there,' the general said, and tried to think what was for the best. The best was to leave it absolutely alone, as the lad's teacher had wisely advised. But he didn't think he could now. He thought he must have been through too much. In the circumstances the best seemed to be to point out not all the things that the boy couldn't know, but the whole range of things – that if he wasn't a cretinous gibbering grinning little bastard who would be much improved by a bloody good hiding delivered not only on the spot but also every hour, on the hour, for the next week or two – that every kibbutz child *must* know.

So he said easily, 'It was the attacks on the kibbutzim, you see, which we put up with for year after year. Until down at Kibbutz Hion, they ran into a spot of trouble. You know it quite well, I suppose, Jonathan. You must have had a run down there – not far from here, Kibbutz

Ha'on, is it? They had to get the beetroots in, you see, on their Plot 52, because it was the season. And the Syrians wouldn't let them, kept on shelling them. So we had to do something about it, and one thing followed another, and the war came about, which is the way wars do come about, for serious reasons of agriculture and economics.'

'Not for the gazelles at all?'

'Not at all,' the general said, smiling. 'That would be silly, wouldn't it?'

'But for beetroots.'

'Well,' the general said. 'Yes. You could say that.'

'All right,' Jonathan said, with a little shrug, and his smile was every bit as warm as the general's.

The general's smile, indeed, faded slightly, at about the same moment that his hands ceased to unbunch, and he said, 'You can go and have another walk now, Jonathan. You can have a longer walk this time,' and sat down for a while in silence after Jonathan had gone.

But they got down to things again presently.

They decided to keep the ravine under observation for a couple of days, and if all was well to send little Jonathan down into it.

# 11
# All About Bargains and Remnants

In the ravine, and for some weeks now, the signs had been coming so thick and fast that Hamud was in a state of almost total bemusement. What bemused him particularly was the non-appearance of the messenger. But when he came to think it over, he saw that this in itself was a sign, and probably a prime one. Hadn't the messenger said that when the time was nigh there would be alarm and confusion? But hadn't he also said that when the time had come he would be there?

A careful reading of the situation inclined Hamud to the view that while the time had not yet come, it was undoubtedly nigh – even extremely nigh. For this reason, he had let things go a bit. He had let the conies go, for he knew he wouldn't be needing them any more. He had let most of his schedule go, and these days merely pottered. He grew a bit of barley and a row or two of onions, but it was more out of habit than anything else. Watering now took several hours, and he didn't hurry it. There was no point in hurrying because the gazelles remained out of doors, anyway. They wouldn't go back in the enclosure since Smith had died.

Smith had died during the first intensive bombardment in April. Hamud had been engaged at the time in removing the end wall of the enclosure in order to extend it, and several of the gazelles had been engaged in giving birth. When the guns had suddenly opened up, all those not engaged in this way had jumped, and Smith had jumped, all four legs in the air, and when she had landed she hadn't got up again, and when Hamud had bent to see why, he saw that she never would.

Smith had been old, of course: she had been a good mature creature upon arrival ten years before, and she had not given birth for some seasons now. But Hamud wept. He had loved Smith. Later in the day he had taken her to the gazelles' cemetery, and had had to climb quite high on the mound of rocks, for Smith had outlived several of her descendants. He had laid more rocks on Smith so that she wouldn't be disturbed, and had remained there for some time thinking over all the years they had spent together.

He had taken to carrying his ear with him – for he didn't want to be caught without it in view of the imminence of things – and thinking now over the history of Smith and of all that had happened to him, he opened the little box and had a look at it. Yes, there was clear meaning here, a line of meaning running through everything that had happened to him.

Hamud knew he must be at the end of the line now, and was not sorry. He wasn't old, but he felt old. He felt antique, an ancient of days, filled with rich experiences. He didn't regret any of the experiences, but he thought he'd had enough of them now, and wouldn't be sorry to become a soul, or whatever else God might have in mind for him.

In the past couple of weeks, when all signs indicated that the time had practically come – skies red and yellow by night and day; uproar in the air unceasing – he had wondered a good deal what God might have in mind for him. He still couldn't see himself in the garden of delights, and thought that was still some way off. But he thought it would be strange to be a soul in the ravine without the gazelles there; and he wondered about the gazelles.

Now that there were six hundred of them he thought

them more beautiful than ever, and he longed to see what seventeen million would look like. He particularly longed to see what they would look like in the holy land. The messenger had given him a fine impression of the place, which seemed a very pretty one: he could well imagine how much prettier it would be with seventeen million gazelles in it. But it occurred to him to wonder who would protect the gazelles. Might it be that a company of the righteous would be appointed to this duty? And if so, who better to join the company than . . .?

Hamud didn't pursue the thought, but he didn't relinquish it, either; and in the past few days, since the sky had resumed its normal colour by day and night, and the uproar had ceased, he had returned to it often – and also to another, of a more urgent nature.

A great-granddaughter of Smith's, who had also been attached to her, had accompanied him to the cemetery, and this gazelle had now attached herself to Hamud. But she was not Smith, and God had evidently not appointed her to Smith's duties, for the other gazelles wouldn't follow her. One of her kids followed her, a rather runtish little male, but this was because she fed him. This bothered Hamud. The fate of Smith, denied entry to the land when the time was so nigh, reminded him of the parallel ease of the prophet Moses, also denied entry to it. But God on that occasion had raised up a Joshua to lead the community into the land. Where now was Joshua?

Hamud thought the messenger would probably have news for him about this. But there again, where was the messenger?

There'd been no predators in the ravine since the uproar had shown the time to be so nigh, but Hamud kept his sling handy, just in case. He had it handy when the messenger arrived, although his keen hearing told him who was coming down.

He prostrated himself and kissed the messenger's hand, and told him all that had been going on, and the pair of them went to the gazelles. The new ones took immediate fright, but were soon calmed when Hamud took the messenger's hand and walked slowly among them. The messenger had brought coffee with him, and they sat and had a few cups, with Smith's great-granddaughter and her kid in attendance. Hamud told all about this, too.

He knew from experience that he shouldn't question the messenger too precipitately, so he waited with some anxiety for him to speak. Presently the messenger did.

He said the time had come.

Hamud at once got down and said his prayers, and when he got up, the messenger said that in view of the situation with Smith's great-granddaughter, and the enclosure, he would like to have a look at the pool, which they went and did.

The messenger did a good deal of pacing in the area of the pool, and he told Hamud God's intention with regard to the gazelles, which was to introduce them a few at a time into the land, in order that they should not be alarmed and affrighted. Hamud found this intention so filled with the spirit of mercy and loving kindness that he said another quick prayer. But the messenger indicated that it was not now a time for prayer but for practical considerations, and when he mentioned a couple Hamud screwed up his eye in the most intense concentration, at the same time seeing fresh aspects of meaning. How extraordinarily intentional that the cistern should have been placed in the narrowest part of the ravine. Everything had been foreseen!

The narrowest part of the ravine, however, was still twenty metres wide, and the problem of building a couple of walls across it, to enclose the area of the pool, and preferably a couple more to seal off the exits up the walls of the ravine, was a tough one. The walls would have to be at least three metres high, for the gazelles could jump over anything less, and of sufficient depth to support such height. So Hamud asked if this was to be regarded in the nature of a test or if there would be Intercession.

The messenger said probably both, but if the test were too hard, God wouldn't write it against Hamud, now that the time had come.

Hamud worked the whole thing out, and he said it wasn't too hard, but it would take him around about three months. So the messenger said in that case there very likely would be Intercession, and he would let Hamud know.

Hamud badly wanted to know about Joshua, but he didn't like to ask; but the messenger said he would be back again pretty soon, anyway.

Jonathan didn't feel happy about any of this, and wasn't sure why. It was hard to stick to the rules now, very hard. It seemed to him that a bit of betrayal was going on.

So when he got back to the kibbutz he kept his account very brief, and severely practical, not mentioning the demise of Smith.

'What if we sent men down to help him?' General Mor said.

Jonathan said he didn't think that would be any good. The gazelles would run.

They all put their heads together to try and think of the best way for a man with a broken back to build four big walls in less than three months, and in the end Esther said it would be a good idea to call in the engineering genius from the machine plant, who very often had inspirations. They called him in, and he had one.

'Bins,' he said.

'Bins?'

'The cotton bins. The grids. Drop a few from a helicopter, and he can bolt them together in no time. The grids weigh nothing at all. If we send down the small ones, he can probably carry a couple on his head.'

The genius took Jonathan to the plant and showed him how to bolt grids, and he picked up the idea rapidly.

When it was all typed out as a series of coordinated operations, the plan was so simple everybody wondered why they hadn't thought of it immediately.

The bottom layer of the four walls would be composed mainly of complete bins to provide stability, A stepladder would be needed to attach the higher single grids. One section would be left open so that the gazelles could enter, and when they had, Hamud would bolt it. It was through this section that he would let out fifty gazelles at a time. By the time he let them out, another bin would be in position – in effect a smaller cage, with a lid – and when they were in it, a party of soldiers would manhandle it down the ravine to a position where a hovering helicopter could lift it off. With ten or a dozen such lift-offs, the entire community could safely and rapidly enter the holy land.

It took Jonathan a few trips into the ravine before Hamud got the idea, but then he became quite adept with a spanner. The helicopter lowered supplies, and they carried them easily to the pool. For the lower course, as arranged, they bolted together mainly complete bins, but for the higher sections, using the stepladder, they simply attached single grids, employing the special strengthening bars advised by the genius.

The gazelles were at first cautious about the grids, but thirst and familiarity soon did their useful work. But when the grids became clearly a cage, they became more cautious still. Supplies of alfalfa were sent down to coax them into the cage, but a section was still left open, so that they could come and go, to familiarize them with the idea.

Jonathan had been coming and going to the kibbutz, on various missions to do with nuts, bolts, and equipment, and on one of these occasions the question was raised as to what was to be done about Hamud. General Mor thought about it and he said the Arab had best come to the holy land too: he sounded rather promising material for the Nature Reserves Authority, particularly that section of it concerned with the welfare of even-toed ungulates.

Jonathan felt rather sick about this, for reasons he didn't bother to analyse.

Hamud had been insistent lately with regard to God's intentions for the future, and also with regard to a Joshua and the company of the righteous. So when he went down again this time, Jonathan decided to answer him. He said God's intentions were known now. There would be a company of the righteous, and Hamud would be joining it.

Hamud gave a sort of sob and a moan, together with immediate thanks, but when he got up again he asked if anything was known about Joshua also.

Jonathan said yes, it was known about Joshua also.

There would be a Joshua.

When he left the ravine this time, Jonathan stopped about halfway and looked down into it. It had been a long time since he'd cried, but he sat down and cried then, knowing that when Hamud joined the staff of the Nature Reserves Authority, The Game would be over. It had been a marvellous game, The Game, in which everything was known, all the mysteries of the universe, of bananas and babies, a most rational magic whose laws all things infallibly obeyed, although the processes were often hard to understand. But now the magic was being bolted up and carted away, and the prime player and exponent was also being carted away to be allotted a part in that irrational and non-magic world where all processes were understood but the reason for none of them known.

It seemed a poor bargain to exchange something magic for practically nothing at all; and recollecting, in the same moment, his father, neatly laid out and filled in, in no position to do back flips any more, he cried a bit harder, realizing he'd got there not because God had decided against back flips, but because some people had wanted to grow beetroots while others didn't want them to, together probably with a few other reasons, of roughly equal value: none of them very magical.

It was hard, but it was also familiar, the world of accident and processes; so he dried his eyes after a while and returned to the kibbutz.

When he got there, he said he was bored with the ravine now, and didn't want to take part in Operation Smith. This caused some consternation. Some thought in terms of offering the boy inducements, and others more in terms of a thick ear. But General Mor had formed his own impressions by now, and he thought in terms of soliciting help. He asked if Hamud could carry out Operation Smith on his own, and Jonathan said he couldn't. It needed two people, one to cope with the gate, and one to cope with the gazelles. So the general asked if Hamud and the gazelles would accept anybody else, and Jonathan said he had thought about this, and they would probably accept Motke.

He made a bargain with the general. If Hamud and the gazelles wouldn't accept Motke, he would do the job himself. But either way once the operation was completed, he didn't want to see Hamud again, and he didn't want Hamud to see the kibbutz. He wanted Hamud flown immediately to a nature reserve.

The general accepted the bargain, and Jonathan took Motke down into the ravine. On the way, he told Motke that he would have to call himself Joshua now. Motke had also formed some impressions by that time, and he didn't argue the point.

Hamud was rather demonstrative on being introduced to Joshua, and Jonathan only stayed long enough to effect the introduction. He didn't explain anything to either of them, and was soon back in the kibbutz, doing back flips. Dina had been hanging around of late, somewhat hesitantly, and he decided to take her in hand again. She couldn't manage back flips, of course, but he got her on the second board, and, after a while, into some kind of shape. He found she wasn't so silly, after all, and presently he didn't think so much about Musallem, although he thought of him.

Motke stayed in the ravine until the gazelles stopped running away from him, and managed to establish a fragmentary though somewhat confusing relationship with the Arab. Motke's Arabic wasn't very good, and neither was Hamud's, so communication was less than perfect, and mainly carried out by hand, although even this was liable to interruption, for whenever Motke raised a hand, Hamud showed a tendency to kiss it. This was one of the things that baffled Motke. Another was the fact that his name was now Joshua; and a third the fellow's excessive enthusiasm – even fervour – at the prospect of becoming an employee of the Nature Reserves Authority. All this was difficult, but Motke seemed to be accepted, which was the main thing; so he went back up to the kibbutz again, and final plans were made.

The first lift-off would take place early in the morning of Smith Day, and watering would be delayed to keep the animals occupied during the course of it. To guard against any possible mishap during the transfer from the larger cage to the smaller, parties of soldiers would make their way down both ends of the ravine, to block it. At the same time, another party would come down the west wall with the equipment needed to carry the loaded cages to the lift-off point. It would only be necessary to put together three or four of these cages, for by the time the operation was well advanced, empties would be returning. An area of the cotton plantation had been marked out for the erection of another large cage to contain the herd while arrangements for their further transfer were organized.

All this took a little while, but in the end everything was nicely buttoned up. Just before Motke went down into the ravine again, he asked Jonathan if he wanted to change his mind about coming, but Jonathan said he didn't. He said he didn't want to go in the ravine any more.


2


Motke and Hamud had the first small cage in position well before daylight, and retired back inside the enclosure, bolting the single grid loosely behind them. Motke gave the word on the radio, with which he had been keeping in contact, and about an hour later, when it was usefully light, the radio reported that the first soldiers had started down.

Motke and Hamud had arranged to share the watering between them, with Hamud having the first stint, so after about half an hour, Motke told him he could begin. Hamud let himself out of the single section of grid facing the cistern, and bolted it behind him, and climbed up to the ledge and knocked the bung out, and the gazelles were soon drinking as the pool filled. About twenty minutes later, sensing the approaching soldiers, they suddenly stopped. At first they merely looked up to the west wall, and huddled rather closer together. Then they began to run about, trying to get out. They couldn't get out, but they managed to knock Motke over a couple of times.

Though well used to the handling of animals, Motke had never been locked up before with a stampeding herd of six hundred normally docile gazelles, and after getting himself badly bruised by the forest of horns, it struck him that the best thing was to call off the operation for the time being, so on hands and knees he made for the radio.

He got to the radio, but he found that it had also been knocked over and was no longer working.

This threw him into a panic, so he commenced crawling in a different direction, towards the stepladder, with the idea of mounting it and signalling to the men coming down to go back. He got it in position and actually had one foot on it before he was knocked down again. The gazelles who had knocked him down scrambled up the ladder, and a dozen of them managed to get over the grid and start off down the ravine before they spotted the advancing party of soldiers whose task it was to block that end of it. They turned around and ran back, and for a minute or two charged in wild circles, not able to enter the grid again, and terrified by the men approaching both along the ravine and down the west wall.

Motke had knocked the ladder over to prevent further escapes, but he saw now what would happen, and groaned, and when able, set it up again and scrambled up himself, and began frantically waving to the soldiers along the ravine to go back. The soldiers, drawing other conclusions, promptly broke into a brisk trot, and the thing Motke was trying to prevent immediately came about. Blocked to the north, south, and west, the trapped gazelles turned east. Three or four of them began scrambling up the wall of the the ravine, and the rest soon followed.

From his perch on top of the ladder, Motke was aware that Hamud was unbolting his section of grid to get back in the cage, and he shouted to him not to. But all in the space of seconds, he saw Hamud hoisting aside the section of grid, and then he had vanished, and where there had been Hamud and a section of grid, there was now a stampede of escaping gazelles.

'No!' Motke cried. 'No! No!' and jumped off the ladder and ran to try and block them. He managed to hang on to a couple of horns, but was soon down and being trampled, and, with his face bloody, had to roll himself out of the way, protecting his head as an avalanche of rock began to descend from the scampering hooves.

From a position of relative safety, he got his head up, and between the crossed arms that were protecting it he glimpsed an extraordinary spectacle. He had a view of perhaps seventy or eighty vertical metres of the wall of the ravine, and all of it was alive with gazelles. The leading animals had found the easiest path and were zigzagging past obstructions. The whole column followed, obeying the same zigzag. Although the sun was up and the narrow slit of sky above now radiant, it was grey in the ravine, and in the grey light, the pale undersides of the gazelles and their tossing horns flowed like water up the rock. It was like, Motke thought, a waterfall in reverse; or an ancient frieze; or a cave painting. But then, watching with awe as the column broke out to a pinnacle, high up, and the magnificent horns showed black against the light, tens of them, and scores, and hundreds, flowing up into the sky, he thought that truly it wasn't like any of these things. It was like nothing on earth.

The falling rock was hitting the lower ranks of the gazelles, and he saw them bowled over and struggling to their feet and continuing, mere eddies in the river. And then they'd all gone. Every living creature had gone. Even the Arab seemed to have gone.

Motke found that he was panting, and moaning, and possibly even praying, and was aware that blood was running down his arms and also into his eyes. But he got to his feet and looked about him in the murk of swirling dust with utter bewilderment. Where could the Arab possibly have gone? Like the gazelles, he seemed, in these fantastic few minutes, to have been spirited away. Motke shook his head to try and clear it, and he had a mad notion that none of it had happened; none of these unbelievable things were true – the enemies of his country had not all been defeated in six days; *Gazella smithii* had not been found fantastically multiplying in the ravine; he was asleep, still soundly asleep in the Wadi Parek. But then he heard the shouts of the soldiers, still approaching, and he knew that it had all indeed happened. And presently through the haze he saw the Arab, and he also saw that not all the gazelles had left the ravine.

Hamud was lying under a boulder, a large one, and a female gazelle was licking his face. Motke stumbled over to him, and the gazelle backed off, at the same time looking upwards. Motke also looked up, and in the cloud of dust he had the impression that another gazelle was there, a small one.

He thought at first that Hamud was dead, but as he bent over him the eye opened and the lips moved. No sound came out, and Motke strained and rolled the boulder off him, and he saw from the look of the ribcage that it was highly unlikely that sound would be coming out again. 'It's all right,' Motke said, hissing, despite himself, at the sight of the ribcage. 'You'll be all right. It's all right. Don't worry.'

The Arab didn't seem to be worrying. He seemed merely puzzled, but in an intrigued way, as though he'd almost, but not quite, remembered something that was on the tip of his tongue, or had just perceived the answer to some mild problem that had teased him. Motke saw that the man was engrossed in his last moments and that there was nothing he could do for him, so he straightened up and in a pleading manner approached the gazelle, who still waited a short distance away. Motke reached out his hand to the gazelle, but at each step he took, the gazelle took one back; and rather desperately, Motke began to run, and the gazelle also ran, up the wall to join the other; and with his mouth open and his hands at his sides, Motke watched them vanish in the haze of dust.

When he got back to Hamud he found that he was quite dead, but the look on his face was not dissatisfied, as though the answer to the problem, whatever it was, was all right. Motke was glad about this, but he sat down and cried, for one reason and another, and was still doing it when the soldiers turned up.


3

Smith's gazelles came out of the ravine and set off at a rapid pace in the direction in which they were already going, which was east. It was still early, but a bit of military traffic was about, keeping carefully to the swept lane. The gazelles didn't like the look of the military traffic and, naturally enough, kept well away from it, turning instead into the minefield. In a very few minutes, most of them had gone up in a series of puffs of smoke, and the military traffic had slithered to a halt to observe the phenomenon.

It was observed, too, from the high ground at the other side of the ravine, where General Mor and his party were gathered. Jonathan was among the party, but the binoculars he'd been given were too heavy and tired his arms, and his eyes didn't seem wide enough apart to look through both lenses at once. So despite the exclamations and groans of the others, he grew bored. It was The Game he had been interested in, and not the gazelles, and since The Game was over, he was glad on the whole that the gazelles hadn't been caught. He lowered the glasses after a while, and as he did so caught a movement and raised them again and was thus able to see, some time before the others, a new development. Not all of Smith's gazelles had gone into the minefield. A remnant had remained. Jonathan thought he recognized the remnant, and when it was joined by another, smaller, one, was quite sure of it.

The arrival of the remnant coincided with a puff of smoke that marked the end of those gazelles remaining in the minefield, so the new arrivals didn't bother going in that direction, but instead turned right, which was the direction from which Smith had originally come.

It was a full minute before the members of General Mor's party noticed the running gazelles and by that time the pattern of the horns could not be identified. Jonathan, watching with one eye, continued identifying quite well, but he didn't let on. He had a rising sensation that The Game might not be over, after all, and that there could still be something to it. But he thought that it was a confusing game, really, very wasteful of participants, and he didn't think he was madly keen to play it any more himself. Still, it was nice to think it might be going on, so he watched quite cheerfully as Smith's great-granddaugter and her little male disappeared from sight, which didn't take long, for the much depleted species always went well when in a hurry, and on the present occasion, as on a former, it went like hell.